"Excellent." —*Booklist* (starred review)

WANTING SHEILA DEAD

"Outstanding . . . Haddam has few peers at misdirection, and she cleverly satirizes the reality show industry while continuing to add depth to her lead."
—*Publishers Weekly* (starred review)

"Haddam's series characters are engaging as always, including Demarkian's quirky Armenian neighborhood, which has enough character to count as one."
—*Charlotte News Observer*

"Her take on reality TV, its egos and backstage battles, is fresh and entertaining, and (as usual) the mystery is sharply plotted. Eventually Haddam may have to deal with the fact that Demarkian's age will prevent him from continuing to solve crimes, but let's hope that's not for a while yet."
—*Booklist*

"Haddam gleefully satirizes reality TV and offers a well thought out appreciation of Agatha Christie's novels, which she lets Demarkian savor for the first time."—*Kirkus Reviews*

LIVING WITNESS

"Haddam offers her typically razor-sharp mystery concerning a highly contentious issue, but also does so without taking sides, treating all of her characters, from devout Christians to agnostics (and all points in between) with respect and understanding. Haddam is a fine writer, exhibiting skills rarely glimpsed in the mystery genre."
—*Booklist* (starred review)

"Haddam's excellent novel takes a nuanced look at the debate over teaching evolution in public schools . . . Haddam makes characters on both sides of the issue sympathetic, explores the inner life of her detective hero—and offers an ingenious fair-play puzzle." —*Publishers Weekly* (starred review)

CHEATING AT SOLITAIRE

"A stellar whodunit." —*Publishers Weekly* (starred review)

"*Cheating at Solitaire* has a sharply satirical edge as it takes on the cult of celebrity." —*Boston Globe*

"Haddam is at her best." —*Library Journal* (starred review)

"This series keeps getting better, each novel just a little more dramatic, more thought-provoking, and more entertaining than the last . . . It's about time she gets the A-list status she so richly deserves." —*Booklist* (starred review)

"Ought to establish Haddam as America's P.D. James once and for all." —*Baltimore Sun*

"Haddam is clearly having a good time."
—*Charlotte Observer*

"Compelling . . . *Cheating at Solitaire* manages a good sense of humor and tight, sharp writing. Haddam lets us ponder celebrity and its meaning, the powerful symbiosis between stars and the public, and our own complicity in the frenzy."
—*Cleveland Plain Dealer*

GLASS HOUSES

"One of those novels that has everything going for it: a crackling plot, an astonishing cast of characters and the best literary exploration of Philadelphia since the works of John O'Hara . . . Haddam has created an elegant, stylish work with great appeal." —*Cleveland Plain Dealer*

"Exhilarating." —*Kirkus Reviews*

and possibly murder in [this] compelling portrait of a closed society." —*Publishers Weekly* (starred review)

CONSPIRACY THEORY

"Devotees of strongly written, intelligent mysteries will be pleased that Haddam remains hard at work." —*Booklist*

"[A] fascinating study in conspiracies and those who adhere to them . . . The book is as up-to-date as today's headlines." —*RT Book Reviews*

SOMEBODY ELSE'S MUSIC

"Fresh . . . suspects and victims who are as fascinating and entertaining as her recurring cast . . . riveting!" —*January Magazine*

"Dazzlingly ingenious, Jane Haddam's novels provide style, humor, and philosophy—they're real spellbinders, sparklingly written and smashingly plotted." —*Drood Review*

TRUE BELIEVERS

"An engrossingly complex mystery that should win further acclaim for its prolific and talented author." —*Publishers Weekly* (starred review)

"Haddam is a fine and compassionate writer, and Demarkian . . . is one of the more interesting series leads in the mystery marketplace. It's a pleasure to find a solid mystery combined with engaging discussions of issues outside the genre. A guaranteed winner." —*Booklist*

SKELETON KEY

"Sophisticated style, excellent delivery, and riveting plot." —*Library Journal*

DON'T MISS THESE OTHER GREGOR DEMARKIAN NOVELS BY JANE HADDAM

AVAILABLE FROM ST. MARTIN'S PAPERBACKS

HEARTS OF SAND

A Gregor Demarkian Novel

JANE HADDAM

St. Martin's Paperbacks

This is a work of fiction. All of the characters, organizations, and events protrayed in this novel are either products of the author's imagination or are used fictitiously.

HEARTS OF SAND

Copyright © 2013 by Jane Haddam.

All rights reserved.

For information address St. Martin's Press, 175 Fifth Avenue, New York, NY 10010.

ISBN: 978-1-250-03695-7

Printed in the United States of America

Minotaur Books hardcover edition / September 2013
St. Martin's Paperbacks edition / August 2014

St. Martin's Paperbacks are published by St. Martin's Press, 175 Fifth Avenue, New York, NY 10010.

10 9 8 7 6 5 4 3 2 1

For Greg and Matt

Chaos is just order waiting to be born.
                                    —Fernando Pessoa

PROLOGUE

As far as is known, ectoplasm does not perspire.
—José Saramago

1

Alwych, Connecticut, is the kind of town about which movies are made, when the movies take place in a small, self-important enclave where Pure Talent lives and pretends to run the country. The grass and shrubs and leaves are greener there, and they hang more heavily in the almost-summer heat. The long, curving arc of Beach Drive is dotted with high streetlamps that glow a particularly purified shade of white. The granite mock-Tudor wings of the Atlantic Club brush up close to the waves of Long Island Sound. Even in the center of town, where there are sidewalks, and parking meters, and a grocery store that has more sales than it should be allowed to, there is an underlying sense of self-confidence. Alwych was here before the country, and many of the people who live in it think it will be here long after the country ceases to exist. Alwych understands what other places don't. There is virtue in being something that refuses to be moved.

Chapin Waring was standing at the landlocked end of Beach Drive. This was the part of the Drive she knew least well. When she had lived in Alwych, her family's house was the last one on the promontory before the Atlantic Club, so that she and her sisters had been able to walk to tennis and parties across the nick in the fence at the back of the property. The house was still there. It was the first thing she had gone to see when she came in on the train this morning, as if just by seeing it, just by knowing it was there, she could change all the things that could not be changed. She had even taken one more risk in a day of taking risks and parked halfway up the drive. The reality had disappointed her a little. She had expected Manderley, ruined and majestic in a jungle of untended shrubbery. Instead, her sisters seemed to have been doing their duty. The grass was cut. The bushes were trimmed. The garden was tended. It was just a big, blank house, shingle-sided and a little weathered by the Atlantic winds. It could have belonged to anybody.

Now she looked beside her on the other front bucket seat of this rental car and tried to remember what she had and had not brought with her from "home." It was a tricky business. The one thing she could not afford was to be seen and recognized. She rummaged through her green and white L.L. Bean canvas tote bag and came up with the gun. It looked innocent and not quite real, like a prop to be used in a murder mystery. She put it back in the bag—there was no point in having it out in the open—and took out a piece of cheese. She didn't want it. She didn't want anything, except to get done what she had to get done and then to get out, before her entire life blew up in her face.

She looked at her watch. It was an ordinary Timex watch. She looked at her shoes. They were wet because she'd walked them right into the ocean. Her mouth was dry, and her head hurt. Her hair was some color it had never been before. She wondered what would happen if she just walked right through the front door of the Atlantic Club and signed the register as a member. She wondered what would happen if she sat down on a bench on Main Street and just waited. Just, just, just. The word kept running around in her head, a truncated version of "justice." If it was justice she wanted, she would have been more likely to get it if she'd stayed away.

She checked her watch again, trying to make herself see

the dial. It was useless. She couldn't concentrate. There had been a time in her life when she was afraid of nobody and nothing, but that time was not now. Now the tension was rising in her body like water in a rain gauge during a heavy storm.

Chapin shifted in her seat. She had been sitting in one position for too long. Her legs were beginning to ache. The radio station she'd been listening to kept promising lots and lots of rain for the end of the week. There was a hurricane coming north in the Atlantic, and so far it had missed all its usual landfalls. Chapin remembered her oldest sister telling them about the flood in 1954, when most of the houses on Beach Drive had had their porches washed away in the mess. There had been another storm, too, in the 1930s. That one had been so huge, entire neighborhoods were washed away, and the Atlantic Club lost its terrace and all its awnings.

I'm stalling, Chapin thought. It had been decades since she thought about her life as a child in this place: the long summer evenings when the light had faded so gradually, it seemed to go on forever; the fall mornings when the roads were covered in leaves and the porches were full of old clothes stuffed with straw; the just-before-dawn darkness in winter when the cold was so bitter, keys froze in locks. Most of the time these days, she couldn't remember a point when she hadn't known the things she now knew. This was the point: herself, lying in the tall grass under the spreading maple tree at the front of the house, feeling the breeze in her hair as she let small kittens climb up her shirt and nuzzle at her neck. *Kittens,* she thought. It was as if she were about to star in an animated Disney movie.

She put her hand in the tote bag one more time, to make sure the gun was still there. Then she turned the key in the ignition and put the car into reverse. The longer she stayed here, the more likely it was that somebody would not only see her, but put two and two together. It didn't matter that it had been thirty years. People remembered things.

She edged the car out onto Beach Drive, made a careful

U-turn, and then made a right on the road that would take her around to the beach by the back way. It was eerie how deserted everything was. Like one of those ghost towns in a Stephen King novel, all the people had been turned into vampires.

She got to that part of the road where the sand started creeping in and pulled over to the side. From here, she would have to walk. She got out and took the tote bag with her, but she didn't bother to lock the car's four doors. Nobody ever locked their doors in Alwych, and besides, she wouldn't be coming back.

2

Out on Beach Drive, Chapin Waring was trying to do the one last thing that had to be done before she could say she'd had a good day. It was hard, because the knife was a long-bladed kitchen one, and it was sunk halfway to the haft under her left shoulder blade. She couldn't reach it, no matter how she twisted. Twisting made her hurt, anyway, and she was losing a lot of blood. There was blood everywhere now. It made a trail across the hardwood floors from the dining room to the hall to the living room. It was in the kitchen, where the tall French doors had been folded back to let in the air from the ocean.

In this house, everything was clean, and calm, and settled, but everything was dead as well. The chairs around the table in the breakfast nook were just far enough away from each other to look as if people had been sitting in them. The Royal Doulton china was stacked behind the glass doors of a double-fronted china cabinet, with pieces to make a service for thirty-four. The long, low hall cabinet had been dusted and polished. The two green-silk–upholstered love seats in the living room sat across the wide square coffee table from each other. The living room ceiling soared out of sight. The tall, gold-leaf–decorated mirror above the fire-place reflected everything and nothing. Chapin would not have been surprised if her mother had walked in wearing her afternoon pearls and carrying flowers cut from the greenhouse.

If it had been afternoon, it would have been easier. In the afternoon there was light. The windows here were so large, there was seldom any need for lights when the sun was up. Now it had to be almost ten o'clock, or later. The twenty-four-foot ceilings only made the rooms feel darker. The small pinpoint lights from the beach were ghost presences that illuminated nothing but themselves. The gun was still on the coffee table, where she had left it. She picked it up and turned it over and over in her hand. It had been fired recently. She could smell it.

If she sat down, she would never stand up again. She was never going to get out of this house alive. If she knew where her cell phone was, she could call 911. She didn't know where it was, and didn't know if she would call, in any case. Dying wasn't the worst thing that could happen to someone. She wished she knew what it was she wanted. Dying wasn't the worst thing, but it might be a thing she didn't want for herself, at least not now.

She could hear the ocean. The French doors led out onto a terrace, and the terrace overlooked the sea. She moved carefully through the room, holding on to furniture when she could. She couldn't hold on with her left hand, because that hurt her shoulder, and her arm wasn't working right. She was dizzy. The air around her had become thick and acquired texture. Moving through it, she had to push it out of the way.

On the night of that last party, the one that took place three days before the world ended, she had worn a blue taffeta dress with blue silk flowers sewn into the neckline, the kind of dress her mother might have worn to come out at the Grosvenor in 1944. She had been so bored, she was barely able to see straight. The air had been as difficult to breathe then as it was now. On that night, everything in her future was settled and transparent. She would go off to Wellesley. She would marry somebody like Tim Brand. She would have a house on Beach Drive and drink double-strength vodka martinis every afternoon at five o'clock. Once a week in the summer, on Friday evenings just before dinner, she would attend a cocktail party where bottles and glasses and ice and drinks were trundled around the garden in a child's red wagon.

The important thing was to be able to hold on to the gun, to hold it steadily. The gun had a kick to it. She'd fired it at least once today. She might have fired it more. She made herself turn, very carefully, so that she was looking at the mirror. She couldn't really see herself in it. The light wasn't good enough.

On the night that the world had ended, at three o'clock in the morning, when she still had Marty's blood across the front of her dress, she came into this room and stood in front of this mirror and told herself it was the one thing she could count on. It would always be here. Even if her family sold the house and another family came to live here, they would not take the mirror down. Then she had thought about Marty and the car in the shelter of the trees off Wykeham Swamp Road, about the blood that went everywhere and the sticky thick clots of it still on her hands. If someone had seen her, they would have known that there had never been a day in her life when she was ever able to tell the truth.

She braced the backs of her knees against the edge of the long couch, the one that faced the fireplace and the mirror. She held the gun in her right hand and raised her right arm. She raised her left arm very slowly and rested her left hand against her right elbow.

The man in the uniform was standing against the plate glass door, barring the way. She had the gun in her hands; the carpet under her feet was thin and beige and close to being worn down by too much traffic in too short a time. She pulled the trigger over and over again. It was easy. The trigger seemed to pull itself. The man in the uniform shot up off the floor and twisted in the air. He came down flat on his belly. She fired again and again, again and again, watching the blood spurting everywhere, watching the glass in the door shatter into pieces. This was what she had been waiting for. She knew it as soon as it happened. This was what she had really wanted when she started out looking for something they could do that would break the spell, that would break the monotony. This was what she had really wanted all along.

The man in the uniform was dead on the floor and his blood was pumping out of his side like someone had turned on a fountain inside his skull. She wanted to reach down and take some kind of souvenir, but there wasn't time. There wasn't time.

"I could have taken a finger," she said out loud, to the dark and the silence of this house that nobody lived in anymore. "I told Marty that. I could have taken a finger."

She didn't know what she was saying. A finger wouldn't have been good enough. Nothing would have been good enough. She would have had to take the whole head.

She got the gun into position. She wasn't sure how. She was swaying. She wasn't going to be able to stand much longer. Time didn't mean anything. Then and now. She closed her eyes and pulled the trigger and heard the glass of the mirror smash just a second before a shower of shards rained down on her head.

She pulled the trigger a second time, and a third, and maybe a fourth. She didn't know and she couldn't tell and it would never matter to her again, because she was falling, falling into the glass and the blood and the coffee table, falling on the antique Persian rug that had cost three thousand dollars in 1873 and now had to be absolutely priceless.

Really, she thought, as she felt herself rolling into blackness. *It was what I really wanted, all along.*

PART ONE

I have never gotten used to the Western notion that women have souls. —Nikos Kazantzakis

ONE

1

On the day that Bennis found the cat, it rained.

It rained in a way Gregor Demarkian hadn't experienced for years—not only heavily but wildly, with thunder that rattled the stained glass windows on the main staircase landing and lightning that cracked across the sky like something out of the old Boris Karloff *Frankenstein* movie. It was only six o'clock in the morning, and it felt like the middle of the night.

It also felt, as Gregor thought of it, impossible. It wasn't the weather that was the problem, but the house. What he agreed to all those months ago, when Bennis had wanted to buy the place, was that they would buy it and fix it up. Then, when it had been renovated, they would move in and put their own knocked-together apartments up for sale. The apartments were just up Cavanaugh Street, and Gregor felt nostalgic for them every waking moment of his life.

Part of the problem, he thought, as he stopped on the landing to listen to the rain, was that the house had not really *been* renovated. It was in the process of being renovated. All the upstairs halls had wood floors that felt oddly sandy when you walked on them. According to Bennis, this was because they had been "stripped," which was something you did to them before you put shiny stuff on them and called them done. All the bathrooms but one had tiles missing from their walls and floors and fixtures that might or might not be fixed. The kitchen ceiling was mostly gone. The living room looked like the back office of a carpet and tile store, where all the samples were kept in a jumble in case anybody needed them right away.

He came down the rest of the stairs and into the front hall. There were little stacks of material swatches lined up against the moldings near the front door and a bigger stack of Bennis's papier-mâché models for her last Zed and Zedalia book lying under the staircase newel. None of this debris was new, but for some reason it felt oddly more intrusive here than it had back at the apartment.

It was a very large house, owned for decades by an elderly woman who had had neither the resources nor the interest in keeping it up. Everything was wrong with the place. They had had to replace the furnace with something brand new. What was left of the old one wasn't even salvagable. They had had to rip out all the old wiring and put in new. It was a miracle that old Sophie Mgrdchian hadn't burned to death in her sleep. It was after they'd replaced the wiring that Bennis decided it was time to move in.

"I'll be right there where I can stay on top of things," she'd said.

Gregor thought that the reality was that they were right here where things could stay on top of them.

He went into the kitchen and opened the small, square "mini fridge" Bennis had bought to do for them until all the new appliances were delivered. The new appliances could not be delivered. The appliances could not be delivered until the kitchen was renovated. The kitchen would not be renovated until it was thoroughly gutted and then refloored. They also needed to find a new stamped tin ceiling and restore it over their heads.

Gregor sometimes had the feeling that a war zone would be less logistically problematic than this place.

He got out a small carton of cream and put it on the round table they used for everything. There were no kitchen counters left. He took a coffee bag out of a box on the table. He found his clean cup in the drainer next to the sink. The sink didn't look entirely bad. It was porcelain, and very old. It had stains and nicks all across its surface. Still, it looked like a sink.

He got the plug-in kettle from the same round table where he'd found almost everything else. He popped the lid open and held it under the high, curved faucet that reminded him of his elementary school. He turned on the cold water tap and watched as the entire fixture started to shake. A second later, the cap at the top between the two knobs flew off, followed by a geyser of water that reached up almost as high as the twenty-foot ceiling.

Gregor turned the water off and stared at the faucet. The metal cap had fallen to a clanking halt in another part of the room.

"I forgot to tell you," Bennis said from behind him. "We're having some plumbing done. The guy was here yesterday. Anyway, you have to hold the cap when you turn on the water or it, you know, does that."

"This was something we had done yesterday?"

"You were out doing whatever. Talking to the people at the Philadelphia FBI office? Something like that."

"Something like that."

"I should have told you," she said again. "I thought this would be a perfect time to do it. You know what I mean. You're going off tomorrow. You'll be away a week, you almost always are. Or longer. I thought it would be a good time to get some of the serious work done."

"What did you intend to do if I didn't go off somewhere?" Gregor asked. "I don't always go out of town to work. Are you going to be able to live in this place on your own if there isn't any plumbing?"

"There will be plumbing," Bennis said. "It just won't be elegant plumbing. I know this seems like a lot of work, and a monumental inconvenience, but it really will be wonderful when it's done. It's hard to find places like this right in the middle of the city. There are only a couple of them right here on Cavanaugh Street. It's just a matter of putting up with a little inconvenience now so that we have something better later. Deferred gratification. You're always talking about deferred gratification."

"It helps to know how long you're deferring it for," Gregor said. "The last I heard, this was going to take a couple of months. I think we may be past that by now."

Bennis ignored this, and took the kettle out of his hand. She put it down on the table and looked around, squinting her eyes in the dim light cast by the floor lamp she'd picked up at IKEA to make do until real lights could be restored. Then she said, "Aha," crossed to the other side of the room, and picked something up.

"Here it is," she said, coming back with the cap. "It would be a really good idea not to lose this if we could possibly manage it." She put the cap back into the center of the faucet fixture, held it down, and then started the water running. "Hand me the kettle," she said.

Gregor handed her the kettle. Bennis stuck it under the flow of water, waited until it was as filled as it was allowed to get, and then handed the kettle back to Gregor. Then she turned off the faucet with her finally free hand.

"There," she said. "It's not all that difficult once you get used to it."

"Ten years at hard labor isn't all that difficult once you get used to it," Gregor said. "But I wouldn't want to try it."

"Oh, Gregor. It isn't going to take ten years. It isn't going to take ten months, not the difficult parts of it, anyway. I know it looks like a mess, but it always does until it's over. And besides. I thought you had work to do. I thought this was a big, important case you were working on. At least, that's the way you made it sound when you got that call about it."

"I don't know that I'd say it was important, exactly," Gregor said. "Not anymore. It's an historical oddity, though. It's important to the Bureau, because the original case was important. It wasn't something I worked on when I was there."

"Still, you're interested in it," Bennis said. "I don't mean to be vague or flippant about it. It's just that I have my mind on other things. It would be a good idea if you had your mind on other things, too. That way, we wouldn't get in each other's hair. Or something."

Bennis had been putting coffee bags into cups and then water on top of them. She handed a cup to Gregor and went to the kitchen door. The thunder and lightning were still going on full blast. The day outside looked darker than it should have for this time of year.

Bennis opened the kitchen door and looked out. Wind blew rain into the house and into her face.

"What are you doing?" Gregor asked. "It's a mess out there."

Bennis was still standing with the door open. "I don't know," she said. "I heard something odd a minute ago. When I was in the bathroom."

"Of course you heard something odd out there. It's an absolute mess."

Bennis closed the door. "It wasn't that kind of something odd," she said. "I don't know what it was. It just sounded wrong."

"That's the kind of thing you say that I never know how to respond to," Gregor said. "Are you coming to the Ararat? I told Tibor we'd meet him."

"I'll come in a bit. Donna's supposed to be here any minute to help me with some things about the wallpaper. I really do hate wallpaper, but sometimes it seems to be the only answer. You can't take apart plaster walls the way you do Sheetrock. I never thought I'd say it, but I'm beginning to feel kindly about Sheetrock."

"I'm not a hundred percent certain I know what Sheetrock is," Gregor said. "I'm going to go on over. Tibor and I will keep you a place."

Bennis went back to the kitchen door, and opened it, and looked out. The wind was making a high-pitched whine.

Bennis closed the door again. "I really wish I knew what that noise was," she said.

Gregor hadn't heard anything to wonder about, so he finished off his coffee and headed back to the stairs to find a Windbreaker and an umbrella.

2

It was June. Gregor was sure it could not be really cold in late June, and that the rain could not be half sleet hitting his face like tiny needles—but that's what it felt like, and the world was so dark, it almost seemed plausible. He kept his head down and his eyes on the sidewalk. He knew his way to the Ararat by instinct, even from this direction. He wished the day were less than terminally depressing, as if it mattered what the weather was.

Through the Ararat's broad front plate glass window, Gregor could see Father Tibor Kasparian sitting in their usual booth, little stacks of papers spread out across the long, wide surface. The wind started picking up again. Gregor pulled the hood of his Windbreaker farther up over his head and went inside.

As soon as he stepped through the door, a dozen heads looked up from half as many tables, noted who had come in, and went back to whatever they had been doing. Linda Melajian rushed out from the swinging door at the back with a coffeepot in one hand.

"There you are," she said. "Father Tibor keeps asking if I've seen you, which makes absolutely no sense, because with where he's sitting, he'd see you before I did."

She went to the booth and unearthed a cup and saucer from under Father Tibor's papers. She filled the cup and looked around for the little metal basket of sugar packets. She didn't find it, and went hurrying off to get another one from the kitchen.

Gregor sat down and pushed the papers around a bit. The little metal basket turned out to be on the stack between Tibor and the window. Tibor picked it up and put it back.

"I needed the space, Krekor," he said, waving at the stacks of papers.

"What is all this?" Gregor asked.

"It's the Problem," Tibor said. "For a while there, I was beginning to think no papers really existed. I thought they'd made up the entire issue of the papers. It would make perfect sense, considering everything."

Gregor picked up one of the papers and looked at it. Long ago—so long ago, he almost never remembered it anymore—he had trained to be an accountant. That was in the days when special agents of the FBI had had to be either accountants or lawyers, which said a lot about what old J. Edgar had thought his Bureau would be doing. It had been a long time, though. His skills were out of date. He had no idea if he had any skills left at all.

"Bennis isn't here?" Tibor said.

"She's back at the house, waiting for Donna to bring something," Gregor said. "I'm not entirely sure what."

"Does the house look like it might be finished soon?"

"The house looks like it might be finished in the twenty-second century. Last night, I found paint samples in bed. And there's something about wallpaper, which Bennis hates, but she thinks we have to have."

"You'll be going away for a while," Tibor said. "Maybe she'll get a lot done and you'll come back to perfection. What is it they say when they work out? No pain, no gain."

"Today, I tried to turn on the faucet in the kitchen sink, and I blew off this little cap thing and water went spurting all over the ceilings. And you know those ceilings. They're twenty feet high."

"Yes," Tibor said. "Well."

Linda Melajian came back to the table. "Do you want a breakfast menu, or shall I just get you your usual cholesterol bomb? Bennis isn't here, so I assume we're going for the whole bacon, sausage, hash browns, three scrambled eggs extravaganza."

"At least I come here," Gregor said. "I could go to

Denny's or IHOP and get bacon ice cream sundaes, whatever those are."

"There isn't either of those close enough for you to get to unless you start driving, and I'm not expecting that anytime soon. I'll be back in a bit."

Linda took off, and Gregor watched her go. She was the youngest of the Melajian girls, but that didn't mean she was very young anymore. And she ran the entire restaurant for breakfast.

Gregor looked back at the papers. "So?" he said.

Tibor nodded. "We're up to six now. The Arkanian family out in Wynne. I remember when they came from Armenia. That was maybe five years ago."

"Speak English?"

"Yes and no, Krekor, you know how it is. They spoke English well enough to get by. And we told them when we came that we would be there to help them if there were things they wanted to do. Things like buying a house. I don't understand why these people don't come to us and ask for help. Russ Donahue would have looked over the loan papers for them. I would have looked over the loan papers. I know nothing about the law, and I could see what was wrong with these."

Tibor pointed his finger at one of the little stacks, and Gregor picked it up. He read the entire page through, stopped, and then read it again.

"This doesn't make any sense," he said.

"That's what I said the first time I saw one of those," Tibor said. "It doesn't make any sense. But of course it does make sense, you just don't believe it. And it gets worse, the more of the document you read. This is not a matter of people taking on more mortgage debt than they could handle, getting greedy for a house bigger than they could afford. I think this amounts to deliberate fraud."

Gregor picked up the stack of papers again, read through the page again, then turned to the next page and read about half of that one. He put the stack down again. "It certainly is something," he said.

"And it gets worse," Tibor said. "There is the matter of the ownership of the loan."

Gregor picked up the papers again. "NationReady Mortgage Finance," he said.

"Maybe," Tibor said.

Gregor cocked an eyebrow. "Maybe?"

Tibor sighed. "For hundreds of years, Krekor, if you bought real estate in this country, you got the deed and you took it to your local assessor's office and you filed it. With pieces of paper, you understand. But these people, these people like NationReady, they did not do that. They used instead a national digital database of deeds."

"All right," Gregor said. "That's not necessarily awful. It's a digital age. Something like that was going to happen eventually."

"Yes, possibly, Krekor, but in this case, it does not seem to have been competently run. The mortgages were all bought and sold in packages, and they were bought and sold very quickly, sometimes several times a day. And not all the transactions were properly recorded. So in some cases, nobody knows who owns the mortgage or who owns the house or who has a right to foreclose."

"Well, that could be good news," Gregor said. "If they can't figure out who owns the mortgage, then it shouldn't be possible to foreclose on the house."

"Shouldn't be, but that is not the way it is working out," Tibor said. "We have been warned by the state attorney general's office that NationReady and some of the banks have tried to foreclose on properties they could not prove they owned. If the buyer and his lawyer are not very sophisticated about these things, they sometimes miss that. People are forced out of their homes by people who have no right to force them out because they don't own the mortgage to begin with, and nobody knows who does. But if you get forced out, it's almost impossible to get back in again."

"My God," Gregor said. "This sounds like a Monty Python sketch."

"Yes, Krekor, I know. But without the funny. And that's not the end of it, either."

"What more could there be?"

"The loan officers who set up these mortgages got paid on the basis of how many mortgages they made. So sometimes, when the buyer didn't have the right credentials for a mortgage, the loan officer would change the application so that the numbers fit. They would change the income, for instance, or say there was no credit card debt when there was."

"You're sure the loan officers did this? People didn't just lie on their applications?"

"First the loan officers tried to get the people to lie on the application themselves, but if they wouldn't, the loan officers would make the changes themselves later."

"That's bank fraud," Gregor said. "You can go to Federal prison for that."

"Yes, Krekor, I know," Tibor said, "but nobody is going to prison for it that I know of, and I have six families in foreclosure, all of them here from Armenia less than a decade. And we helped to bring them to America, Krekor, we are responsible to them. Two of these families are out on the street already, and we've had to find them accommodations elsewhere. And everybody has been very good about pitching in, but this is getting to be more than we can handle. And the legal things—*tcha*."

Linda Melajian came back with two plates, both of them the full cholesterol extravaganza, as she put it. She looked at the papers strewn everywhere and hesitated. Gregor and Tibor hurried to push papers out of the way.

"Don't worry about getting them out of order, Krekor," Tibor said. "There is no such thing as 'in order' with these things."

Linda put the plates down and looked into their coffee cups. "I'll be back with the pot," she said, "and if that's the mortgage stuff, I still say you should just dynamate Nation-Ready and get it over with. We've got a whole family staying in our back apartment, and the grandmother keeps threatening to commit suicide. Not that I think she means it, mind you, but this is ridiculous."

"It is criminal," Tibor said.

"Be right back," Linda said.

Gregor watched her go and then looked back at the papers. "You'd think there would be something you could do about outright fraud," he said. "I know half a dozen first-rate Federal fraud investigators from at least four agencies who would love to bring down a big operation like NationReady."

"NationReady has been bought by CountriBank."

"They'd love to bring down that, too. You don't know what these guys are like. Woman, in one case. They live to bring down big operations, especially if the operations are supposed to be respectable banks. They really hate banks."

"They can hate banks all they want, Krekor, but that will not get these people back into their houses. And we are now stuck trying to make sure no more of them are forced out. It is not so simple as it sounds like it ought to be."

"Maybe I'll go talk to one of those people for you," Gregor said.

"I would much appreciate it," Tibor said. "I don't think you will do much good, you understand, but I would appreciate it."

"Of course it would do some good," Gregor said positively, picking up his fork and attacking his sausage.

He always went for the sausage first, because it was the first thing Bennis wanted to take away from him when she saw he wasn't breakfasting on fruit.

3

An hour later, with no sign of Bennis or Donna at the Ararat, Gregor walked back home to pick up his briefcase. The storm had died down. The wind was no longer violent. There was no more thunder. There was no lightning in the sky. The drizzle was still coming down, though, and it still felt cold.

Gregor went in through the front door of the house, because that was the place where the house looked most "done." It was a beautiful entry, really, with a glass-inlaid door and a brass knob and knocker. As far as he could tell, Bennis didn't intend to do anything at all about the building's facade.

He let himself into the foyer, stepped over a stack of tiles, and took his Windbreaker off. There was an old-fashioned coat stand right there in the corner. Bennis had picked it up at an antique store somewhere or the other. He put his Windbreaker over that and headed for the back of the house.

"Bennis?" he said. "Are you all right? You never made it to the Ararat."

He went past little mounds of bathroom fixtures, puddles of carpet samples, stacks of "home plan ideas" magazines that he was sure Bennis had never read. He let himself into the kitchen and heard a sudden, inhuman shriek.

Bennis was sitting on one of the chairs, holding a small, impossibly frantic animal in her lap. It looked like nothing Gregor had ever seen before. It was skeletal and matted. It was twisting around like it had no bones at all.

Bennis stood up and thrust it under a pile of blankets on the table. When Gregor looked again, he could see that the pile had actually been shaped into a little blanket cave. Shrieks came from the center of it, and the whole pile seemed to shake.

"What was that?" Gregor asked.

Bennis sat down again. "It's a cat," she said. "It's a very small cat, and it's half dead. Donna and I found it under the back porch with what was probably its mother and two litter mates. They were all dead."

"All right," Gregor said. "So you brought it in here. I didn't think you liked cats."

"I don't mind them," Bennis said. "And we couldn't just leave it out there to die. We called the vet, and we've given it something to eat, but Donna went to get a cat carrier so that we can get it some medical attention. The vet says it sounds like it might be feral."

"Which means?"

"Cats that have gone back to the wild, who have never lived with people. But if the mother cat had the litter under our front porch, the kittens might not have seen people but the mother cat might have, so—"

"All right, I can see that."

"It is all right, Gregor, I promise you. I don't intend to stick you with a cat. We're just going to take it to the vet's and then when it's all right medically, we'll feed it for a while and find somebody to adopt it. Maybe Tibor can adopt it. He likes cats. And the apartment is big enough."

"You'll have to ask Tibor about that," Gregor said. "And the cat seems to be reemerging."

Bennis got up to look. The cat was coming out on very wobbly legs. She picked it up and held it close to her chest, stroking its head. It curled up against her, and its shaking seemed to get less violent.

"Well," Gregor said.

"Oh, I know," Bennis said. "You think I've gone completely out of my mind. But it's really not anything like that. And I promise you, the house will not take forever."

The kitchen door rattled and Donna Moradanyan Donahue burst in, carrying three cat carriers and another pile of blankets, and being trailed by a small boy who looked as if his day had suddenly become not boring.

TWO

1

Gregor Demarkian always thought of Patrick Hallihan as living "in Philadelphia." Technically, however, Patrick lived in a township just past the proper city limits, in a big apartment complex that stretched out across blocks like an upscale housing project. The name of the apartment complex was Drexelbrook, and Gregor tended to think of the entire town by that same name. He had no idea if this was right or not. The cabdrivers knew how to get him to Drexelbrook, and that was all that mattered.

Of course, a cab all the way out here was enormously expensive, but for some reason Gregor didn't care this morning. This morning the sky was black and everything looked apocalyptically dismal. Gregor was sure that somewhere, somehow, Cassandra had returned in the flesh to warn the populace about the coming doom.

The cab left him at the curb. The building was a bit of a walk down a narrow concrete pathway. Gregor wished he'd brought his Windbreaker as well as his umbrella.

He went down the path and into the foyer. The fresh flowers were really there. The air-conditioning was on much too high. He went to the call board and buzzed Patrick's apartment, only to get a lilting female voice saying, "If that's you, prove it."

Gregor said, "Good morning, Lillian. I don't know how to prove it."

"Honestly, Gregor," Lillian said. "You wouldn't know you'd been in the FBI for twenty years. You wouldn't know it about Patrick, either. Don't either of you ever watch television?"

Gregor made his way across the lobby to the elevators. When the elevator doors opened, he punched the button for the third floor. The lobby itself was absolutely empty, and it had been absolutely empty every single time Gregor was ever in it. In fact, now that he thought of it, every apartment building lobby he had ever been in was empty, except the ones with doormen, and those didn't count. It made him wonder why there were apartment building lobbies.

When he came off the elevator, Patrick was standing in the hall waiting for him, holding open the door of his apartment. Gregor shook the water off his shoulders and hurried up a little.

"I think I'm losing my mind," he said. "I'm thinking about apartment building lobbies."

"What?" Patrick said.

"And Bennis has a cat," Gregor said.

Patrick stepped back to let Gregor through the door. "I wouldn't have thought Bennis was a cat person," he said.

"She isn't," Gregor said. "She found it under our porch. It looked half dead, so she brought it inside. It was pitiful."

Lillian was putting out a coffeepot and cups on the living room coffee table. She was all dressed up like a housewife in a '50s sitcom.

"You two should watch television," she said. "You'd find out how you're supposed to behave. I've never known a law enforcement officer in my life who knew how to behave."

"She watches *CSI*," Patrick said. "I try to talk her out of it."

"I left all that stuff on the wingback chair," Lillian said. "I'm going to run out to the grocery store. You'd think once you people retired, you'd stay retired."

Gregor and Patrick waited while Lillian went through the door to another room and then reemerged in a good London Fog raincoat. She waggled her fingers at them and headed out the front door.

Then Patrick looked at Gregor and shrugged.

"You might as well sit down and have some coffee," he said. "I don't know how much use I'm going to be able to be to you. It's been a long time."

Gregor sat down on the love seat. Patrick sat down on the couch. They both looked at the stack of papers and notebooks and journals on the wingback chair. Then Patrick picked up the coffeepot and started pouring.

"So," he said, "I take it this is official. You've been hired to look into this."

"I've been hired as a consultant by the Alwych Police Department, yes," Gregor said, "to help them look into what really does seem to be the deliberate and planned murder of Chapin Waring. The deliberate and planned murder of a ghost, was what the police chief told me when he called. Then I got a call from the Bureau's New York office, asking me to be their liaison, or something. I insisted that Alwych had to know up front. Nobody was happy, but everybody's going forward at the moment."

"Well, you can't really blame the New York office," Patrick said, handing Gregor his full cup. "It was one of the most famous cases they've had since the sixties, and the best anybody will say about it is that they botched it. That I botched it. You do know that was the reason I retired?"

"I'd heard something about it."

"Elizabeth may have been sick then," Patrick said. "I always forget that you spent the last year on the job more than a little distracted. Even though part of me says that there wasn't anything we could have done that we didn't do. You don't come into a bank robbery case thinking that the bank robbers are a couple of rich kids who happen to be bored."

"Is that what you think happened? Chapin Waring and this other person—"

"Martin Veer."

"Martin Veer. They were bored?"

"Well, Gregor, what else would it have been? We looked into them at the time it all blew up in our faces, but there wasn't any indication that either of them needed money. And then, you know, the whole thing was just bizarre."

"The whole thing?"

Patrick nodded vigorously. "The Bureau got called in on the bank robberies on the third one. Not that we weren't investigating the first two, because we were, but the third one was what started the special investigation. Before that, it looked to us like normal bank robberies. Except it didn't."

"This isn't making sense," Gregor said.

"There were two bank robberies in two different towns in Connecticut, Fairfield and Greenwich. Two perpetrators, both dressed head to toe in black like they were in some commando ops movie. They went in. They waved guns around. They got the money and put it into their own bags. That was interesting right there, because we were just starting to use those paint things that blow up and turn all the money blue, and they knew enough to protect themselves from it. Anyway, they got their money and then they shot up the place. They put a bunch of bullet holes in the ceiling and the walls. Then they got out. The whole thing, both times, took less than three full minutes. And when they were gone, they were gone."

"Nobody saw two people dressed all in black like commandos wandering around in the streets?"

"Nope. Greenwich is pretty built up for a suburban town, and it was even then. But nobody saw a thing."

"What about surveillance cameras?"

"This was thirty years ago," Patrick said. "They had them, but they didn't have nearly as many as they do now. We did get some surveillance footage. I've included whatever is in the public domain in that stack of stuff over there. I'm sure New York will give you the rest. There isn't much of it. But that's weird, too."

"Why?"

"Because"—Patrick shook his head—"it's hard to put

your finger on. The cameras weren't as good then. So maybe I'm just fussing around about nothing. Try to get New York to give you the actual feed. Look at the film so that you can see them in motion. That's all I'm going to say. I never knew if I was actually seeing something or if I was imagining things. You tell me."

"What happened with the third one?" Gregor asked.

"They crossed state lines," Patrick said. "The third and the fourth ones were in New York State, in Westchester. Not that that's much of a drive. Greenwich is right on the border with Port Chester. The third robbery was a bank in Rye, the fourth was a bank in Armonk. Armonk was a bit of a drive."

"Same routine?"

"Yep. Same routine, and same problems for us. You'd think somebody would have seen something somewhere. It was the middle of the summer, for God's sake. Who walks around in black turtlenecks in summer? You'd figure we would have gotten something. But there was nothing. Then there was number five."

Gregor nodded. "The one where somebody got killed."

"Two people," Patrick said. "Same routine, same complete lack of anybody seeing anything, but when they got to the part where they shot the place up, they ended up hitting two people, a bank guard and a high school kid waiting in line to make a deposit from his first job. Their names are in all that, too. It was in Westport, Connecticut. The Fairfield County Savings Bank."

Gregor considered this. "You're sure it was accidental, that somebody died?"

"It was either accidental, or it was done just for kicks. We've never been able to find out. We didn't have a single lead as to who killed them, or who had been robbing those banks. It would have been the biggest news story in town, if the accident hadn't happened the same damned night."

Gregor tried to process this. "Accident," he said. "I did hear something about an accident."

"Of course you did," Patrick said. "When a bunch of rich Fairfield County teenagers smash up a car and one of them is killed, it's going to be bigger news in the New York ADI than the bank robberies were, even with two people dead. There were six people in the car. Martin Veer was driving. Chapin Waring was in the backseat. Then there were four more, don't remember the names off the top of my head. Martin Veer was killed. Two of the others were treated for injuries. There was a big, enormous explosion, and four days later there was a funeral. It was a big funeral. It made all the local news stations and it made CBS in New York. There was this one clip they kept running over and over again, of Chapin Waring putting a rose into the ground where the casket was. And that's what did it."

"Did what?"

"We had a special agent then—she died a few years ago, unfortunately, breast cancer—her name was Sarah Havermack. She was watching one of those clips when she realized that the Waring girl looked familiar. She checked it out, and sure enough, there was no mistaking it. Chapin Waring was one of the two people in the bank surveillance footage. It wasn't even hard to tell."

"You say one of them," Gregor said. "The other was Martin Veer?"

Patrick hesitated. "Martin Veer is very definitely the other one in the fifth robbery film."

"You think he wasn't the one in the other robberies? It was her every single time, but not the same second person every single time?"

Patrick shrugged. "I don't know. I wish I did. Look at the video yourself and see what you think. But we never found any evidence that any of the other kids in that car, or any of the kids Waring and Veer hung around with, had anything to do with any of it, so the official explanation has always been that it was just those two."

"Did you go after Waring right away?"

"As soon as Sarah figured it out," Patrick said. "We just weren't fast enough. We got there two days after the funeral, and by then Chapin Waring had disappeared into thin air. She was gone. Completely gone. And so was all the money."

Gregor considered this. "It's not that easy to drop out of sight carrying—what? A couple of hundred thousand in cash?"

"Two and a half," Patrick said.

"Okay, two and a half," Gregor said. "People are suspicious when you show up with wads of bills, and they were just as suspicious thirty years ago. She couldn't have just waltzed off and thrown the money around. She had to have help."

"I know."

"But?"

"We never found any trace of it," Patrick said. "And we've been looking. We've been looking for years. We've never caught any communication between her and her family. We've never caught any communication between her and the other kids who were in the car that night. And that's not all."

"Could this actually get worse?"

"Indeed it could," Patrick said. "We've had her featured a total of five times on *America's Most Wanted*. We came up absolutely blank. We didn't even get any false reports."

"Seriously."

"Absolutely. And you've seen pictures of her, Gregor. She's a striking-looking woman. It's not like she looks like everybody else on the planet, or has the kind of face you wouldn't notice. She was just gone, vanished, transported to another dimension. That's the joke we used to make about it. I always thought she was dead."

"But here she is," Gregor said.

"Right," Patrick said. "With a knife in her back."

"Do you think the Bureau knows where she's been?"

"If they did, they would have announced it," Patrick said. "I've still got contacts where it matters. I'll guarantee you there's been nothing to find. She disappeared. She stayed disappeared. She showed up one day in June and ended up dead in her own family's living room. And nobody has any idea where she's been or what she's been doing, and when she finally did show up, she was armed."

"We're sure it was her gun she had on her when she died?"

"Well," Patrick said. "It wasn't registered to anybody, if that's what you mean. I've heard it had her fingerprints on it. Like I said, I've still got contacts where it matters."

"What's that over on the chair?" Gregor asked.

"Those are my notes," Patrick said. "Including the diary I kept at the time. I've got copies of all of them, don't worry, and I've scanned them into the computer. I was thinking I might write a book on the case. It would be a good case to write a book on, don't you think?"

"It would be better if we could figure out what happened."

2

Gregor hailed a cab and the driver was adamant about how much it would cost to get him to Cavanaugh Street. But Gregor could afford it and a bus ride would be bumpy and uncomfortable. Once the cab took off, he opened his briefcase and looked at the material in it briefly. There was a little manila envelope full of pictures, and he took that out to look through them. Most of the pictures were close to useless, grainy old-time surveillance photographs that had been taken from above the crowd and were therefore only minimally useful. Gregor thought the actual moving surveillance tapes had to be better, or he couldn't see how anybody could have recognized Chapin Waring, or anybody else. As it was, some of the pictures looked odd—in a way he couldn't put his finger on. He wondered if that was what Patrick had meant about there being something wrong with the photographs of the second robber.

There were also other pictures in the envelope, pictures of Chapin Waring and Martin Veer from their senior year high school yearbook, pictures of them at what notes on the backs indicated was Chapin Waring's coming-out party, pictures of them with a group of other kids their own age at some beach somewhere. What wasn't from their high school yearbook seemed to have come from newspapers. The *Alwych Town Times* had produced a lot of them.

Gregor gave some of his attention to the other kids in the photographs. They were almost always the same other kids. Hope Matlock. Kyle Westervan. Tim Brand. Virginia Brand. On one of the photographs, Patrick had circled the picture of Virginia Brand and written: *VB Westervan, USHR.*

Gregor was about to go looking for what that meant when the neighborhood around him began to look more familiar. He pushed the papers back into his briefcase and locked it up. They passed his old building, which looked as if nobody lived there anymore. With three of the five floors now unoccupied, Gregor wasn't surprised.

They passed the church, which also looked unoccupied, but that wasn't unusual for a midweek afternoon. They passed the Ararat, which looked very occupied indeed. All the lights were on. Linda Melajian and one of her sisters were rushing back and forth between the tables. The tables were packed. Everybody on Cavanaugh Street seemed to have decided that a stormy day was a good day to get out of the house and have a little lunch.

Gregor had the cab take him to his own front door. The place looked almost as deserted as everything else did, except that there was a dim light shining in the front window. Either Bennis was home, or she had left a light shining for him, as if he were in danger of being lost at sea.

Gregor got out of the cab and paid the driver. The rain fell down on the back of his neck in drips and drops that made his skin crawl more than just a little. He ran up the front steps, tried the doorknob, and found that it was open.

It never failed. He could never get the people of Cavanaugh Street to understand that the fact that Cavanaugh Street felt safe did not mean that Cavanaugh Street was actually safe.

He let himself inside and looked around. He checked the living room and the dining room and the hall closets. He looked into the kitchen. Nothing seemed to have been disturbed, and there were no bodies lying anywhere, bloodied and half dead. Of course, there might be a body upstairs, but Gregor had a better idea.

He stopped in the kitchen and sat down in one of the chairs near the overloaded table. He took out his cell phone and punched in the speed-dial number for the Ararat. It was old Mrs. Melajian who answered the phone. She was too frail to wait tables these days, and much too frail to cook, but she oversaw the kitchen and answered the phone.

"I will go look," she said when Gregor asked her if Bennis was there.

Gregor waited, looking at his briefcase as it lay on the table. Bennis had bought him that briefcase one year—he couldn't remember whether it was Christmas or his birthday. He often had a difficult time remembering things about what he had done with Bennis, and when. He found it odd, because he had no trouble at all remembering those things about his life with Elizabeth. Sometimes the differences made him uncomfortable, as if he was still committed to his first wife and hadn't completely come over to his second.

Of course, he could also remember a lot of what it had been like when Elizabeth was dying, and he had never even once forgotten she was dead.

Old Mrs. Melajian picked up the phone on her end and coughed into it. "Bennis is here, Krekor," she said. "She's here with Donna. I was born at the wrong time. I tell my daughter that every day."

Gregor had no idea what this meant.

"I will tell her you are coming," old Mrs. Melajian said. "If you are coming. If you are not coming—"

"Yes," Gregor said. "I'm coming. I'll be there in a minute."

Then he put down the phone and went out to the hall for his Windbreaker. He didn't have to dress up and look professional in the Ararat. Everybody there knew him already.

They liked to sound impressed about him to people outside the neighborhood, but they would never be impressed about him to his face.

He got the Windbreaker zipped and went back to the kitchen. He looked at the briefcase lying on the table. He considered taking it with him, to show Bennis the pictures. Bennis had been a debutante herself once. There were things she knew that other people didn't.

On the other hand, Bennis would be coming back to the house before the afternoon was over. There was no need to drag the briefcase to the Ararat now.

He left the briefcase where it was and headed out.

3

Ten minutes later, soaking wet from an angry cloudburst, Gregor was easing into the front booth next to Bennis and across from Donna Moradanyan Donahue. They both looked dry. They both looked impossibly depressed.

Gregor looked at his Windbreaker hanging from the coat tree. It was dripping thick drops of water on the floor.

"So," he said.

Bennis and Donna had coffee. They didn't seem to be drinking much of it.

"So," Bennis said. "We took the cat to the vet."

"I bought a cat carrier," Donna said. "Cats hate to ride in cars. You have to be very careful. And we didn't know about this one."

"It could have had rabies," Bennis said. "But the doctor doesn't think so. There are tests, you know, and he's going to run them, but he says he doesn't look like it. The cat doesn't look like it. It's a male cat."

"We thought we'd name it George," Donna said.

"Assuming we can name it anything," Bennis said. "It's in really bad shape."

"Half starved," Donna agreed, "if not all the way starved. And it's got fleas and all kinds of things like that. And it just looked so pitiful."

"And this is what the two of you are so depressed about?" he asked. "A cat? I didn't think either of you liked cats."

"We don't hate them," Bennis said. "And it's like I told you before, it was just such a—he was just so wretched. I don't know. People shouldn't do things like that. I mean, you've got a responsibility."

"What did people do?" Gregor asked, mystified. "Who has a responsibility."

"It makes perfect sense," Donna said. "Cats and dogs and other domesticated animals. We made them the way they are. We have a responsibility."

"Okay," Gregor said as Linda Melajian's older sister came rushing up to him with a pot of coffee. He tried to remember her name and couldn't. She turned his coffee cup right side up in the saucer and started pouring. "Start from the beginning."

"Do you need a menu?" the Melajian girl asked. "The lunch menu is pretty much like the dinner menu."

"Bring me some *yaprak sarma* in broth," Gregor said. He looked from Bennis to Donna. "Who domesticated them? And who has a responsibility for them?"

Bennis let out a long sigh. "Okay," she said. "It's really simple. Human beings took some animals and bred them deliberately to be good at living with human beings. Or for being good for being food for human beings. Cows in the wild wouldn't be that stupid, but there aren't any cows in the wild anymore, because we bred cows and now they're dumb and live on farms so that they can become hamburger."

"And sheep," Donna said.

"And cats and dogs," Bennis said firmly. "They're not really equipped to go back to the wild and fend for themselves. We've bred those traits out of them. So we're responsible, you see, to make sure they're taken care of, because we're what made them unfit to fend for themselves to begin with."

"Except that Father Tibor doesn't completely agree with

us," Donna said. "He says what we're suggesting is collective guilt, and guilt can never be legitimately collective. Guilt is always individual."

"We got a lecture on good and evil and guilt and innocence and tribalism and I don't know what else," Bennis said.

Donna nodded. "He even quoted Kant in German."

"So you see," Bennis said, "the one thing we didn't figure out was whether he'd be willing to take the cat if it turned out to be all right. Or, you know, take it later, after I'd fed it and stuff for a while so that it was stronger. He was stronger. Did we tell you we're going to name it George?"

"Yes," Gregor said.

"It really was awful to look at it," Bennis said. "It was so small, and so miserable, and it was shaking, and it was scared to death, and nothing we did seemed to make things all right. And then we got to the vet's and it really went crazy. It didn't like the vet at all, and it liked the vet even less when the work started, and then we had to leave it overnight."

"It's going to be longer than that," Donna said. "I think it's something like four days before they're sure it isn't sick, and it could be sick a lot of ways. Even if it doesn't have rabies, it could have feline leukemia, and I don't know what else. And that was what was getting to both of us, don't you see? The mother cat and the other cats out there under the porch dead because somebody abandoned them somewhere."

"Tibor said the mother cat could have wandered away and gotten lost," Bennis said, "but that's no excuse, is it? They've got chips they put in animals these days so that you can be sure to find them, and if you can't afford something like that, you can always afford a collar and a little tag with information on it. I mean, really, Gregor. It's just ridiculous."

"He quoted Aristotle in Greek," Donna said. "And then he quoted Jackie Collins and Stephen King. I didn't know what it was about by the time he was finished."

Linda Melajian herself popped up at the table, carrying an enormous bowl of *yaprak sarma*. She put it down in front of Gregor and then handed him a soup spoon.

"I hope you can cheer these two up," she said. "They've been driving me crazy for an hour."

THREE

1

On the last Saturday morning in June, one week after Chapin Waring was murdered, Hope Matlock woke up to the sound of the phone ringing. She had been lying more or less asleep on the pullout couch in her living room. The mattress in the pullout was thin and full of sharp pricks where the metal springs had begun to poke through the covering.

The phone rang and rang and rang.

Finally, the answering machine whirred on. Hope heard her own voice asking whomever to leave a message. Then there was a pause, and a chirpy little female voice said,

"Steve? This is Dr. Martinson's office. We're just calling to remind you that your appointment is at nine tomorrow morning, and it's important that you not be late. This kind of thing is manageable if we catch it in time, but it can get tricky. We'll see you in the morning."

The answering machine clicked off.

Hope lay still. She was not Steve. There was no Dr. Martinson anywhere in Alwych. Doctors' offices did not leave chatty little messages about dire medical problems.

Hope sat up on the couch bed and swung her legs off the

side of it. She never slept upstairs anymore. It was too hard to make the climb.

She stood up and braced herself against the side table. The side table wallowed.

The genius of using a doctor's office for the calls was that the urge to call back and explain that this was a wrong number was almost irresistible. You didn't want somebody to miss a doctor's appointment.

Hope was fairly sure there was a law against this kind of thing. Bill collectors in the state of Connecticut were supposed to announce who they were and that they were attempting to collect a debt.

Hope walked through the back of the house, through the dining room, into the kitchen. She let herself into the big bathroom next to the pantry and the back door. She washed up and looked very carefully at herself in the mirror. She looked terrible.

She went back to the kitchen. The newspapers were spread across the peeling surface of the laminated wood table. Most of them had stories about chapin Waring's murder, complete with big inside spreads about the case all those years ago. There were pictures of Martin's car smashed up against that tree out on Wykeham Swamp Road. There were pictures of Chapin herself and the rest of them the year before in their Harvest Ball getups. There were even pictures of Chapin standing at the graveside at Martin's funeral.

Martin. None of them had ever called him Martin. They had always called him Marty.

Some of the newspapers were more recent, and these contained stories about Gregor Demarkian. Hope had heard of Gregor Demarkian. God only knew she watched enough television. He was on all those truTV shows. *American Justice. City Confidential.*

She looked over the papers again. There would probably be another paper waiting on her front walk.

Hope went back into the foyer. There was sun coming in through the window next to the door.

One of the pictures in the newspapers in the kitchen was of Chapin Waring on the floor of her family's old house on Beach Drive. You could see the knife sticking up out of one shoulder.

Hope stopped at the telephone. There was a stout boxy stool near the television stand. She sat down. She picked up the metal flip address book. She pushed the little level to w. She hesitated between "home" and "cell" and finally picked cell. This was an emergency.

Kyle Westervan's voice came on the line sounding both angry and hungover. She cleared her throat a little.

"Kyle?"

"Oh, for Christ's sake," he said.

"I haven't been stalking you," Hope said. "I haven't called at all."

"But you were going to," Kyle said. "I knew you were going to. Why can't you leave it the hell alone?"

Hope hesitated. "That isn't what I was calling about," she said.

"Really?" Kyle said. "Because it's what everybody else has been calling about. I've had Virginia up my ass like some gay man's chipmunk. And she's not even supposed to be talking to me."

"Yes," Hope said. "Well."

"Well, what?"

"I've been thinking about that conversation we had. About your offer. If it's still open."

"What?"

"I know I said no before, but circumstances have changed."

"Circumstances have changed," Kyle said. "For Christ's sake. Yes, of course circumstances have changed. That ass-hole is arriving any day now, and the place has been crawling with feds ever since Chapin's body hit the floor. Chapin was always a pain in the ass. She was a pain in the ass from the day she was born."

"I thought you said that whatever this is hasn't got anything to do with Chapin."

"It hasn't got anything to do with Chapin."

"Well, then."

There was a long silence on the other end of the line. When Kyle's voice came back, it didn't have the flippant nastiness Hope had come to think of as "normal." It was low and hard and very serious.

"Listen," he said. "Forget about it. Forget we ever talked about it. You never knew what it was about anyway."

Hope took a deep breath and closed her eyes. "You mean the offer has been withdrawn."

"The offer has to be withdrawn," Kyle said. "Like you said, the circumstances have changed."

"Then it was about Chapin Waring," Hope said.

"No," Kyle said. "It wasn't, but everything is about Chapin Waring now."

The phone went dead in her ear. Hope hung up at her end.

She got up off the stool and headed back to the kitchen. She didn't have a lot in the refrigerator, but she had some, and she needed to eat.

She was going through the dining room when she felt her heart begin to squeeze. It wasn't bad this time. She'd get to her pills in the kitchen and that would take care of it.

She got to the kitchen and stopped. The newspapers were still spread out on the kitchen table. Chapin Waring's face still stared up at the ceiling from almost every page.

The squeezing in her heart stopped. Her lungs filled with air. It wasn't her heart, or her weight. It was the fear.

And now that the fear was gone, she felt just fine.

2

From the beginning, Caroline Waring Holder had been convinced that she could make everything come right if she could only get herself to concentrate.

"If you're going to have a funeral for her out there, I'm not coming," Caroline's sister Cordelia had said before Chapin's body was even cold.

Cordelia was in Chicago, and she called herself Dr.

Cordelia Frame. If she had any connection to the infamous Chapin Waring, nobody had to know about it.

"It's not like I'm going to be able to get out from under this completely," she said. "They'll figure out who I am sooner rather than later. That doesn't mean I have to make it any easier for them."

Caroline wanted to scream. "It's not like I asked her here. It's not like I wanted her here. The two of you have seen more of her than I have over the last thirty years."

"I haven't seen anything of her," Cordelia said stiffly, "and if you tell anybody I have, I'll sue you for slander."

"I've worked very hard myself," Caroline had said. "I hate it when you act like you're the only person in the world who has anything to lose."

"Well, playing fifties housewifey in the Connecticut suburbs isn't exactly in the same league as making a name for yourself in medicine."

"The first I heard of it was when I went to a meeting that night, and Lisa Freedman and Deirdre Nash kept going on and on about how they'd seen her all over town. By then she must have been lying dead in the house on Beach Drive."

"We've been very careful to make sure it's well kept up. You can't fault us for that," Cordelia said.

Caroline could fault her sisters for a lot of things, and she did not exclude the fate of the house on Beach Drive.

"You two should have sold it," she said.

"It was what Mother wanted," Cordelia said. "We wouldn't have kept it otherwise."

"Whatever."

"I'm not coming to a funeral," Cordelia said. "I don't care what you do with her body. I'm glad she's dead. Maybe the FBI will take the taps off my phones."

Caroline had wanted to say that she wasn't going to hold any funeral, and that Cordelia had no proof that the FBI had ever tapped her phones. But Cordelia had hung up, and Caroline was left sitting at her own kitchen table, looking down at nails she had bitten to the quick.

Her other sister had called last week.

"Don't listen to Cor," Charlotte had said. "Of course we'll have to bury her. It will make a bigger stink in the press if we don't. And of course we'll have to do something to keep the funeral from turning into an absolute zoo."

"We can't have her cremated at the moment," Caroline had said, "and we can't have her buried, because the medical examiner's office still has the body. There has to be an autopsy, and if the two of you think I'm arranging and running a funeral neither of you have any intention of showing up to attend, you're both crazy."

"Of course I'll attend," Charlotte said. "Why wouldn't I attend?"

"According to Cordelia, attending would ruin her life."

"Oh, for God's sake," Charlotte said. "You've got to arrange the funeral. You're the one that's there."

"Come back here and arrange it yourself."

"Don't be ridiculous. Just get it done and we'll come out and support you."

"I'm not going to arrange the funeral," Caroline said again.

By then Charlotte, too, was off the line, and Caroline was back at that same kitchen table, looking at the double ovens and the granite countertops, wanting to scream.

This morning she didn't so much want to scream as want to melt. The phone had been busy the entire seven or eight days, and none of the messages had been what Caroline would call "supportive." Most of them were from the women she knew from the organizations she participated in. The women from the League of Women Voters, the PTA and the Enrichment committee, the Food Pantry in Bridgeport and the Literacy Volunteers of America in Norwalk.

Caroline hadn't realized that she knew so many women, or that she was as distant and antagonistic to them as she'd ever been to the girls she'd known at Miss Porter's School.

Now it had been a week, or eight days, or whatever, and she was still sitting at that kitchen table, as if she'd never moved. The young officer from the police department was standing in front of her, holding his hat in his hand. She'd asked him to sit down, but he had refused. He had come with a big sheaf of papers he had put down on the table when he first came in.

He looked like he was squirming.

"We don't want to be insensitive," he said, clearing his throat for the fourth or fifth time. "We do have to follow procedure. We will be ready to release the body on this coming Thursday—"

"Why Thursday?"

"It's because of the consultant we hired," he said. "Just in case he wants to, you know, look things over himself."

"This is this Gregor Demarkian person."

"Yes, ma'am."

"Is he a pathologist?"

"I don't know, ma'am. But he will be here on Monday, and then we need to ask him what he needs. It's for your own good as well as ours. If we don't get this thing cleared up—"

"This thing hasn't been cleared up for thirty years. What makes you think you're going to clear it up now?"

"I think the point is to clear up the murder," the officer said. "The thing is, we have to release the body to the next of kin. That's the law. And you're the next of kin. I'm sorry to intrude on what I know must be a difficult time."

"Do they teach you to say things like that at the police academy?"

"Excuse me?"

"Never mind," Caroline said.

"I'll just be going," the officer said.

"What happens if I won't take the body?" Caroline said.

The officer stopped his slow backward crab walk to the door. He looked totally flabbergasted. "But you have to take the body," he said. "You're the next of kin. The next of kin always takes the body."

"Surely there are some bodies that have no next of kin," Caroline said. "Surely you run across murder victims or accident victims you can't identify. I'm sure you don't let them just sit in a cold box in the morgue for fifty years."

"Oh," the officer said. "Oh. No. We have procedure for John Does. But those are John Does. Nobody knows who they are."

"And nobody wants this one," Caroline said.

"Oh," the officer said. He took a great, big breath. "You don't really have to decide until Thursday."

"Once the body's gone, I can finally get that woman out of my life forever," Caroline said. "It's a nice idea, but the Internet is eternal. Chapin Waring is going to be a cult figure for a generation and some idiot is going to put up Skycam footage of my front yard on their Web page for all that time. Welcome to the twenty-first century."

"Still," the officer said.

Caroline waved him away. "I'll talk to my sisters. Maybe they want to do something. I don't know."

"That's a good idea. Talk to your sisters." He'd started backing up again.

Caroline watched him get into his police cruiser and listened to the engine gun up, and the car began to move.

She didn't move herself, because she didn't see any need to.

Then something in her head broke, and she stood up abruptly.

She had Babycise and two soccer games and a trip to Home Depot to worry about.

She had a life that was made up of events on a schedule board, and she would have to live it.

FOUR

1

Gregor Demarkian had always liked New York City—sort of. It was closer to the truth that he had liked every version of it he had ever seen, and that he liked this one, too, at least as it appeared in the morning. That was the trouble with New York, as far as he was concerned. It never stayed the same from one visit to the next.

Of course, it didn't help that the city had a thousand hotels or more, so that he never found himself staying in the same one. The one for this trip was in Greenwich Village, and he was here because Bennis picked it out for him.

"My publisher is always trying to check me into the Hilton," she'd told him when she printed out the reservation confirmation on her computer, "but I prefer the Village. It's calmer, for one thing. And it's manageable. Of course, in a way, it's a bit like Paris. You think you're walking into a world of great writers and genius painters, and what you find is tourists and lawyers."

Gregor didn't know about the tourists and lawyers, but his appointment at the FBI wasn't until afternoon, and what he wanted to do more than anything was walk around. Part of him was a little miffed that he was too far from Midtown

to walk to it. There were bookstores up there he liked, and
he would have been happy to see if the Mysterious Book-
shop was still doing business at the same old stand. Of
course, it wasn't. Bennis had told him something about the
store moving to TriBeCa, wherever that was.

The hotel was a good one, although Gregor had some
trouble finding it on the map Bennis had given him as a
guide. It wasn't large and shiny the way an uptown hotel
would have been, but Gregor was willing to bet it had cost
the earth. He had a bedroom and a sitting room with a window that looked down on a street that might have been part
of the last century, if it weren't for the fact that everybody
walking on it was talking on a cell phone.

Gregor kept his opinion of cell phones to himself and
went downstairs in search of coffee. The hotel itself did not
run a restaurant, but there were a few open places just down
the block, and more across the street. Gregor picked one that
looked less determinedly artful than some of the others and
ordered a cup of coffee that cost less than a parking space.

The coffee shop was full, and loud, and the longer he sat
there, the more he felt as if he shouldn't. There were people
waiting for tables. He couldn't settle in.

He went out onto the street and began to look around. He
went to Washington Square Park and sat down on a bench.
He checked his watch. He really had managed to waste a fair
amount of time. It was nearly noon. He looked at his notebooks and wished he'd managed to get something done.

He got up and started walking again. He was restless.
He didn't like all these consultations and conferences, all
these different people wanting different things from him.
It was never a good idea to put yourself in a position where
you couldn't tell where your loyalties should lie. The town
of Alwych had hired him. He wished he could just leave it
at that.

He was coming around a corner when he saw a young
woman busily unhooking and unlatching things on the
street. He stopped where she was and found himself in
front of a long expanse of plate glass, very bright and very

clean—so clean, he wondered if they washed the glass daily. He looked across at the books in the window.

"You're a bookstore," he said to the young woman.

"Partners and Crime, Mystery Booksellers," she said brightly. "Haven't you visited us before?"

"I don't visit New York all that often," Gregor said. "I almost never get down here."

"Well, if you have the time, you should come in and look around. We're the largest mystery bookstore in New York. And we carry, really, just about everything."

"True crime?"

"Of course true crime," the young woman said. "Although I've got to admit, I prefer fiction. But lots of people want true crime these days. It's a very hot subgenre."

The young woman flashed Gregor a smile and went back inside.

Gregor backed up a little to look at the facade. The name of the store was painted in gold letters across a black expanse that reminded him a little of the old Scribner building.

He went closer to the windows again. The young woman was fiddling with what looked like a cash register. He made up his mind and went through the front door.

"You've decided to come in," she said, looking up. "That's excellent. I've decided to sell you at least five books, all in hardcover. Is there anything special you might want to see?"

Gregor said, "Do you think you can get me something about a crime that occurred thirty years ago, a series of bank robberies in suburban Connecticut—"

"Oh, that," the young woman said. Then she peered at him, suddenly seeming uncertain. "You know, you look very familiar. I'm not sure why. But the Waring case, with the murder and all the publicity—well, I do have some items you might find of interest."

"Already?" Gregor asked. "It's been—what? A week?"

"They're not new books," the young woman said. "But we stocked up. And I've got one that you might be interested in."

"Which one is that?"

The young woman moved out into the store, waving at Gregor to stay where he was. She came back only moments later with a large coffee table–sized volume that was obviously a picture book.

"There's not a lot of text," she said, putting the book down on the counter, "but a year from now, we're going to be inundated with very good work. We've heard that Ann Rule is doing something on the case, on the murder case, of course. And then there's always the chance that Gregor Demarkian will finally decide to write one of his own. I figure someday, he's almost going to have to."

"Maybe he doesn't like to write," Gregor said.

"Maybe. Still, if he wrote one, that would be the one you'd want. Anway, this book has got literally hundreds of pictures from the time when the robberies happened, family pictures of some of the people involved, or people the police thought were involved. That kind of thing."

Gregor flipped through the wide tall pages, past one grainy black-and-white print after another. Every once in a while there would be a photograph in color that looked like an amateur snapshot.

He closed the book.

"All right," he said. "I'll take it. You take American Express?"

"We take everything," the young woman said. "Let me ring this up for you. You really do look very familiar. If you hadn't said you were just visiting, I'd have thought you were one of our regulars."

2

When the time came, Gregor took a cab to the FBI office.

Sitting in the cab, he leafed through the book. It was not only large and ungainly, but haphazard and sort of oddly printed. The title was *Gone: The Real Truth About Chapin Waring and the Black Mask Robberies,* but there was virtually no text among the pictures.

Gregor stopped at one that took up an entire half of the page. There were six people, lined up more or less by height. He looked at the caption and found that the two enormously tall men were Kyle Westervan and Tim Brand, that the very tall woman just after them was Virginia Brand. That would be Tim Brand's sister and, according to Gregor's notes, later Kyle Westervan's wife. Then the heights dropped off significantly, so that Martin Veer, who was next, barely made it to Virginia Brand's shoulders, and Hope Matlock, who followed him, was almost as tall, but not quite. The two of them looked oddly out of place. They were boxy and lumpy instead of tall and willowy. They looked like members of a different species.

The last figure in the line was Chapin Waring, and she was very small indeed. There was, however, nothing boxy or lumpy about her. She was like an exquisite miniature of a pedigreed dog.

Gregor looked on the back of the book and found: KNIGHT SION BOOKS. He looked at the copyright page and found Knight Sion Books again, along with an address in Queens.

He put the book back in the bag and got out at his destination, feeling the suddenly unmuffled sounds of city traffic as vaguely hostile. He went into the building and took out his authorization letter. The guard in the lobby looked it over and handed him a visitor's badge.

The elevator opened at his floor, and a young woman was waiting for him, holding a file folder. She was pleasant and bland and not particularly interested in him. She stepped forward and held out her hand to be shaken. Gregor shook it.

"Mr. Fitzgerald is this way," she said without bothering to give her name. "He told me to show you right in."

Gregor was glad not to have to wait. They went down one corridor and passed through a room of cubicles. The office they were going to was down a side hall. The hall was windowless. The office was small.

Darcy Fitzgerald rose up from behind his desk as Gregor and his escort approached, and held out his hand.

"Mr. Demarkian," he said. "I know we've never met, but I've heard a lot about you. And not just from Patrick. Why don't you sit down."

The young woman waited expectantly.

Fitzgerald said, "Coffee is probably a good idea," and she took off.

Gregor took one of the two padded visitors' chairs in front of the desk and put his bag from Partners and Crime on the floor. Fitzgerald raised his eyebrows slightly, and Gregor brought the bag up onto the desk.

"I was wandering around the city earlier," Gregor said. "I found this and picked it up. The clerk at the bookstore recommended it."

Gregor took the book out of the bag and put it on the desk. Darcy Fitzgerald's face lit up.

"Oh, God," he said. "Well, I suppose it's not all that surprising. The damned things are all over the city."

"This book is all over the city?"

"All over the tristate area, probably," Fitzgerald said. "You've got to give the guy credit. He's got an obsession and he's made it pay."

"What guy? And what obsession?"

"Ray Guy Pearce," Fitzgerald said. "He's a—I don't know what to call him. A conspiracy theory nut, that's for sure. He's been running Knight Sion Books out of his dining room in Queens for decades—all kinds of conspiracies, the government covering up alien landings, the government being manipulated by the thirteen richest families in the world, who aren't really humans, but some kind of reptiles, and Clinton was one of them, they only made him look as if he'd grown up poor so that the rest of us would be fooled. That's the kind of thing."

"And he does all this out of a dining room in Queens?"

"It's probably a lot easier now than it used to be," Fitzgerald said. "Everything's digital now. He's got a couple of Web sites. But, yeah, Knight Sion is the largest publisher of conspiracy books in the country. Bigger even than Feral House. This murder must have been a godsend to him."

"The murder of Chapin Waring?"

"Sure. She's part of the conspiracy, or the robberies were, or something. I'll admit I was never able to straighten it out. Knight Sion has been publishing books on the Waring case since maybe two or three years after Chapin Waring went missing. One of my predecessors took it seriously and looked into good old Ray Guy, but I don't think he ever found anything that would link the man to the case. Except, you know, an obsession to see conspiracies in everything. We've got notes about Ray Guy and Knight Sion Books in the file, if you want to look into it yourself."

Gregor picked up the book and turned it over in his hands. "Maybe I will," he said.

Fitzgerald laughed. "The one you've got came out the first time a few years ago. When the news hit the wires, Ray Guy probably had a ton printed, along with a ton or two of the other titles on the case."

"And this man has no connection to the case at all?"

"Not that we could tell," Fitzgerald said. "He's been sitting out there on his rear end for fifty years, just getting this stuff into print and trying to convince as many people as possible that we're all being secretly prepared as sacrifices to the Antichrist by a cabal of—I don't know. I never understood it."

"He writes all these books himself?" Gregor asked.

"Nope. He's got a whole stable of writers who do this stuff. Most of them specialize. And there are new ones coming in all the time. You've got to ask yourself how many of these people there could possibly be, but the answer is—an infinite number. And I do mean infinite. He writes the stuff about Chapin Waring, though."

"I'd think it would be difficult to put five bank robberies and a flight from justice into the context of an international conspiracy of—did you say the Antichrist?"

"I did indeed."

"Somehow, I don't find Chapin Waring plausible as an agent of the Antichrist."

"I don't either," Fitzgerald said. "But she sure as hell is

plausible as a reincarnation of Houdini. It's been thirty years, and nobody caught so much as a glimpse until she turned up stabbed in the back at Alwych. That's got to be some kind of record."

There was a noise at Gregor's back. He turned to see yet another young woman coming in with coffee, faux cream, and sugar on a tray.

"Here it is," Fitzgerald said. "And now we can get down to the serious business of finding out what happened to all that money."

The young woman put the tray down on the desk and left. Fitzgerald handed Gregor a cup of very black coffee. Gregor reached for the faux cream and a spoon.

"The money," Gregor prompted.

Fitzgerald shook his head vigorously. "Over two hundred and fifty thousand dollars. Quite a bit of it in bills we had serial numbers for. Gone without a trace for thirty years, just like Chapin Waring herself. Not a single bill has ever turned up anywhere. Not even once."

"Which means nobody was spending it," Gregor said.

"That's what it means," Fitzgerald said. "It also means that wherever Chapin Waring went, she either didn't take the money with her, or she didn't need to use it for anything. The best we can come up with is that it's got to be sitting somewhere in a pile. It might be a couple of piles. But we want it back."

"I can imagine," Gregor said. "It's a lot of money for only five robberies."

"Yes, well, what we're worried about now is that you're going to go out to Alwych and solve their murder for them, and then that's all you're going to do. We'd appreciate it if you would look out for our problem while you're there. We've got reason to think that at least some attempt may be made to keep you from doing anything but dealing with the present."

"Really?" Gregor said.

"Really," Fitzgerald said. "Do you remember the name of the person who hired you to go out to Alwych?"

"Jason Battlesea?" Gregor said, thinking about it. "I think he's the chief of police."

"Well, this guy may have called you, and he may have made the arrangements, but he couldn't have hired you without the permission of the mayor. And it's the mayor who worries us. Her name is Evaline Veer. Martin Veer was her brother."

3

On the way back to his hotel in the cab, Gregor tried looking first at the picture book he'd bought, and then at the paper file of everything Fitzgerald thought he might need to help the FBI with what they wanted. There was also another file, firmly fixed in Gregor's laptop, but it might take him a while to get to that.

The book was more interesting every time he looked at it. Gregor had never seen a more eclectic collection of pictures. The photos with credits were all grainy in the way newspaper photographs were thirty years ago. The uncredited ones ran the gamut from posed school photographs to family snapshots to a few that looked as if they might have been taken by a telephoto lens.

That was an interesting point. The Waring case was so famous by now that nobody thought twice about the idea that some investigative journalist manqué had been following Chapin Waring around with a camera and taking pictures of her in secret. But at the time these photographs had to have been taken, there was no Waring case. If Chapin Waring was "famous" at all, it was only among a small group of well-off teenagers on the Connecticut Gold Coast.

In fact, until the case did break, Chapin Waring looked to be on track to be just another one of those women: house in the suburbs and two kids by the time she was thirty; drinking problem (if not worse) by the time she was forty.

There was no reason for anybody to have been stalking and taking pictures of Chapin Waring before she was revealed as one of the two people who were robbing those banks.

And yet, as a slow page-through of this book made clear, somebody had been doing just that. It had been a fairly thorough stalking, too. There were pictures of Chapin Waring in a bedroom, getting ready for bed—although no nudity, and no pictures of her prancing around in her underwear. There were pictures of Chapin Waring in what looked like a breakfast room, having orange juice and coffee. There were pictures of Chapin Waring sitting in the driveway of a big house in the driver's seat of a little convertible.

He put the book aside and picked up the file. He wondered if the FBI had checked out Ray Guy Pearce as well as Fitzgerald had said they did. Had they noticed the stalking photographs?

Gregor put the file back in his attaché case. More than $250,000 just gone into thin air.

Which left the question of where that was. In that thick file folder, Gregor had the reports of all the search warrants over the years, and there had been plenty of them. Houses had been searched. Cars had been searched. Safe deposit boxes had been searched. Leads had been followed up.

Nothing.

The cab came to a stop under the canopy of Gregor's hotel. Gregor paid the fare and got out, handing the driver a tip as he went. He went in through the lobby and stopped at the desk. There were no messages for him.

Gregor went to his room and put the book and his attaché case on the little table in the sitting room. He went into the bathroom and washed his face until it didn't feel full of grit. Then he went back into the sitting room. Sometime while he was out, somebody had sent up a bottle of Johnnie Walker Blue. It was sitting on a tray next to an ice bucket and some glasses.

There was only one person who would send Gregor a bottle of Johnnie Walker Blue.

Gregor opened the bottle and poured himself a short glass neat. Then he got out his cell phone and called Bennis.

"I keep telling you I'm not enough of a scotch drinker to know the difference between Black and Blue," he said when he got her on the line.

"I know the difference between Black and Blue," Bennis said.

"Yes, and you take a drink every couple of years. Thank you for the bottle, anyway. I'll carry it around in my suitcase like a private eye in a forties novel. Are you all right?"

"Of course I'm all right," Bennis said. "I wasn't going to leave the cat in the snow. It's going to be back here tomorrow morning. Then it's going to stay awhile until Donna and I can find somebody to live with it. Didn't I already tell you that?"

"I think so."

"Well, anyway, Donna's got her sights set on Hannah Krekorian. Old lady. Lives alone."

"She's no older than I am," Gregor said. "She and I went to school together."

"Oh, I know that," Bennis said. "I didn't mean to imply anything. But she's older than you are in spirit, if you know what I mean. And her landlord allows cats."

"Howard Kashinian?"

"Let's just say he'd better allow cats, or Donna will make his life miserable for an eternity. Anyway, that's where that is now. Are you sure *you're* all right."

"I'm fine. The case is a mess, and I haven't even gotten to the part I'm supposed to be investigating. Let me ask you something. You were a debutante, right?"

"Do we really have to do this again?"

"I'm not trying to dredge up your embarrassing past. I want to know something. Can you think of any reason why somebody would stalk a debutante? Or would have, in Chapin Waring's day? Followed her around. Taken her picture."

"On a personal level, or a professional one?"

"There's a professional one?"

"Well, considerably before my day, debutantes were to the general public what celebrity twits are now. They were celebrity twits. People like Brenda Frazier. They came out in big spectacular parties that were reported in the press. Photographers followed them around the way the paparazzi follow Paris Hilton now."

"Did Chapin Waring have that kind of coming out?"

"Not that I remember," Bennis said. "The last real celebrity debutante I remember was Cornelia Guest, and that was 1982. And it never quite reached the level of a Brenda Frazier or a Gloria Vanderbilt. Time has moved on, Gregor. I don't think anybody cares anymore."

"What about the personal?" Gregor asked. "Would it make sense for some lone guy, or woman, I suppose—for somebody to follow around a local debutante and take pictures of her with a telephoto lens, for private reasons?"

"You mean ordinary stalking? That can happen to anybody at any time, last I checked."

"Yes, but would Chapin Waring, as a debutante, have gotten the kind of publicity that would have drawn in somebody from the outside, maybe way from the outside—not even in the same state?"

"I don't think she would have had national publicity, if that's what you mean," Bennis said. "I think I'd have noticed that. But there's always *Town and Country*."

"The magazine?"

"Exactly. *Town and Country* always covers all the deb stuff, and a fair amount of the subdeb stuff. If you're talking about someone who was following the circuit, then he or she would have probably been able to read about her coming out in *Town and Country*. And then there would be the local newspapers. Although, to tell you the truth, Gregor, there's not a lot of coverage even in those anymore. Time really has moved on."

"I'm not sure it had moved on thirty years ago."

"Well," Bennis said, "maybe it hadn't. But it really wouldn't have been the kind of thing it used to be, not even the kind of thing it was in my day. What's the matter? Did Chapin Waring have a stalker?"

"I think so."

"And you think it's connected with everything else? With the way she died? And with the bank robberies?"

"I don't know," Gregor said. "I just find the whole thing very odd. I don't suppose you've ever heard of a guy named Ray Guy Pearce."

"Sure I have," Bennis said. "Knight Sion Books. The gold standard in conspiracy theories. Don't tell me he's involved in this, too."

"He seems to be publishing books about the Chapin Waring case. The old one."

"Of course he is," Bennis said. "But, Gregor, for God's sake. You can't take Ray Guy Pearce seriously. He thinks the world is being run by reptilian life-forms who are the descendants of the coupling of human women with Satan's demons. I don't think he's entirely sane."

FIVE

1

Evaline Veer was not a stupid woman, and she was not nearly so naïve as some people thought she was. When the reappearance of Chapin Waring in Alwych had been nothing more than a series of rumors about sightings up and down Beach Drive, she'd had reason to hope that the whole thing was just mass hysteria. Alwych had never gotten over the Waring case, and probably never would. Schoolchildren talked about Chapin Waring as if she were a cross between a ghost and a bogeyman. Girls at Alwych Country Day pretended she was their role model.

As soon as the body had turned up, Evaline knew she would have to go ahead whether she wanted to or not. It had been odd, getting that phone call. Chapin Waring was back, but she wasn't wearing big black sunglasses at a fruit stand out on Route 7 or stopping for ice cream at the little place next to Lanyard's. No, she was dead, with a knife up to its hilt in her shoulder blade. Evaline had known, as soon as she heard that, that all the reports would say that Chapin had been "stabbed in the back."

It's more like she stabbed us all in the back, Evaline thought, pulling into her space in the Town Hall parking lot.

She walked around to the steps leading to the Town Hall's side door. Jenny's car was parked right next to the steps.

Evaline let herself into the building. The Town Hall wouldn't be officially open for another half hour. The tax collector's office was empty. The long plastic shade was pulled down in front of the payment window. The probate judge's office was empty, too.

On the second floor, there were finally signs of life. The door to the Office of the Mayor was open, and inside Jenny was singing something to herself about how all you had to do was put a drink in her hand. She stopped at the door to Jenny's office and looked in. Jenny was wearing heels high enough to be stilts and a tight, straight skirt so short, it could have served as shrink-wrap. The skirt was sky blue. Her hair was neon green.

Evaline knocked against the doorframe to get Jenny's attention. Jenny looked up and took the earphones out of her ears.

"I don't understand what the point of the earphones is," Evaline said. "I can hear everything you play. You must be blasting your eardrums to pieces."

"It's a good thing you're in," Jenny said. "I already have a pile of messages on your desk. The FBI called again."

"What did they want?"

"They never want anything," Jenny said. "They just go on and on about cooperation and being on the same side. Are we on the same side? I can never tell when we're talking about Chapin Waring. I wish I was old enough to have known her."

"There was nothing to know," Evaline said. "She was like every little snotty party girl you'd meet at Alwych Country Day."

"I didn't go to Alwych Country Day."

Evaline let this pass and went through into her own office. Light was streaming in through the two tall windows at the back. Her desk was pristine except for the little pile of messages. Evaline looked through them.

"Jenny?" she said.

"What's up?" Jenny appeared in the doorway.

Evaline passed on the opportunity to give a lecture on the proper way to respond to a superior in a business setting.

"There's nothing here from Gregor Demarkian," Evaline said.

"Oh, I know," Jenny said. "It was the police department who contacted him, so his messages go there. I don't think we've ever talked to him directly, have we?"

"Not yet."

"Well, you don't have to worry. He's coming in on the noon train, and the chief of police himself is going to meet him."

"Has anybody told him that the state forensics lab lost its certification?" Evaline asked.

"I don't know. Do you want me to call the police and ask?"

"No, really, that's all right. If he doesn't know already, he'll know soon enough. Did we remember to get him his car and driver?"

"Yes," Jenny said. "Of course. You checked all that out last week."

"I just want to make sure everything is in order," Evaline said. "When this is over, I never have to see any of it again."

"Right," Jenny said, teetering a little. "There's something I forgot. We got a call from the Office of Health Care Access."

"The Office of Health Care Access. That's one we haven't dealt with before."

"The woman who called is sending over some papers," Jenny said, "so I suppose we should read those. It was something about something being wrong at Tim Brand's clinic."

"Something being wrong that has to do with health care access? Really? The man provides free health care services to strays who wander in from Bridgeport."

"She said something about the rules for emergency rooms."

Evaline had been leafing through the messages, putting aside the ones she thought might be important. When she heard "emergency rooms," she looked up.

"Somebody called from something called the Office of Health Care Access, talking about Tim Brand's clinic and emergency rooms?"

"Exactly," Jenny said. "But Tim Brand runs a clinic, not an emergency room. There's an emergency room at the hospital. I tried to explain that to her, but she wasn't listening, and then she said that she'd send over these papers. So I figure we just have to get the papers and read them."

"It makes perfect sense," Evaline said.

"I don't see how."

"I knew she was going to do something," Evaline said. "I just didn't know what. I wonder if she really thinks she's going to get away with this."

"Who's going to get away with what?"

"She can't imagine nobody will trace it back to her," Evaline said. "The only hope she's got is that it will take longer to trace than it takes her to get elected to the United States Senate. And I wouldn't bet on it."

Jenny brightened. "Oh, you mean Mrs. Westervan. Is she head of the Office of Health Care Access?"

"No," Evaline said.

She got up from behind her desk and started pacing.

Evaline Veer had never much liked Virginia Brand Westervan, and she liked her less and less as the years went by.

"Damn," Evaline said, sitting down again.

Jenny looked uncertain. "Are you all right? Can I get you something?"

"Yes," Evaline said. "Get me Tim Brand. Get him out of bed. I don't care. If he knows what's good for him, he'll be in this office in under half an hour."

2

There were two times in the last two weeks when Kyle Westervan thought he might have pushed this thing too far, and both times he turned out to be wrong.

The first time was, of course, the night Chapin Waring had been murdered. There was no scenario on earth that started with Chapin Waring being murdered—even thousands of miles away in a brothel in Bangkok—that didn't end in a hailstorm of Federal agents from one end of Connecticut to another.

He'd sat in his office in New York for days, waiting. He'd ridden home in his Saab every night very late, waiting. He'd woken up every morning in his bed at home, waiting. The waiting had felt like one of those long, slow nightmares where you know you're asleep, but can't make it out the other side no matter what you do.

And then nothing had happened. The Waring house was cordoned off as a crime scene. There were two officers stationed at the end of the drive at all times. There was another officer stationed on the patio in back, where the house overlooked the sea. People came and went, but nobody knocked on his door or called his office to ask anything about where he had been at the time of the crime.

The other time Kyle had been sure everything was about to fall on his head was last Saturday, when Hope Matlock called. Kyle got the impression that Hope was living hand to mouth these days. She was obviously not skipping any meals, but he thought that might be because she was skipping out on the utilities or making some other accommodation he found completely outside the pale. She was also very nervous. Talking to her was like plucking on a taut elastic band. She jumped if you did anything unexpected. She always seemed on the verge of tears.

In a way, it was because of all that—because he felt sorry for her—that Kyle had suggested the arrangement to begin with. At that point, Chapin Waring had just died, and he thought it made a certain amount of sense to stop carrying so much cash on him all the time. In a lot of ways, it couldn't be helped. For a certain kind of client with a certain kind of problem, cash was all that would do.

Kyle regretted making the suggestion to Hope as soon as he'd made it. He regretted it even more on Saturday morning, when she'd gotten him out of bed and sounded completely hysterical. Hope was not a person who could be trusted in any situation in which stress was involved. She lost her nerve almost immediately.

For a couple of days after Hope woke him up that morning, Kyle had waited. He had waited at home and in the office, just as he did after Chapin Waring was killed. There was nothing but the usual.

Finally, Kyle had had to accept it. The Alwych Police Department didn't think he was enough of a suspect to interview, never mind to demand an alibi from. He didn't know if this was because they really hadn't considered the obvious, or maybe they just didn't want to bother the congresswoman's ex-husband. The hiatus had given him just long enough to make sure he had nothing on him that could lead to the wrong kind of questions.

This morning, he had risen and packed up his briefcase and driven to the train station. He usually drove into the city, but he was running late. Just for once he didn't want the bother of traffic and rush hour and Manhattan parking.

If anybody had opened his briefcase, they would have found it a model of rectitude. It had his phone, court documents from a bankruptcy filing that was being entered against his advice, a copy of *Forbes* and a copy of *The Economist*.

He found himself a seat alone near a window. The train car was almost empty. There was a buzz in his briefcase. He opened it and took out the phone.

"Yes," he said, leaving the briefcase on the empty seat beside him.

"Where the hell are you?" Walter said. "I've been looking for you for the past hour."

"I'm running a little late." This was not an explanation. Kyle knew it. "The train is just leaving the station. I'll be in in about an hour and a half."

"You're taking the train? You never take the train."

"I couldn't handle the traffic. Is this actually about something? Has there been some kind of crisis in the office?"

"Listen." Walter was whispering. His voice was so low, Kyle almost couldn't hear it. "I'm a little worried about this phone. Your phone. We need a secure connection. We could get picked up."

"For God's sake," Kyle said again. "Those people would need a wiretap warrant. And to get a wiretap warrant, they'd need probable cause that a crime had been committed, or was being committed, or was about to be committed. What kind of crime do you think is being committed here?"

"Everything is a crime these days," Walter said.

"For God's—never mind. Walter, just tell me who it is so I'll know what to expect when I get there."

More hemming and hawing. Another cough.

"Walter," Kyle said.

Walter gave one great, last cough and said, "It's the guy from Washington. He flew in this morning. He's at the Hilton."

The train started to move. Kyle watched as he rolled slowly by cars and people and buildings.

"Kyle?" Walter said.

"I'm here," Kyle said.

"He's blowing steam out his head. I'm supposed to call him as soon as you get in."

"You should both calm down."

Kyle looked out the window again. The train was picking up speed. There was a billboard that said: VIRGINIA WESTER-VAN FOR U.S. SENATE. Kyle wondered for the hundredth time why she hadn't gone back to her maiden name after their divorce.

"Kyle," Walter said.

"I'll be there when the train gets in," Kyle said, and then slid the phone shut.

With the phone shut, the world was silent.

3

Tim Brand had been born into a lot of money. He had as much in a trust fund on the day after he was delivered than most people would see in a lifetime. He had money he was not allowed to touch except for the income. He had money he could do anything he wanted with.

Even so, he didn't have enough money to run a full-service free clinic 24/7/365 unless he was very, very careful.

The letters from the Office of Health Care Access and the Office of the Healthcare Advocate had come Saturday. Tim hadn't been able to get a full night's sleep since. He'd pushed himself at the clinic until he thought he was going to fall over. It didn't matter. He got home and lay down and found himself staring at the ceiling.

Part of being careful in the founding and running of the free clinic was his choice of where to live. He hadn't been silly enough to think he could afford a house in Alwych at the same time he was telling single mothers they didn't have to worry about getting a bill for Susie's flu vaccination and Tommy's set leg. Tim Brand lived in a "condominium town-home," which had been ridiculously expensive, but at least within the realm of basic sanity.

This morning, he had gotten up and showered as soon as he accepted the fact that sleep was over for the night. Then he had gone to Mass at Our Lady of Perpetual Help.

After Mass was over, he went out to stand on the steps and look down the hill at the town. The priest stopped and asked him if he felt all right. He brushed it off.

He took his run the long way. He went down by Beach Drive and the Atlantic Club. He watched the waves coming up on the shore.

He ran down the Drive and up again. Then he headed off through the houses and the stores toward the hospital and the clinic. The hospital was not a Catholic hospital. It hadn't had to do anything ridiculous when the law was passed that required all emergency rooms to provide the morning-after pill to rape victims. The hospital emergency room was so close to the clinic, he could walk there in under three minutes. Ambulances arrived at the doors of the emergency room all the time. No ambulances arrived at the clinic. There were good reasons why, if he went toe to toe with the Office of the Health Care Advocate and the Office of Health Care Access, he would very certainly win.

The problem, of course, was that winning—that way—was not the issue here.

Tim got to the clinic parking lot. The clinic was open, because it always was, but there was almost nobody waiting.

Tim let himself in through the front door. He nodded at the volunteer on reception and went on through to the back. He passed the door to the room where Maartje was sorting mail. She looked up and waved to him. He waved back and kept on going.

He went past empty examining rooms and empty offices. He got all the way to his own office and stopped. Marcie was in there, going through the paper records of their books. They always kept paper records as well as computer records, just in case.

Marcie looked up when he stopped at the door and gave him a faint smile. "I couldn't sleep," she said.

"I couldn't either," Tim said. "We'd better start finding ways to sleep, or we're going to start making mistakes when we really can't afford to. Did you really buy one of those silly books about the Waring case?"

Marcie picked it up and looked it over. "It was at the checkout this morning when I went into the pharmacy to buy aspirin. I bought the aspirin, I bought the book, and I bought a little Fourth of July teddy bear to give to the little Desini boy the next time his mother brings him in."

"Did we talk to Yale about that?" Tim asked. "I thought we were going—"

"I got a call from the financial department about his insurance."

"Ah," Tim said. "Maybe we should try Saint Raphael's."

"They're merging with Yale."

"Mary Desini is absolutely never going to let us do a public appeal."

"I know."

Tim came all the way into the room. Marcie was sitting in his chair behind his desk. He took one of the other chairs and sat down.

"We're going to need lawyers," he said finally.

"Well," Marcie said. "That was the idea, wasn't it?"

"I think the idea was for Virginia to be able to tell her hard-core base that she was moving against 'theocracy.' Not that she's ever going to admit in public that she's behind this thing. If she did, she'd kill any chance she had of being elected, even in Connecticut. But there are ways to get the word out without admitting anything, and Virginia knows all of them."

"It's ridiculous," Marcie said.

"It's ridiculous, but it's just plausible enough so that we can't count on its being thrown out the first time we appear before a judge. And that, Marcie, means we're going to need lawyers."

"Does she really think the world would be a better place if this clinic shut down?"

"I think she thinks the world would be a better place if nobody in it thought like us," Tim said. "I've never really understood Virginia."

"She's a rich girl who wants to go on being rich."

"If that was all it was, she could have stayed married to Kyle Westervan and devoted her life to giving parties. There's something else driving that woman. There always has been, even when we were both children. And I've never known what is it."

"Are they going to walk in someday next week and shut us down?"

"No," Tim said. "They're not going to shut us down at all. They're going to give us a time frame, and when we don't comply, they're going to start levying fines. Once the fines get high enough, they'll put a lien on the clinic. This could take years."

"Oh," Marcie said. "Years. But a lot could happen in years."

"One of the things that could happen is that they could bleed us dry."

"I hate lawyers," Marcie said. She looked down at the papers and ledgers spread out over the desk. Then she picked up the paperback about the Waring case—*The Secret Files of Chapin Waring!*—and turned it over in her hands.

"I suppose it is going to be a silly book," she said, "but I get curious. Did it upset you very much, when Chapin Waring died?"

"I think it mostly disoriented me," Tim said. "I think I unconsciously assumed she'd been dead for years. If there are things you really want to know, I could probably tell you more about that case than anything you can get out of a book. Especially a book like that."

"I didn't like to ask. I didn't know if it was—something, you know. A painful something," Marcie said.

Tim got up out of the chair. "I don't know if 'painful' is the word I'd use," he said. "That case made me a Catholic, although it took about a decade."

"Maybe this Gregor Demarkian will find all the answers," Marcie said. "Maybe having him here and having all this fuss will take everybody's minds off of us, and this whole Health Care Access thing will fall into the sea without a trace."

Tim thought that was as likely to happen as fig trees sprouting green cheese.

SIX

1

Gregor Demarkian got his first glimpse of Alwych, Connecticut, from the windows of the Metro-North train. Alwych was much as Gregor had expected it to be: high-end suburban, complete with dozens of little shops with highly erudite names, all their facades framed with very real wood. Going out from the center of town there would be houses, most of them on streets with sidewalks and set well back from the road, but there would be no subdivisions. Towns like Alwych had serious zoning.

Gregor had spent the trip out from Manhattan going through Patrick's diary and Fitzgerald's presentation and even the picture book he'd bought in Greenwich Village. He had no more insight into the robberies than he'd had before he started.

The robbery case looked, on the surface, like nothing particularly complicated. Except for the difficulty the police and the FBI had had in pinpointing the perpetrators, and possibly the intelligence with which the perpetrators had demanded and taken their money, it was like a thousand other bank robberies over the years.

Even the two things that seemed like anomalies weren't really. In the ordinary course of events, police didn't go looking for upmarket teenagers to solve their bank crimes. All Chapin Waring and Martin Veer needed to do was to get around a corner somewhere and ditch the black clothes, and they would have looked like hundreds of other innocent citizens of those suburbs. Nobody would have looked at them twice.

As for the intelligence—it was a fantasy to think of robbers as really smart guys with lots of skill who were doing this instead of attending Harvard because they'd had bad breaks in their lives. Most criminals were bone stupid, and most were outright thugs. Gregor had met intelligent criminals in his life, but they were nearly all sociopaths.

The train did a little jerking bounce and stopped moving. Gregor put his papers and the big book away. At the last minute he looked at the big picture in the middle of the book cover. It was a security camera shot of the robbery in Fairfield. He could recognize the slim figure as belonging to Chapin Waring right away. The other figure still looked odd. Gregor wished he had a better picture of Martin Veer in civilian clothes. There was something wrong about that second figure in black.

Other passengers were up and moving down the aisle. Gregor got his suitcase from the rack above his head, and went down the aisle and to the claustrophobic little vestibule where he could get out onto the platform. He looked around. The station had a little waiting room, heavily done in dark wood.

Gregor was about to go into the waiting room when a man approached him, wearing the livery of a limousine company. He had his hat in his hand and a note folded up in one fist. He was small and square and thick around the neck.

"Señor," he said, thrusting the note at Gregor.

Gregor took it and had a moment of panic that the police department of Alwych, having been asked to get him a car and a driver, had misinterpreted that to mean a limousine and a chauffeur. There was no possibility in the world that he could work on a case while being driven around like Jackie O on a night out.

He opened the note. It had been typed out, very neatly, on Alwych Police Department letterhead.

This is Juan Valdez, the note said. *He'll be your driver while you're in town. I've told him to take you directly to the Switch and Shingle as soon as you get in. He can bring you out to us when you've gotten settled. Thank you again for coming. Jason Battlesea.*

Gregor read the note through twice. What in the name of God was the Switch and Shingle? He looked up at Juan Valdez.

"Is the Switch and Shingle close to here?" Gregor asked.

Juan Valdez stared at him. Then he bent over and picked up the suitcase. He did not touch the attaché case. He said something in Spanish that Gregor didn't understand. Then he headed through the doors to the waiting room.

Gregor grabbed his attaché case and followed as quickly as he could. Juan Valdez was moving through the doors on the other side as Gregor got to the waiting room benches. Gregor tried moving faster still.

He got out of the waiting room's front doors and found himself on a little sidewalk with cabs parked along it. The only car that wasn't a cab was a brown Volvo sedan. Juan Valdez was standing next to the sedan, closing the trunk. Then he came around and opened the back passenger door closest to the curb.

"Por favor," he said.

Gregor hesitated a moment, then got in. At least it wasn't a limousine. Juan Valdez closed the door next to him and went around the car to get behind the wheel. Then he pulled out as if there were no other cars in the area, and pulled out onto Main Street.

Main Street looked, from the ground, pretty much as it had from the train. There were dress shops and restaurants, a little local bookstore with a cat in the window, a drugstore with a big cardboard sign in front in the shape of a gigantic puppy. They passed a hospital and, right next to it, a building announcing itself as a FREE CLINIC. They passed a small park that sat deep in a well in the ground, so that you had to go down a steep grassy hill or an equally steep ramp to get to it. It had slides and swings and places where the grass had been removed to make way for sand.

A couple of minutes later, Gregor began to feel the sea. The car was running the air-conditioning at full blast, but he put his window down anyway. As soon as he did so, he could most definitely hear it. He could smell it, too. There was ocean here.

They took another turn, and they were on a wide, nearly straight boulevard flanked by the sea on one side and huge, secretive houses on the other. The houses were all behind hedges. Gregor turned around and looked out the rear window. All the way at the end down there, getting smaller and smaller, was an even bigger building, houselike but without the quasi-protection of hedges, and with terraces making a wide sweep over the beach. That, he thought, must be the Atlantic Club.

The houses never got smaller, but they did get farther apart. The beach was empty, even though the day was beautiful and it was almost July. They glided past it all as if none of it had any significance to Gregor's being here, even though he knew this had to be Beach Drive, and that meant that this had to be where Chapin Waring had died. He tried to concentrate on the houses, to see if he could pick out the one. There was nothing out in the open that indicated that any house was any different from any other. There weren't even any people. For some reason, Gregor found that very disturbing.

The road made another little sweeping turn, and Gregor suddenly found himself being driven through the gates of a big Victorian with wide terraces facing the ocean. He just caught the sign that said THE SWITCH AND SHINGLE BED AND BREAKFAST as they passed it.

Juan Valdez pulled the car up in front of the front door. Gregor opened his door and got out. The driveway under his feet was gravel. The house in front of his face was big enough to be a girls' school.

Suddenly, the front doors opened and a woman came out. She was tall and heavyset and out of breath, and she was wearing the muumuu to end all muumuus. It was mostly purple, but it had some flamingo pink in it, and some neon orange. She was, however, wearing neither makeup nor jewelry, and she had never dyed her hair.

She came down the steps from the front door and walked right up to him.

"Are you Gregor Demarkian?" she asked.

"I most definitely am," Gregor said.

"Well, we got something right, at any rate," she said. "I'm Darlee Corn. I was born and brought up right here on Beach Drive, in this very house, and if you think I spend my time wishing I hadn't been, you'd be right. Jason Battlesea is having the vapors about putting you up here, and Evaline don't-say-my-last-name-too-loud Veer is doing worse, but there aren't any hotels in Alwych. I gave you the best room in the house and I think you're going to like it. You'd better come right in now. If you take too much time, we're going to have Jason over here foaming at the mouth."

2

The room Gregor was shown to was spectacular. It had a curved wall of windows and glass doors. Through the glass doors was a curved balcony that looked right out over Beach Drive and, beyond it, the sea. It was Long Island Sound, not Maui, but impressive all the same. The suite was even more so. The broad, high-celinged bedroom let in more light than Gregor thought he could stand. The sitting room had a stained glass window that made everything look like it had been dipped in rose food coloring.

Darlee Corn waited for him. When he had stopped pacing back and forth and looking in closets, she moved in, her hands crossed over her chest like freckled tree trunks.

"It's not for tourists," she said, looking around as if she

were doing housekeeping inspection. "You get tourists in the Hamptons, but you don't get them out here. This place doesn't like flashy."

"I can understand that."

"You're flashy, though," Darlee said. "You're on television all the time."

"And that makes me flashy?"

"It makes you something I wonder about. You'd think that after all this, the last thing the people in this town would want would be publicity. And now here you are."

"Sometimes publicity is impossible to avoid," Gregor said. "Sometimes you can't get rid of it. Then the best you can do is to manage what publicity you're forced to have."

"Maybe," Darlee Corn said. She did a tour of the bedroom, checking the way the quilt lay on the bed, checking the notepad and pen on the night table. She stopped when she got to that big curved wall of glass. "You know how they're always saying things like, don't bother with the rich twits, the *real* Green Acres is a lot different? Well, the real Alwych is the rich twits. This town was founded by rich twits. The real Alwych is a woman with a four-thousand-dollar handbag the size of a feed sack, drinking a seven-dollar latte, driving a BMW, and believing with her entire heart and soul that nobody really wants to eat at McDonald's, they're just duped into doing it by evil corporations who brainwash them."

Gregor was intrigued. "And?" he said.

Darlee dragged herself away from the window. "As I said, we don't get tourists here. It's not usually very busy. But it's busy now. The only reason you got this room was that Jason Battlesea asked me first and Virginia Westervan asked me later. And that makes me very nervous."

"I think it's probably fairly normal," Gregor said. "You've just had an unusual crime. It's gotten a lot of publicity. People come to see. To tell you the truth, I was a little surprised not to pass a clutch of tourists on my way here."

"On your way here? Why?"

"Isn't the Waring house on this road?" Gregor asked. "Beach Drive."

"It's just up the road, back the way you came."

"Exactly," Gregor said. "I did assume that there would be people there, people who'd come to get a look at a murder house, maybe even some reporters. I didn't even see a place with crime tape."

"They had to take the crime tape down from the end of the driveway," Darlee said. "There were too many people—" She stopped. "Oh," she said. "I see."

Darlee paused, as if trying to figure out how to proceed. "I wasn't of that generation, but I remember the crimes happening. I remember all the fuss on television. And every once in a while, they do those retrospective things on television, you know. So it's not like I'm clueless. I do get what's going on here."

"And?" Gregor said.

Darlee shook her head. "The problem is that I wouldn't, I couldn't, recognize Chapin Waring right off the bat the way a lot of people here could. I wouldn't just know, if I saw her. But on the day of the murder, I did see her. And I knew it was her."

Gregor tried to be careful. "A lot of people saw her," he said. "The notes I got of the initial investigation are full of reports—"

"Well, there are always *reports,*" Darlee said. "I was out on the terrace, and I saw her walk onto the beach. I saw her, and I thought that she looked a lot like Chapin Waring. And then I wasn't sure, so I came in the house and looked through some of my History of Alwych scrapbooks. The guests like the scrapbooks, and I've got one that's almost nothing but pictures of the Waring case. I looked at these pictures and then I went back out onto the terrace to see if I was right, but she was gone. And that's when I got to thinking. I'm probably the only woman in this town of my age or older who wouldn't recognize Chapin Waring when they saw her. And that explains why I didn't recognize her."

"But you just said you did."

"I didn't recognize her the first time. About five years ago. She was out on Beach Drive that time, just walking along the side of the road with a dog. And when I went by her, the first thing I thought was that these people ought to stop walking their dogs on the road. It could be dangerous. And then there was something about her that just bothered me. So I looked back in the rearview mirror and slowed down a little. And she looked familiar. And she gave me a bad feeling. But I couldn't figure out why, and so I sped up and just kept going. But the more I've thought about it since the murder happened, the more I'm sure. That was Chapin Waring on the side of the road. It had to be."

3

Chapin Waring was not standing on the side of the road when Gregor climbed back into the perfectly ordinary car with its ridiculously uniformed driver and headed to the Alwych Police Department. The drive back through Alwych was about as interesting as the first drive through it had been. Juan Valdez didn't speak English, and Gregor wasn't even sure he knew much about the area. Beach Drive was still an empty landscape of big houses and wide lawns. If women did walk their dogs here, they weren't doing it now.

This time, when he passed the Waring house, he knew the property from Darlee's description. He asked Juan Valdez to slow down, and the driver did so. Either his passive English vocabulary was better than his active one, or he had some reason not to want to talk to the people he drove.

Gregor peered up the long drive as they went slowly by. It was gravel all the way up to where it went out of sight between the trees.

"Wasn't there a fire?" Gregor asked.

Juan Valdez said nothing. He didn't even look into the rearview mirror to acknowledge that Gregor had said anything. Gregor looked through his notes and found nothing that helped him out. He took one last look down the drive as they glided all the way past. The landscape showed no signs of a traumatic fire.

They drove to the end of Beach Drive and then began meandering again through town.

The police station was a plain, squat brick building with a low band of windows that ran in an uninterrupted line across its facade. Valdez pulled into a parking space right in front of the front door. Gregor got out and looked around. There were four patrol cars sitting in a line a little farther down the building. There were six civilian cars on the other side of the lot.

The front door opened and out came a short, squat man in a business suit that looked as if it had been custom-tailored for someone else. He was a youngish man without being really young. He was also bone-cold bald.

The man came forward, squinting. "It's Gregor Demarkian. I recognize you from TV. I'm Jason Battlesea," he said, coming forward with his hand held out. "They called me to tell me you'd arrived. We're very glad you're here. I hope you found the accommodations acceptable. If they're not, we can always put you up in the Radisson on Route 7, but it's a bit of a drive."

"The accommodations are fine," Gregor said. He shook Jason Battlesea's hand. It was a mechanical process. There was the contact. There was the shake. Then Jason Battlesea dropped his arm as if it were a dead weight.

For a moment, they stood there in the bright summer air. It was as if neither of them knew what to do next.

"We do know about the FBI," he said finally. "And we're not going to complain. They've got legitimate interests in all this, and we know it."

"But?" Gregor said.

Jason Battlesea looked uncomfortable. "I don't think you can just assume that, because the victim is Chapin Waring, the murder has to belong with the FBI."

"There were two people killed in the last robbery," Gregor said.

"But this murder happened here," Jason Battlesea said. "It happened in Chapin Waring's old childhood home. It happened in a town where one of her sisters still lives. It happened in the town where she grew up and got to be—like she was, which was a first-rate spoiled brat and a world-class bully. Chapin Waring always had a lot of enemies in Alwych."

"The kind of enemies who would hold a grudge for thirty years?"

"I don't know," Jason Battlesea said. "I don't even know if it's been thirty years. We don't know where she's been. She could have been anywhere. She could have been here."

"Fair enough," Gregor said.

"I suppose Darlee's been on to you about how she saw Chapin Waring in town five years ago."

"She said something about it."

"Well," Jason said, "once you've been here for a couple of days, you'll realize one thing. She's not the only one who thinks she's seen that woman wandering around on and off over the years. We've got an entire file of sightings in the office. We passed every single one of them on to the FBI, except Darlee's, of course, because she didn't say anything about it before last week."

"Do you think any of those sightings were real?"

"I think Chapin Waring was to this town what Bigfoot was to everyplace else. I think now that she's dead, we're going to start getting sightings of her ghost."

"All right," Gregor said.

Jason Battlesea looked him up and down and up and down again, as if Gregor were an actress trying out for a role where the physical fit had to be perfect. Then he shook his head slightly and sighed.

"You're not what I expected you to be," he said.

The next sigh he took was very deep, as if he were trying to suck in all the air in the universe.

"Thank God," he said.

SEVEN

1

One of the things Virginia Brand Westervan liked best about being a member of the United States Congress was the geography. No matter where you came from, no matter whom you were supposed to represent, you had to spend most of your time in Washington, D.C. It made the ritual returns for constituent contact feel like bad vacations.

This morning, though, what was striking her was that she was not going to be able to stay this far south for too much longer. She had to go back to Connecticut to campaign, and she had to go back soon because July Fourth was coming up. Nobody stayed in Washington on July Fourth, except tourists who came in to see the monuments and watch the fireworks.

Virginia leaned over her desk and buzzed Susan in the outer office. It always astounded her how old-fashioned all the technology in the Capitol building was.

Susan stuck her head in the door, her eyebrows halfway up her forehead.

"Have we heard from Alwych yet?" Virginia asked.

Susan came all the way into the office and closed the door behind her. "Sara in the constituent office called to say that Gregor Demarkian has arrived. She said he got picked up at the train station by a plain car driven by a man in a chauffeur's uniform. It's all right, Virginia. We had him thoroughly checked out when Jason Battlesea first said he was going to hire him. The only thing I found interesting in that entire file was that his first wife died of cancer and he just married again a little while ago, to this woman who writes fantasy novels."

"Bennis Hannaford," Virginia said. "I know. You know what I'd like to know?"

Susan shook her head.

"I'd like to know just how good he is at his job," Virginia said.

"Oh," Susan said. "I don't think you have to worry about that. He's solved a number of high-profile cases, and practically everybody who's ever hired him has thought it was worth it."

"Is he staying at the Switch and Shingle?"

"Yes."

"Has there been a press conference down in Alwych? Or is there going to be?"

"No word on that," Susan said. "I can call down and find out."

"That would be a good idea."

"I still think you're worrying unnecessarily," Susan said. "Isn't it better to have somebody who doesn't have a stake in the outcome? You can't even say that about the FBI anymore. Everybody has some way they want it to turn out."

"I suppose," Virginia said.

She made a face and stood up.

"I take it that there's been nothing at all on the other thing," she said.

Susan took a minute to process that. "I'm not sure what you're talking about," she said. "If you're talking about Kyle, we've still got the same intelligence on him and we're doing the best we can, but he just does what a lawyer does. He meets with clients. The only way we could get any better intel on him is if we bugged his client conferences, and you know as well as I do that we couldn't do that. If anybody found out about it, we'd be dead."

"I don't mean Kyle," Virginia said. "Although, God only knows, I expect him to get hit with insider trading charges any minute. And now with this Gregor Demarkian in the picture—"

"I don't know why you've got so much trouble with Gregor Demarkian," Susan said. "You liked the idea when you first heard about it."

"I know I did. I still like the idea. It's just—I don't know. Maybe you just had to have been there at the time. It was a very strange time, the weeks right after Chapin disappeared. I think we were all under suspicion, the four of us who were left. Nobody ever said so out loud, but we were. And there was a lot to be suspected of. There were two people dead. And the rumors were—the only word for them would be insane."

"Did any of them turn out to be fact?"

"I don't know," Virginia said. "I expected that people would look into them now that things had started up again. But nobody seems to be very interested."

Virginia sighed. Her desk was clean. There was no reason she had to be here at all. She just didn't feel like moving.

Susan coughed politely. "I'm nearly packed up," she said. "We can go back to Connecticut anytime you're ready."

Virginia made the strangled noise she saved for agreeing to something while she was feeling frustrated.

"It's very odd," she said. "I was thinking about all of this the night Chapin Waring died. We had that fund-raiser at the Atlantic Club."

Virginia let it go. Most of the time, she did not express her deeply held conviction that her brother was not only not a saint, but some kind of Machiavelli with an agenda none of them had figured out yet. Virginia was just as committed to the things she believed in as Tim pretended to be about the things he did. And over the last several years, those things had coalesced in Virginia's mind as: putting a stop to everything Tim is doing.

Tim's motives always seemed to get a pass, and nobody questioned the saintliness of what he was doing even though so much of it was damaging and hurtful. If it was left up to

Timothy Brand, no woman would ever again be able to get a safe and legal abortion, no gay couples would ever again be allowed to marry or adopt children, and—she wasn't sure what the "and" was.

Susan had started to busy herself taking files out of filing cabinets, probably in order to take them off and copy them.

"You know," Susan said. "You're not going to be able to get out from under this forever. You have to go back to Connecticut to campaign, and you have to go back to Connecticut to talk to Jason Battlesea. He isn't going to let you get away with nothing more of a statement than the one you made on the night they found Chapin Waring's body."

2

For about an hour that morning, Hope Matlock felt better. In fact, she felt positively happy. Summers these days were always bad news, because there was never any teaching to be had in the summers. Summer courses went to full-time people who wanted to make a little extra money on the side.

She thought she would read e-mail and look around a little before she performed her ordinary summer-morning ritual of checking the bank account and counting the money. There was not a lot of money to count, but she thought she might be able to get through July without any actual problem. That was what was stopping her from doing anything drastic.

She made coffee from one of those coffee pods. She had another six in the box, and after that she would have to get the freeze-dried stuff. She logged on to her computer and then on to the Internet. She thought she was probably one of the last five people on earth who still had dial-up. The computer made those weird connecting-to-the-Internet noises that AOL seemed to think would make users less frustrated and angry with how long it took. Then the Welcome Screen came up and the little voice said, "You've got mail!"

Hope opened her e-mail to find just what she was expecting, plus one from Caitlin Hall. Caitlin Hall was, nominally, her boss. Letters from Caitlin at odd times of the year were never good news. Hope had her contracts for the fall. This probably meant that she was going to lose one of them.

Hope took another long sip of coffee and waited. She still had the material she'd collected a few days ago. It was lying on the dining room table. She could go in and get it and start doing something about it today. It might be dangerous, what with this Gregor Demarkian arriving today—but what did she mean by dangerous? Half the people she thought of as her friends barely spoke to her these days.

She moved her mouse and clicked on Caitlin's e-mail. She waited while it took forever to open. If she called AOL to complain about how slow her service was, they would tell her she should move off dial-up and sign on to broadband, or whatever it was these days.

The e-mail form came up blank. Then it sort of shivered. Then there was a message, although not much of one.

> *I've got an ADP, Thursday nights 6 to 9, eight weeks, English 101, starting next week.*
> *2100.*
> *Can you do this?*

Hope stared down at the e-mail.

It was, in a way, a kind of miracle. Part-timers never got summer courses. And never meant never. Hope had been teaching at the same place for close to fifteen years. She'd had exactly one summer course in all that time. ADP meant "accelerated degree program." The courses lasted only eight weeks, and there was a lot on the Internet. Hope loved working on the Internet.

She clicked on the Reply button and said:

> *Of course! Yes! I'd love to!*

Twenty-one hundred dollars might not sound like a lot of money, but it was twenty-one hundred more than Hope usually had in the summer. She could stop worrying about paying her gas and electric bills. She could start thinking seriously about doing a massive Costco shop.

She thought about the papers out on the dining room table, and mentally imagined them dissolving into air. There were people she needed. Tim Brand was one of them. She could just imagine what Tim would say about all that.

She got up and went out into the kitchen to see if there was anything going on. Sometimes she fell into a stress-induced sleep before she'd remembered to put away the mayonnaise or clean up the stove after dinner.

She looked into the refrigerator and didn't like anything she saw. She looked into the freezer and found a large bag of Pizza Rolls. She took this out and arranged twenty of them on a plate. She shoved the plate into the microwave and set it for two minutes and fifteen seconds. Then she went back to the refrigerator and got a large, three-liter bottle of IGA cola.

The microwave beeped. Hope took the plate of Pizza Rolls and the bottle of cola and went through the dining room into the living room. She sat down on the couch and put the plate and the bottle on the coffee table. The coffee table was covered with books and magazines and take-out menus from half a dozen restaurants. The menus came in the snail mail, and Hope kept them all just in case something came along that meant that she could use them.

She was feeling a little dizzy again. She needed to take the medication Tim had given her. She preferred to get her medication from Tim rather than the emergency room, because Tim never looked at her funny or asked her to make a plan to pay.

She finished off the Pizza Rolls and thought about making another plate. She decided against it and went upstairs to shower. The stairs were hard. She was hyperventilating by the time she got to the top of them, and she was dizzy again.

She showered, and washed her hair, and gave some thought to the world out there, if only in Alwych. This was the day Gregor Demarkian was supposed to show up. She didn't believe the man would be able to make any more sense out of the life of Chapin Waring than anybody else had. It was silly to think of Chapin as a force of nature. She had only seemed like that to Hope when Hope was very young, and it was part of being very young that you overestimated the lightweights with charisma.

She went down the hall to her proper bedroom, the same bedroom she had had when she was growing up. She went into her big wardrobe and found some summer clothes. One of the wonderful things about being up here on the second floor was that she had access to all her things.

She found a skirt and a T-shirt she particularly liked, and some almost-new underwear. She got dressed and then she looked through the wardrobe again. She got T-shirts and skirts and big, stretchy dresses.

She went back downstairs again, carrying the big pile of clothes, humming a little. She put the clothes on the dining room table, on top of the papers she had spread out there.

She was just about coming to the decision that she needed that extra plate of Pizza Rolls when she heard the sharp click from the computer that meant that she had new mail. She went in to see if it was something important.

She found a new e-mail from Caitlin Hall. That would be Caitlin confirming she'd gotten Hope's message, and probably promising an attachment with a syllabus template as soon as possible.

Hope opened the e-mail. She stared at it for a minute.

Oh, Hope, it said. *I'm so sorry. I sent that last night, and I was under a lot of pressure to fill that immediately if not sooner. I'll let you know if anything else shows up.*

The dizzy thing was back again, right there at the top of her head. Her entire skull felt numb.

It would be crazy to think Caitlin had done this on purpose, but that was what Hope did think. There was just something about this that felt deliberate, like the bait and switch children used to make fun of other children. Lucy taking the ball away before Charlie Brown could kick it. Kids at a junior high school dance pulling a chair out from under someone trying to sit down near the wall.

Hope closed the e-mail. She got up and walked away from the computer. She walked into the dining room. The clothes were still there, spread out across the papers.

She leaned forward and picked up some of the clothes. She moved them carefully to another part of the table. She looked at the papers underneath them and made a face.

She had to ask herself, when she found herself in these situations, if the people who believed in karma had it right. Maybe she had been something terrible in her last life, something that deserved everything she was getting now.

Maybe she had been Caitlin Hall in her last life, and the gods that controlled that sort of thing would never let her forget it.

EIGHT

1

The Alwych Police Department was the model of modern suburban law enforcement—suburban in the old sense of the word, when suburbs were places rich people went so they didn't have to live next to all those other people in the city. The building was small but very, very clean. All the surfaces gleamed as if they had never been used. There was a big open area at the front, with a counter staffed by a woman in a crisply immaculate uniform and, beyond her, a sea of uncluttered desks. There was a corridor that looked completely blank going off toward the back. There wasn't anything that looked like it could be a jail, or the gateway to a jail.

Gregor could see Jason Battlesea looking at him as he looked around the room.

"Are you waiting for me to ask?" Gregor said.

"Sort of," Jason Battlesea admitted. "There's another entrance, around the back. It goes to the lower level. The holding area is there, and about a dozen cells, including two isolation cells. If we have to lock up people, we have a place to put them."

"That's good to know," Gregor said. "Do you ever have to lock up people?"

"Sometimes. We have a fair amount of crime here in the good weather. Burglary and car theft mostly. We're not all that far from Bridgeport, which means we get a fair influx of the kind of people who tend to make a career of that kind of thing."

Gregor considered this. "You don't get anything local?"

"Sure we do," Jason Battlesea said. "Lots and lots of drunk driving, especially in the spring. That's the party season here for the high school and the kids home from college. We get a lot of marijuana, although we don't tend to pursue those."

"Why not?"

"Because the town doesn't want us to," Jason Battlesea said. "The parents here, they don't just want their kids to go to college, they want them to go to Harvard. And the kids are not going to get there if they've been busted for weed. When we catch them with it, we don't make a big deal out of it, and we don't make it official."

"What about other drugs?"

"Other drugs, we get more serious about," Battlesea said. "On that one, the parents are adamant. They're scared to death of heroin and cocaine. But even with that, we have to go slow sometimes."

"Was this the first murder you've had?"

"The first in fifty years, yes," Battlesea said. "The two people killed in the last bank robbery weren't killed here. None of the robberies were even done here. But I looked it up. About fifty years ago, a woman named Grace Lewison shot her husband on the front lawn of their house on Sands Street at eight o'clock in the evening. She'd caught him sleeping with the maid."

"Is Sands Street a good part of town?"

"There isn't really a bad part of Alwych," Battlesea said, "but it's no Beach Drive. In case you're wondering, it was the definition of an open-and-shut case. It was a nice summer day and the neighbors were all out on their lawns. They saw the guy run out of the house, they saw Grace run out after him shooting, and then when she got him she stood there and kept plugging him until the bullets ran out. Of course, this is Alwych, so she tried to plead temporary insanity."

"Do you have anybody here who's trained in homicide investigation?"

"Oh, we've got them trained," Jason Battlesea said. "The town funds the hell out of it. It funds the hell out of all its public services. The public high school here will give you an education to out-Exeter Exeter. It's got Latin and Ancient Greek as well as Spanish, French, German, Russian, and Chinese. The hospital offers cancer services to rival Yale–New Haven. So, yes, we've got people here who are trained in homicide investigations. They've been sent on training courses. They've been sent on refreshers. They've done all that kind of thing."

"They've done everything but work on an actual homicide investigation," Gregor said.

"I've got two detectives," Battlesea said. "Both of them did liaison advisory stints with the Bridgeport police. That means they went down there and spent three months apiece working for the Bridgeport PD and going along on homicide cases with seasoned homicide cops."

"That's not a bad idea," Gregor said.

"No, it isn't," Battlesea agreed. "Unfortunately, it doesn't help us here. Bridgeport has a real police department, if you don't mind my putting it that way. They deal with a lot of crime, and a lot of violent crime, and they deal with it every single day. The problem is that it's not this kind of violent crime. They have carjackings. They have home invasions. They have gang murders. People get stabbed in the street and robbed at gunpoint, and you couldn't get me to work in a liquor store or a convenience store in Bridgeport on a bet. But it's not this kind of thing. To tell you the truth, Mr. Demarkian, I didn't think this kind of thing existed outside of *Murder, She Wrote*."

"Are your two homicide detectives here now, by any chance?" he asked.

"They're downstairs," Jason Battlesea said. "We can take the elevator."

Battlesea gave a little nod to the uniformed woman at the counter and led Gregor down the blank hall to an opening at the back, with elevator doors on both sides of it. The doors were wide enough to accommodate gurneys if they had to.

Battlesea pushed the call button, and as soon as one set of elevator doors opened, he ushered Gregor in and pushed another button.

The elevator bumped to a stop and Gregor followed Battlesea out and found himself confronted with what was, in a way, a more comforting atmosphere. It did look as if somebody had tracked dirt through here on and off, and there were people, many of them rumpled. Most of the rumpled ones were in the back, in open holding cells. They all looked tired.

There was another woman at another counter. She was also in uniform, and also looked crisply efficient, but she had strands of hair coming out of the shiny metal hair clip she was using to hold it all back. She looked up when Battlesea approached and said,

"They're in the common room. They've got some files for you."

"Thank you."

Battlesea led Gregor through the hatch door in the counter and across the broad room with even more desks in it.

At the other end of the room, there was a door left slightly open. Battlesea pushed it in, and there were two men sitting at a cheap, wide table, drinking coffee.

Battlesea gestured at Gregor.

"Gregor Demarkian," he said.

"Damn," one of the men said.

The men were both white and in their thirties. They both had brown hair and brown eyes. They were so much alike, Gregor wasn't sure he would have been able to pick one over the other in a lineup.

The one who hadn't spoken stood up. "Mike Held," he said, holding out his hand. "This is Jack Mann."

Gregor shook Mike Held's hand. Mike Held waved at the chairs around the table. Gregor sat down.

"We're really glad you're here," Mike Held said. "We really don't know what we're doing."

"We don't even know where to start," Jack Mann said. "And then there's all that trouble with the state crime lab."

"What trouble?" Gregor asked.

Now it was Jason Battlesea who sat down. "Not to put too fine a point on it," he said, "they lost their accreditation."

Gregor tried to take this in. "How did they lose their accreditation?"

"They say it's mostly about not being fast enough and that kind of thing," Mike Held said. "They haven't had a full-time person over there for ages, and they weren't getting the forensic evidence processed as fast as they should have. We're beginning to think that even if we find the murderer and arrest him, even if you find him, it won't matter, because the prosecutor will get into court and the defense will start going on about how you can't trust any of the forensics because the lab is unaccredited, and that's going to be that."

"You said 'the lab,'" Gregor said. "There's only one."

"There's only one," Jack Mann agreed. "For the entire state. And they couldn't even put on a full-time person there."

"Let's leave that for a moment, all right? You are the two who have been investigating this crime up to now?" Gregor asked.

"Absolutely," Mike Held said.

"And it was copies of your notes that were sent to me when I agreed to come out here?"

"We sent all the notes, not just ours," Mike Held said. "We sent the notes of the uniform who responded at the scene."

"All right," Gregor said. "Uniforms responded at the scene. These were—"

"A woman," Mike Held said. "She was doing a patrol around Beach Drive. She saw what she thought was a light where there shouldn't be any, and she pulled into the drive. You've got to wonder how stupid anybody had to be to leave a light on in that house."

"Maybe not," Jack Mann said. "The family has timed lights for security. It's not impossible for there to be lights on there."

"Maybe not," Mike Held said, "but everybody on the force

knows which lights those are. So if there are other lights, we're going to go right ahead and check."

"The uniform didn't know what to think when she got in there," Mike Held said. "She didn't know it was Chapin Waring. She's much too young, even Jack and I are much too young, to have been around when all that happened. So in the beginning, we just went at it like any homicide case. And then—"

"It was the ME's office that figured out who it was," Jack Mann said. "They got the body, and the guy who was supposed to work on it knew all about that case, and they called us immediately. And then we did what we were supposed to do to confirm it. It was bad enough having a murder case. Now we've got this, and we don't even know where to start. Hell, the FBI doesn't know how to solve this thing. How do they expect us to solve it?"

Gregor was getting that feeling he had sometimes, that it was going to take infinite patience to get through the next fifteen minutes.

"Solve what?" he asked them.

2

The scene would have been funny, if Gregor had been in a mood to laugh. The three men sat around their cheap table, staring at him as if he'd just told them that something they'd always believed to be true—that the world was round, for instance—wasn't. Two of them actually had their mouths open. Jason Battlesea's face had gone more than a little red.

Gregor took the attaché case he'd been carrying and put it on the table. He snapped it open and went through the four bound stacks of paper he had there.

He found the bound sheaf he was looking for. He had written "Alwych PD" across the front of it. He took it out and put it on the desk.

"Do you know what that is?" he asked.

Jason Battlesea looked a little uncertain. "You had us investigated?" he asked. "Do you do that with all your clients?"

"I did not have you investigated," Gregor said. "I did ask around, because that's only sensible. If I'm going to take a case, I want to be sure that the people I'm working with are capable of being worked with. But this is not that. This is a hard-copy printout of the computer files you sent me outlining this case. And do you know what's wrong with it?"

"Did we leave something out?" Jack Mann asked. "We went over it and over it. We really did."

"You may have left something out," Gregor said, "but it would be hard for me to know what. What's wrong with this is this: Four-fifths of it concern the robberies, or Chapin Waring disappearing at the very moment when she was identified as one of the people involved in those robberies, or about the people Chapin Waring did or didn't know in the period when those robberies were taking place. There are even six solid pages about debutante parties."

The three men looked more and more bewildered. It wasn't stupidity. They were all bright enough. It wasn't even entirely lack of experience. There were experienced agents of the FBI who were making this same mistake, but they had the excuse that this case was not actually theirs. Jason Battlesea, Mike Held, and Jack Mann had no excuse at all.

Gregor tried very hard not to let his exasperation show.

"No matter what happened with those robberies," he said, "you have a case here and now. You have a body in the morgue. You have a crime scene. You have an act of violence. A woman was murdered in a house on Beach Drive. She was stabbed in the back with—with what? I presume a knife, but your report to me doesn't actually say so. I can find out more about a thirty-year-old bank robbery in these pages than I can about your actual case."

"But," Jason Battlesea said.

"Yes?" Gregor said.

"But aren't they connected?" Jason Battlesea said.

"I don't know," Gregor said.

"But they have to be connected," Jason Battlesea said. "She disappeared because of the bank robberies, and because those two people got killed in the last one. She wouldn't just come back here for no reason. She knew the FBI was looking for her. And why would anybody kill her if it didn't have something to do with the robberies? It's not like she'd been here all the time, making enemies."

"Maybe," Gregor said, "but I don't know, and you don't know either. What if this hadn't been Chapin Waring who'd been killed? What if it had been some unknown woman? How would you have gone about it then?"

"Well, we'd have tried to identify her," Mark Held said. "But we have identified her this time. There were fingerprints and that kind of thing. The identification isn't in doubt."

"If it had been an unknown woman," Gregor said, "I presume you would have gathered all the forensic evidence and sent it to the lab. And yes, I know the state lab lost its accreditation. But you'd have done that. Have you done that?

"All right," Gregor said. "Then I would presume you'd cordon off the scene and keep going over it. You'd check out the rest of the house. You'd talk to the neighbors."

"We did all those things," Mike Held said.

"And you didn't put that into your report," Gregor told him. "She was stabbed. I assume with a knife. Where did the knife come from? Was it part of a set in the house? Was it brought in from outside?"

"It wasn't part of a set from the house that we could see," Mark Held said. "We looked in the kitchen, and there were three or four knife sets in those wooden blocks, but they were all full. It could have been in the house in a drawer or something, not part of a set, but we've got no way of knowing. Nobody has lived in that house for decades."

"It's still owned by the Waring family?"

"Owned, but not occupied," Jack Mann said. "The parents up and moved away less than a year after Chapin disappeared. The impression I get talking to people is that they couldn't stand it. People were always coming around, invading their privacy."

"And the parents are now—?"

"Dead," Jason Battlesea said.

"And the house still isn't sold. And nobody lives in it."

"There are three other sisters," Mike Held said. "Caroline lives right here in town. She and her husband have a place over in the Sheepwoods section of town. The other two—"

"Charlotte and Cordelia," Jack Mann said.

"Right," Mike said, "Charlotte and Cordelia. They're not local anymore. I think one of them lives in Chicago, but I'm not sure."

"And the house has never been up for sale?"

"Not that I know of," Jason Battlesea said.

"Well," Gregor said, "did you ever ask yourself why?"

The three men looked nonplussed.

"But aren't you doing the same thing?" Mike Held asked. "Aren't you just concentrating on the old crime? I mean, okay, they kept the house like that all these years and it's really odd, but isn't the reason they did that something having to do with the older crime?"

"Maybe," Gregor said. "But unlike reports of the witness statements of the bank robberies, it's also something that has an immediate relevance to this crime. Chapin Waring was found dead in her family's home, which has been maintained—has it been maintained?"

"If it hadn't been, there would have been complaints from the rest of Beach Drive," Jason Battlesea said. "I've driven by that place dozens of times, and the lawns always look really great."

"What about inside the house?" Gregor asked.

"Oh, that looks really great, too," Mike Held said. "Except for the stuff that was shot up when the murder happened. Or maybe later."

"Do you know if the murder actually occurred in that house?" Gregor asked. "Do you know if Chapin Waring was stabbed there?"

"No," Mike admitted.

"But you do know she had a gun?" Gregor tried to sound encouraging.

"She had a gun in her hand when the body was found," Jack Mann said.

"And that doesn't set off alarm bells in your heads?" Gregor asked.

"Alarm bells about what?" Mike Held asked.

"Well," Gregor said, "here's a woman who has been stabbed in the back. But she also has a gun in her hand. If somebody was trying to kill her, why didn't she shoot?"

"She did shoot," Jack Mann said. "She shot up the entire living room. She shot a bunch of holes in this big mirror. She took out most of a really huge chandelier."

"Those were all bullets from the gun she was holding?"

"They were," Mike Held said, "so maybe she was shooting at the person who stabbed her. Maybe that person snuck up behind her when she didn't know he was there—or she was there—and then she turned around and tried to get them with the gun."

"Okay," Gregor said, "that's not entirely implausible, but I don't like it much. We have to presume she knew she was in a place where she was at least potentially in danger. I'd think she'd be on her guard. But let that pass for the moment. What time of day was the body found?"

"It was at night," Jason Battlesea said. "Maybe nine o'clock at night."

"And when she was found, she was dead? Do you know how long she'd been dead?" Gregor asked.

"You know better than that," Jason Battlesea said. "This isn't *CSI*. We can't pull magic out of our hats."

"You can usually tell if a body is a couple of minutes or a couple of hours cold," Gregor said. "There's nothing wrong with the state medical examiner's office, is there? Isn't that Henry Lee?"

"There's nothing wrong with the medical examiner's office, no," Jason Battlesea said. "We must have all this information somewhere. I'm not sure why we didn't send it to you. Why don't we sit down and go through the computer files and see what we can find."

"Didn't you say the first person on the scene was a uniformed patrolman?" Gregor asked.

"Patrolwoman," Mike Held said.

"I want to talk to her," Gregor said.

"Of course," Jason Battlesea said. "She's—what, she's still on night duty? She ought to be coming in around six."

"I want to talk to her now," Gregor said. "Even if you have to get her out of bed."

3

It took Angela Harkin nearly twenty minutes to get into the station, and when she arrived she was not in uniform. What she was wearing instead was one of those sundresses whose tops were made out of something ruched and elastic, with thin spaghetti straps and a hemline that ended above her knees. Gregor noticed first that she did not have the kind of body usually associated with that kind of dress. She was stocky and short, built more like a man than a woman in many ways. The next thing he noticed was the way she walked. She kept her back very, very straight. She always looked straight ahead.

"Military?" Gregor asked her as she threw her huge tote bag down on the table in the middle of them.

Angela Harkin nodded. "Army, ten years. MP the last six. Then my knees gave out. I felt like an idiot, you know? I mean, what do MPs do if they're not in a war zone? Mostly, they pick up drunks who're overstaying their leave or causing some kind of trouble. You'd think anybody would be able to handle that kind of thing. Well, one of my drunks had a baseball bat and went right for my knees, and a couple of months later another one tried to drive over me, and here I am. Not that I mind being here. It's a great place. It's just that I always intended to make a career out of the service."

"Angela gets a little bored," Jack Mann said.

"There's a lot to get bored about in a place like this, Jack," Angela said. "Nothing ever happens here that can't be cleaned up by a call to Bridgeport or a call to Hartford, and I much prefer Bridgeport."

"There are always the calls to Washington," Mike Held said.

Angela Harkin rolled her eyes and sat down. "I take it this is Mr. Demarkian," she said, turning to him and holding out her hand. "You have no idea how glad I am to see you. You been over to Beach Drive yet?"

"He's staying at the Switch and Shingle," Jason Battlesea said.

"Good," Angela said. "Then you know what it's like. Great, big houses, set back, with their backs to the sea, and then on the other side with their faces to the sea. The ones that are right on the beach itself are more expensive. The Waring house is one of the expensive ones. So I patrol that, and I start at six o'clock. It was June, so it was light out. I made maybe three turns that night without seeing anything. And I mean not anything. I didn't see any cars on the road. I didn't see any people walking. Then I had to stop in at the Atlantic Club and check that out."

"What was going on at the Atlantic Club?"

"Fund-raiser for Virginia Brand Westervan's Senate campaign," Angela said. "Virginia Brand Westervan is the congresswoman from this district, and now she's running for Senate against an absolutely brain-dead jerk whose idea of fiscal responsibility is to eliminate homeless shelters."

"That's not true," Jason Battlesea said, "and you know it."

"All right, I'm exaggerating a little," Angela said. "But not my kind of guy. Anyway, there was a huge fund-raiser over there and there was lots of security. We had a couple of guys on extra shifts, and Virginia had her own private security people. So I was supposed to stop in and look around and make sure everything was going okay. And I did."

"And everything was going okay?" Gregor asked.

"Everything was fine," Angela agreed. "Virginia came out and talked to me herself, and then she got this waiter to get me a bunch of these canapé things with lobster that were absolutely stellar. And I don't want to hear one thing about what I was or wasn't supposed to be doing on duty. I didn't drink the champagne."

"If this was a serious police department," Jack Mann said, "you'd have been fired months ago."

"I don't like to hear that this isn't a police department," Jason Battlesea said. "This isn't a high-crime area, but—"

"Trust me, this is a high-crime area," Angela said, "it's just Federal crimes and they're all financial. We've already had five people from Alwych go to Danbury for fraud, three of them for mortgage fraud, which, as far as I'm concerned, is as bad as it gets. But anyway, I took a little time eating the canapés and then I got back in the patrol car and started another round."

"And was it still light out?" Gregor asked.

Angela nodded. "It was a little," she said. "It wasn't full dark, and wouldn't be for a while, but the lights in the Atlantic Club were all on, and the lights were on in most of the houses I passed after that."

"That included the lights in the Waring house," Gregor said.

"Absolutely," Angela said, "but that didn't mean much, because the lights there are on a timer. They go on and off at set intervals, and the intervals are changed every once in a while. I'm not sure what the Waring girls think they're doing, though, because it's not like everybody on earth didn't know that that house was empty. It's been empty for decades."

"But well taken care of," Gregor said.

"Oh, yeah," Angela said. "Really well taken care of. If you didn't already know, you'd never guess from looking at the place from the outside. They've got people who do the snow in the winter. They've got people who do the grass in the spring and summer. They've got a cleaning service that comes in once a month to dust things. They've got a repair service that checks every week. They repaint the house every three years. They take care of it as if they were going to move back in, but they never have."

"Do they have a security system?"

"Yep, and a good one, too," Angela said. "One of those private outfits you pay significant money to so that if the alarm goes off, they call the police."

"But nobody called the police on this night?" Gregor asked.

"Nobody called the police from the security service,"

Angela said, "and nobody called the security service. Those two checked. But somebody on Beach Road did call earlier in the night, to say she thought she saw odd lights there, and then heard something she was sure was a gun going off. If it had been anywhere but the Waring house, somebody would probably have been sent over immediately. But the Waring house is our own private haunted house. We get a lot of calls about that house that turn out to be nothing."

"The way you get a lot of calls from people who think they've seen Chapin Waring?" Gregor asked.

"Absolutely," Angela said again. "And it had been that kind of day, from what I'd heard. People calling in, saying they saw her, I mean. So, when I made the round, I slowed down and looked hard at the house."

"And?" Gregor asked.

Angela looked uncomfortable. "And I don't know," she said. "There were different lights on than what I thought ought to be there, but it's like I said. They've done this well, and it's not always the same lights. It was just—I don't know. It felt wrong. So I pulled into the driveway, way up until I was near the house, and I got out to look around."

"There's no security in the drive?" Gregor asked. "There's no outside alarm system?"

"No," Angela said. "I walked around the house for a while and there didn't seem to be anything. I stood on the terrace in the back and looked at the beach. There were footprints on the beach, leading up to the house."

"You're sure of that?" Gregor asked.

"Yeah, positive," Angela said. "There were footprints coming up, but none going down. And I didn't know if I was supposed to think that was odd or not. People have private beaches here, but they're not really private. They run into each other, and all you have to do to walk along the shore is just walk. There are chain fences, but they don't go very far out into the water, and at low tide you'd have a great big open space to walk in. And I'd bet anything that people walk along those beaches and then come up to the Waring terrace to look inside."

"But there were no footsteps leading away from the house," Gregor said.

"No, there weren't that I could see," Angela said. "But I just might have missed something."

"Do you really think you missed footsteps going away from the house?" Gregor asked.

"No," Angela said.

"All right," Gregor said. "That's good. What next?"

"I didn't want to jump the gun. The house is empty, but it has owners, and one of them lives in town. The family does come in on and off and check the place out."

"They never stay there?"

"I don't know," Angela said, "but I wasn't going to barge in there before I knew what was going on. I was on the terrace, and the terrace has this big wall of glass looking out onto the ocean. It's also got curtains, but I went up to the glass to see if I could see anything at all, and it turned out I could. I could see a foot in a pair of canvas espadrilles. And right then, I thought it was going to turn out that I only thought I saw a foot, and it was really just an espadrille on the floor. So I looked again, and it still looked like a foot. So I decided that it wouldn't hurt to check it out, that maybe somebody had gotten in there and started squatting, so I went around to the front door."

"There was a reason you couldn't get in from where you were?" Gregor asked.

"I probably could have, but we've got keys to the security system at the front door, and it causes a lot less fuss if I do things officially," Angela said. "I went around to the front and let myself in."

"The front door was locked?"

"Yes, it was," Angela said. "I had to jimmy it to get it open, and then I had to do a sprint to keep the alarm system from going off."

"But the alarm system was on?"

"Yes, it was," Angela said. "I stood in the foyer for a while and there was nothing to see. I called out and nobody answered. Then I went toward the back of the house, and there it was."

"It?"

"The body," Angela said. "She was lying on the floor, the knife was sticking out of her back, and the place was a complete mess. She had a gun in her hand. The whole room was shot up, the mirrors, the chandelier, everything. There was glass everywhere. But that isn't the detail you want."

"What detail do I want?" Gregor asked.

"She wasn't wearing espadrilles," Angela Harkin said. She sounded almost triumphant. "These two have been telling me I must have been mistaken about the espadrille I saw when I looked in from the back, but I'm not. It was an espadrille I saw. But the body of Chapin Waring was wearing tennis shoes. And they weren't anything like the same color."

The door to the room opened up, and the uniformed woman from the front desk looked in. "You haven't been answering your beeper," she said to Jason Battlesea. "You're needed out here for a minute."

Jason Battlesea got up and left the room. Gregor turned his attention back to Angela Harkin.

"This foot you saw," he said. "Was it the foot of somebody standing up? Lying down? What?"

"Not standing up," Angela said. "It was up off the floor."

"Like somebody was sitting on the couch or on a chair?"

"Something like that," Angela said.

"But there was glass everywhere?" Gregor asked. "You said everywhere. There was glass on the furniture, too?"

"Yes, there was glass on the furniture," Angela said. "Lots of it. Lots of it everywhere. Furniture, rug, floor, hearth, the body, everywhere."

"So that if somebody was sitting or kneeling on a piece of furniture, they would have to have been sitting or kneeling on glass?" Gregor said.

"They'd have to have been sitting or kneeling on a lot of it," Angela said.

The door opened and Jason Battlesea came back in, looking harassed.

"Here's something," he said. "The burglar alarm has just gone off at the Waring house."

PART TWO

A genius is the one who is most like himself.
                                    —Thelonious Monk

ONE

1

The Waring house turned out to be one of the ones with a high hedge near the road, so that Gregor couldn't have seen it if he'd wanted to while he was being driven to and from town. It was yellow.

They climbed out of the almost unmarked town car now parked in the driveway of the Waring house.

There was a young patrolman in full uniform standing near the side of the house, looking uneasy and very inexperienced. He had the palm of his right hand resting on the butt of the gun in his holster. He was rocking back and forth on the balls of his feet.

"Stewart!" Mike Held called.

"This is Stewart Crone," Jack Mann said. "Stewart, this is Gregor Demarkian."

"Are you guys going to want to come in and look around?" Stewart asked. "I've been in already once and there isn't anything. I mean, there really isn't anything. It's spooky."

"We got a call from the security company?" Mike Held asked.

"Oh, yeah, exactly," Stewart said. "And I didn't expect to find anything. We get calls all the time. People come snooping around and trip the alarm, or the help does, or sometimes it's animals. But this time the front door was open. It was just open. Maybe an inch or two."

"Had it been forced?" Gregor asked.

"It doesn't look like it," Stewart said. "I was very careful. I moved it back and forth with a pencil so I wouldn't smear much in the way of prints. And the other thing is, I'm pretty sure it's unlocked."

Gregor thought about it. "Could it have been left unlocked after the investigation?"

"No," Jack Mann said. "Every time we've come to this house, I've locked and unlocked it myself. And I've always been careful to check."

"There aren't dead bolts or that kind of thing for backup?" Gregor asked.

"You don't use dead bolts when you leave a house," Stewart said. "That's for when you stay in. Anyway, this door has one of those locks that turn with a little half circle key. I'm pretty sure horizontal is locked and vertical is unlocked, and it was vertical when I got there."

"Anything disturbed?" Mike Held asked.

"I wouldn't know how to check," Stewart said. "I did a quick tour and nothing seemed out of place, but any number of things could have been taken that I wouldn't notice."

"Tell me you took an inventory the night of the crime," Gregor said.

"It was the day after," Mike Held said, "but we took it. And we've got a copy at the station and another one we gave to Mrs. Holder."

"Mrs. Holder is—?" Gregor said.

"Caroline Waring Holder," Mike said. "She's the youngest sister."

"We get your drift, Mr. Demarkian," Jack Mann said. "We should double-check against the inventory. We will."

"Let me just make sure I have this part straight," Gregor said. "The security company called in to the police station to say that the alarm had gone off in this house. When Officer Crone got here, he found the front door open and probably unlocked. The door had been locked by the police when they last investigated the scene of the crime. Could anybody else have been in this house legitimately between then and now?"

"The sister could have," Mike Held said. "Mrs. Holder."

"All right," Gregor said. "Then we've got two possibilities: Either this Mrs. Holder came into the house for reasons of her own over the last few days and accidentally left the front door unlocked when she left, or somebody with a key to the front door let himself or herself in and then let the alarm go off, and then left."

"Why does that sound ridiculous when you say it?" Mike Held asked.

"Because," Gregor said, "you have to assume that anybody who legitimately has a key to this house must also have the code for the security system. Without it, the key is pretty much useless. There is always the possibility that somebody has an unauthorized key to this house, but then we run into the same roadblock. The key without the security code is worthless. And anybody who actually knew anything about this house would know that."

"So, what are you saying, exactly?" Jack Mann said. "Nobody tried to get into the house? Because somebody seems to have tried to get into the house."

"Why?" Gregor asked.

"To tamper with evidence," Mike Held said. "Isn't that why people usually do these things?"

"Yes, that's why they usually do them," Gregor said, "but in this case, we're back to the problem. Anybody who knew anything about this house would know there was a security system here. I'd assume that most of the houses on this road have security systems."

"All of them," Mike Held agreed.

"But on top of that," Gregor said, "this is a house with a history. Everybody in town knows about it. People five states away know about it. Even someone who stole a key, or managed to get a copy, would at least be able to guess that there was a security system here. And that means that if somebody who didn't have the security code wanted to get in to tamper with or remove evidence, they'd have to know exactly where that evidence was and it would have to be easy to tamper with it or remove it. There wouldn't be any time for mucking around, looking for it. The alarm would go off in a minute or two, and the police would be here sooner rather than later."

"Maybe whoever it was was desperate," Jack Mann said. "Maybe he decided to take a chance because it was now or never."

"He'd have to be desperate enough to get stupid," Gregor Demarkian said, "and that's a lot of desperate for a case that, until now, has generated not a single suspect that I know of. Unless I missed that part in the notes."

"There are suspects," Mike Held said, "sort of. But not—you know what I mean. We know a lot about the people Chapin Waring knew when she was here thirty years ago. Those people are at least possible suspects."

"My point exactly," Gregor said.

He took his cell phone out of his pocket and used it to push the front door open. He walked into a high-ceilinged, expansive foyer. A staircase with a heavy carved wood banister rose up to the right. The walls on the left had a small cluster of framed prints on the clean white wall. The prints looked like copies of things by Braque.

Gregor went back outside and looked at the door again. Stewart Crone was right. There was no sign that the lock had been jimmied. Of course, it was also possible that the front door was not the point of entry. That idea opened up yet another can of worms.

He started to walk toward Mike Held and Jack Mann, to explain the alternate-entry idea, when there was a noise on the road and a long, black Volvo Cross Country station wagon came barreling up the drive, screeching to a halt just millimeters from the back of Jack and Mike's municipal car.

A second later, the driver's door opened and a tall, thin woman with wild hair jumped out, looking ready to kill somebody.

"For God's sake," she said. "Can you people get anything done right?"

2

There was a small moment when Gregor felt as if he'd seen this woman a hundred times before—and then he knew, of course, that she was Chapin Waring's sister. What he was looking at was mostly Chapin Waring's face, but much older than it had been in the newspaper photographs and memorabilia from the time of the robberies. There were four sisters. He wondered if the two he hadn't seen resembled each other as closely as these two did.

This one was loaded for bear.

"The one thing in the entire universe that you're supposed to do," she said, advancing on Mike Held and Jack Mann, "is to keep people away from this goddamned house. You were supposed to do it before, but by God, you'd think that with a murder in the living room, and having to haul Gregor Demarkian out here to save your asses from not being able to detect tapioca pudding, you'd think you'd be able to do it now. What's wrong with you? I thought you were supposed to have a guard out here twenty-four/seven."

"Now, Mrs. Holder, you know we weren't going to do that," Jack Mann said. "We explained it to you. The department doesn't have the kind of manpower we'd need to keep this place under surveillance twenty-four/seven. If that's what you want, you're going to have to hire your own man."

"I'm going to have to hire a good lawyer to sue your asses off sooner rather than later," the woman said. "I'm going to do something, because I'm sure as hell fed up. First Chapin turns up out of nowhere when all of you were supposed to be looking for her—"

"We weren't looking for her," Mike Held said. "It's the feds that have been looking for her."

"—she turns up here when you were supposed to be looking for her. She's seen by half the people in town. You do absolutely nothing about it and then she turns up dead. And do you know what's happened to me, seriously? My life has become one long defense against my telephone. I've got reporters staking out my house. I've got my children being asked God only knows what at school and now it's all over the television again. And you can't even keep the tourists out of the house."

"We don't know it was a tourist," Mike Held said.

The woman looked at him as if he were pond scum clinging to her Wellingtons. "For God's sake," she said. "Who else would it be?"

Gregor gave a little cough. The group all turned their heads to him. The woman blinked.

"Who's this?" she asked.

"This is Gregor Demarkian," Mike Held said. "He just got in this morning."

"He doesn't look like much," she said. "Maybe it's not such a bad idea. Maybe if you don't look like much, people tell you things they shouldn't."

"Mrs. Holder—" Mike Held said.

Caroline Holder ignored him. "Are you actually going to do something about this mess?" she asked Gregor Demarkian. "Or will you say you're going to do something about it and then you never do?"

"I'm going to try to do something about it," Gregor said. "I'd like to know why you're so sure the alarm was set off by tourists."

Caroline Holder looked infinitely tired. "Because it always is tourists," she said. "Even before the murder, it was tourists—there were just fewer of them. God, I hate those cable channels. It was bad enough before, what with 'retrospectives' and all that other crap every few years. And then there was *America's Most Wanted,* which for a minute or two I was stupid enough to think might do some good. Now there's *American Justice* and *City Confidential* and *Deadly Women* and all the rest of them, rehashing the case and rehashing the case and rehashing the case until you'd think it had become some kind of cult. And then there was the murder, and the town is full of people who just want to get a look. Even Darlee Corn's full up, and the prices she charges ought to be illegal."

"We came out here to investigate," Mike Held said. "We came, not just the patrol officer. So if you would just—"

"Just what?" Caroline Holder said. "Just trust you to know what you're doing? Well, I don't. I don't trust you to have the brains to pick your own noses. And I don't see why I should. You've got to keep this place under surveillance, or that alarm will go off every other day and by the time you get here, whoever it was will be gone and taken a little souvenir to say they've been here. I'm sick to death of losing half the kitsch from my childhood because you won't face reality."

"Mrs. Holder?" Gregor asked.

"What is it?"

"I just want to get a couple of things straight. Tourists come, you say, and break into the house. How do they do that?"

"How do they do what?"

"How do they get into the house?" Gregor asked.

"Oh," Caroline Holder said. She put a hand in her wild hair. It didn't help. "Well," she said. "Mostly, they come up by the beach. The house on that side is right on the beach. There's a terrace, and then past the terrace there's sand. And Long Island Sound. They walk along the beach and then come up from there."

"And how do they get in?"

"There are sliding glass doors to the terrace," Caroline Holder said. "Except we've got rods in the slider slots now. It didn't used to be very hard. Even if they were locked."

"And you changed that so that there were rods in the slots?" Gregor said. "When did you do that?"

Caroline Holder blushed. "It was after the murder," she admitted. "Before that, it hadn't been absolutely impossible for a while. Even with the television shows, you know, the crimes were so far in the past, and nobody saw or heard from Chapin—"

"I thought lots of people saw her," Gregor said. "I thought people in town saw her fairly often."

"Well, they *said* they did," Caroline Holder said. "But really, Mr. Demarkian, how could that possibly have worked? You had half the Federal government trying to find out where Chapin was. Do you really think she could have shown up here in town half a dozen times in the last thirty years, been identified and called in by dozens of people, and they would never have caught her?"

"No," Gregor agreed. "What I want to know about is this house. Why keep it all these years, when nobody was living in it? And I take it nobody has been living in it."

"Nobody's lived here since—maybe since a couple of weeks after Martin Veer's funeral," Caroline Holder said. "We couldn't, really. There was a nationwide manhunt for Chapin. There were reporters everywhere you looked. People came right up to the front door and knocked. My parents decided we'd be better off somewhere else, so they moved us all to this place we had in the Adirondacks for the summer. Then, when the summer was over—" Caroline shrugged. "When the summer was over, my parents didn't want to come back. And I can't say I blamed them."

"Where did they go?" Gregor asked.

"Out to California for a while," Caroline said. "They put us in school out there and kept their heads low. Then, when I left for college, they traveled. And then they died."

"And they never tried to sell the house?" Gregor asked.

"I think they did try, once," Caroline said. "I was still very young, but I seem to remember something about it, except all they got was people who wanted a look."

"And when they died, the house came to—who, exactly?" Gregor asked.

"To me and my sisters," Caroline said. "We all got equal shares of everything."

"All?" Gregor asked.

"If you're asking if Chapin also got an equal share, then the answer is yes, Mr. Demarkian. And that should answer your other question. Charlotte and Cordelia and I would have been happy to sell the house, but we couldn't do it without Chapin's agreement, and we couldn't find Chapin. We couldn't even have her declared legally dead. And we tried. The United States government intervened in the case and the judge refused to do it."

"So you've kept up the house ever since?" Gregor asked.

"Charlotte and Cordelia pay for most of it," Caroline said. "I'm the one who gets stuck here on the ground, dealing with the day-to-day stuff. The break-ins. The periodic vandalism."

"It's been years since there's been any vandalism," Mike Held said.

"It doesn't matter how many years it's been," Caroline Holder said. "It matters that it's happened at all. And then there's the management. We have a maid service that comes in once a month and a lawn service that comes in every week during the spring and summer and repair people for specific jobs, like painting and that kind of thing. Somebody has to hire and fire those people and make sure they're doing their jobs. And I'm here."

"Yes," Gregor said. "You are."

"If you're thinking that one of us came in here and killed Chapin because we wanted to sell the house—well, it's not possible. Charlotte and Cordelia both live out of state, and I don't know if I would have recognized Chapin if she came right up to me and told me who she was. It had been thirty years, Mr. Demarkian, and I was only eight."

"But you did identify the body," Gregor said.

"I went down to the morgue and looked," Caroline Holder said. "What I saw was a woman who looked a lot like me. So I stated the obvious. I told them I thought it could be Chapin. I think they finally made the definitive identification some other way."

"And you were where on the day the murder happened?" Gregor asked.

Caroline Holder smiled. "I've been waiting for somebody to ask me that question. On the evening when I think they've decided it happened, I was at my children's school. I'm part of a group that helps to bring musical instruments into the schools. We were discussing a harpsichord."

"And earlier in the day?"

"Earlier in the day," Caroline Holder said, "I was doing what people do earlier in the day. I did some shopping. I did some housework. I did some gardening."

"You don't work?"

"No," Caroline Holder said. "I don't need to work, financially. My husband does well enough even without my money. I thought I'd give my children the kind of childhood I'd always wanted to have."

"The one that was interrupted by your sister," Gregor said.

"Oh, the mess started long before that," Caroline Holder said. "You've got to grow up in a place like Alwych to know just how awful that can be."

Gregor raised his eyebrows slightly. Caroline Holder put her hands in her hair again.

"I think I'll get out of here before you can start the whole 'poor little rich girl' thing," she said. "Yes, I know. There was always enough money and none of us ever wanted for anything."

"Except love?" Gregor said.

"Don't be maudlin," Caroline Holder said. "That's not what I'm talking about, and you know it. Now for God's sake, let's not have this happen again."

"You're going to have to hire your own security man," Mike Held insisted.

"One more thing," Gregor said. "Who has keys to this house?"

"Keys?" Caroline said. "Well, I do. And my sisters do. The cleaning service has a set. They have to, or I'd have to let them in every time they need to be here. And the police have a set."

"That's since the murder?" Gregor asked.

"No," Caroline said. "As far as I know, the police have had a set at least since my sisters took over caring for the house. We want them to be able to get in and out of here if there's a problem."

"And all those people also have the code for the security system?" Gregor asked.

"I suppose so," Caroline Holder said. "I do and the police do and the cleaning service does. I'm not sure about my sisters."

"How about the family lawyer, say, or the repair people—?"

"The lawyers—and it's plural—do not. If there are repairs

needed to the interior of the house, I let the repair people in myself."

"Interesting," Gregor said.

"You really do think one of us killed Chapin," Caroline said. "Well, I suppose I can't stop you thinking it. It might have worked if we could have done it and hidden the body somewhere, but that isn't what happened. Now there's all this, and it's not going to make anything better. It's making everything worse. And besides, why would any of us want to kill her? You don't kill someone you haven't seen in thirty years. You don't have enough in common."

3

Caroline Holder left without spewing gravel, which Gregor told himself was a good thing. He wouldn't want to have to deal with the woman in that state of anger for very long.

He waited until she was all the way out of the driveway and then went back into the house, through the foyer and into the large living room beyond. He went to the sliding glass doors and checked the sliders for the rods. They were there. He moved from room to room, checking every door he found. None of the doors to the exterior looked as if it had been in any way tampered with. He went back to the front door and checked that again. It still looked pristine.

"Well, that's interesting," he said.

Mike Held and Jack Mann waited for him to go on. Officer Crone looked positively entranced.

"Sometimes," Gregor told them, "you have to pay attention to the obvious. Can't you see the obvious here?"

"Nothing about this case looks obvious to me," Mike Held said. "That's why you're here. If you see something that tells you exactly who committed this crime and why they committed it, you ought to come right out and say so."

"I don't see who committed the crime," Gregor said, "but I do see a circumstance that's interesting. On the night of the murder, the alarm didn't go off, and the security service wasn't alerted."

"No," Jack Mann said.

"So," Gregor said, "on the night of the murder, both Chapin Waring and at least one other person got into this house without setting off the alarm. It's possible they got in from the sliding glass doors, which didn't have the rods at that point, but even if they did, someone had to have entered the security code, or the alarm would have gone off. If Chapin Waring had a key to the house and the security code, then the other person or persons could be anybody at all. If she didn't, then the other person or persons had to be among the people who did have those things."

"How could Chapin Waring have the keys and the code when nobody had seen her for thirty years?" Jack Mann asked.

"We only have Caroline Holder's word for it that nobody in the family had seen her sister for thirty years. She could be lying. Even if she isn't, her sisters could be lying to her. There's been nonstop Federal surveillance, and that would have made contact a lot harder, but it wouldn't have made it impossible. And then we come to today."

"What about today?" Mike Held asked.

"Today," Gregor said, "either whoever came here didn't have the security code but did have a key, or they had the security code but didn't use it. Why would they not use it if they had it?"

"Maybe it was tourists," Mike Held said.

"A tourist wouldn't have had the key," Gregor said. "No one would have the key but not the security codes, unless, as I said before, the key had been stolen. And no one could use the key without having the security codes."

"I'm getting dizzy," Officer Crone said.

"I'm getting dizzy, too," Gregor said. "I can see why everybody around here wants to concentrate on a thirty-year-old crime. At least we know what happened in that one."

TWO

1

The fourth call of the day from Jason Battlesea came through at just about three o'clock, and Evaline Veer almost didn't take it.

She stared at the blinking light on her telephone and sighed. A part of her had never been happy at the idea of bringing Gregor Demarkian into this case. She'd never said that out loud, to anyone, but it was true.

She picked up the phone and punched the flashing button to get the line. She said "Yes" without giving out any other kind of information, on the assumption that Jason knew whom he'd called and recognized her voice.

Jason's voice boomed out over the wire, loud and steady.

"Evie!" Jason said, "I've got another update for you! He wants to know about the keys!"

"Are you using a bullhorn?" she asked Jason. "You sound like you're standing on Main Street, trying to disperse rioters."

"I'm at the station," Jason said just as loudly. "Hell, Evie, where would I be? I thought you'd like to know that he's asking about the keys to the Waring house. If they've ever been changed. How often they've been changed. When was the last time they were changed."

"Well, of course the keys have been changed," Evaline said. "What does he think the Warings are, hillbilly hicks? As for the last time they were changed, I don't know. Do you?"

"Yeah, it was back in January," Jason Battlesea said. "Caroline Holder came over and gave us a set. I don't know what prompted it that time. Sometimes I think that that woman has the locks changed on a random basis, you know, so nobody can get an idea."

"That wouldn't be stupid," Evaline said. "Although God only knows who wants to get into that house now. Or did want to get in it before the murder. I blame it on the Internet."

"He's sitting in the conference room, going over the notes with Mike and Jack," Jason said. "It's a little depressing. I don't know what I thought he'd do, but I guess I thought it would be something different from the usual."

"You expected him to come and pull a rabbit out of his hat?" Evaline asked.

"Maybe. Something."

"I really do have something I'm working on here," Evaline said.

"I think Mike and Jack are going to go crazy if he keeps on like this," Jason said. "He's going through those notes line by line. There are a lot of things we didn't think of, apparently. Really basic things. It's going to make us look like idiots if it gets out."

"I doubt he makes a habit of making his clients look like idiots," Evaline said.

"He doesn't have to make a habit of it. Somebody just has to hear about it."

"Like what?"

"Like Caroline Holder telling them about it," Jason said. "You know how she gets when she gets mad."

"Yes," Evaline said. "I know how she gets. I've known her all my life. I knew her before you did."

"I wouldn't put it past her to call *The New York Times*."

"Could I please get back to work now?"

"I'm just keeping you updated," Jason said. "You said

you wanted to be updated, and I'm doing it. If you don't want to be updated anymore, you can always just say so."

"No," Evaline said. "No, of course not. Of course I want to be updated. I need to be updated. Maybe just not every four seconds."

"He wants to meet you."

"Fine. He can meet me anytime. It's just that now—"

Jason hung up.

She put the receiver of her own phone back into the cradle. Then she got up, walked to her office door, and locked it.

There was, she thought, absolutely nothing that she knew anymore that could hurt anyone. It had all happened so long ago, and then things she had known and never told could not reveal where Chapin Waring had been for thirty years, or why she had decided to mastermind those robberies, or where the missing money was. The things she knew were personal, and of importance only to herself. There was still something about the whole thing being raked up again that made her neck feel as if it had been injected with cement.

Sometimes she just wanted to be away from people, away from talking, away from the endless gossip that was the core of Alwych.

It was bad enough having to deal with Tim and Virginia.

It was worse having to deal with something that should have died a few decades ago.

Evaline got up again, went back to her door, and unlocked it.

She had no idea what she'd been doing when she did that, but she did know it was entirely ridiculous.

2

It was only four thirty when Kyle Westervan showed up at Tim Brand's clinic. It was only an accident that Tim was here this early himself. There was nothing at the clinic Marcie couldn't handle if he let her.

Tim watched Kyle walk up the long driveway to the clinic.

Kyle was looking the clinic over as he came. He did not seem to be surprised by anything he saw, and he didn't seem to be put off by it. Tim sent up a thank-you to God for both those things, and then just waited at the top of the rise for Kyle to get to him. He also checked out the suit. The damned thing had to have cost four thousand dollars if it cost a dime. It broke all of what Tim had always thought of as Kyle's rules.

Kyle reached the top of the rise and took off his sunglasses. He lifted his briefcase in the air and said, "I've come loaded for bear. You told me to."

"I didn't know if you'd ever been here," Tim said. "Most everybody else has been at one time or the other. I hit them up for donations."

"Is that what I'm here for? You're hitting me up for donations?"

"No," Tim said. He looked up and down the line. "Let's go back to the office. I really didn't expect you this early. It's a miracle I'm here myself. Don't you have to put in hundred-hour weeks to get that salary they're paying you?"

"Most of the time. I've been having a rather odd day."

"I've been having a rather odd week," Tim said. "Come around back. We can actually get some peace and quiet, if not for long."

"Are they always this patient, the people who stand in line? I've seen bank lines that have been more agitated."

"They're calm this time of the day," Tim said, leading Kyle between gurneys and equipment and nurses and cubicles to the corridor in the back where the closest thing to quiet was. He opened the door to his office and stood back to let Kyle pass.

Kyle walked in, looked at the cramped space, and smiled slightly. "I was wondering where the hair shirt was," he said.

Tim walked in, too, and closed the door behind them. "It's not a hair shirt, it's a matter of necessity. You need a big office to impress clients. I have no clients to impress. We need space for other things."

"You could always spring for a desk," Kyle said, sitting down at the little round laminated table.

Tim went to one of the big cardboard boxes he used as filing cabinets when he needed to keep paper records. This was a new cardboard box, with almost nothing in it. He opened it up and took out the letters from the Office of Health Care Access and the Office of the Health Care Advocate. He threw them down on the table in front of Kyle.

"Take a look at those," he said. "I know this isn't the kind of law you do. And I don't expect you to handle this case for me. But you're a smart lawyer. And I was hoping you'd give me your thoughts."

Kyle picked up the first of the letters and read through it. Then he picked up the second and read through that. Then he put them both back down on the table.

"Well?" Tim said.

"It's Virginia," Kyle said.

"I know it's Virginia," Tim said. "The only thing I've known for sure since those letters came is that Virginia was behind them."

"You won't find her fingerprints on them," Kyle said. "You won't find a scrap of paper to so much as hint that she knew this was going to happen, or that she talked to anybody about it before the fact. Or am I stating the obvious again?"

"Somewhat," Tim admitted. "I guess what I was hoping for was some kind of legal strategy that would allow us to resolve this without going to court. I've been advised that if this does go to court, the state will not be able to prevail. That's a wonderful word, isn't it? Prevail. But they don't have to prevail, and I think Virginia knows it. If they did, I would shut the clinic down voluntarily. I wouldn't operate it if I was required to give out morning-after pills to rape victims or anybody else. The court case will gut us. Even if we walk out in victory, we'll also walk out dead broke and unable to go on. I've got a fair amount of money, but not enough money to fund half this clinic and a major court case at the same time."

"Do you really fund half the clinic?"

"Just about," Tim said. "Donations have gotten better and better over the years, but every time donations get better, I think of four more things we need to have."

"I was surprised when I heard you were opening this up in Alwych," Kyle said. "I kept thinking it would make more sense to open it in Bridgeport."

"If you think there isn't need out here, you're crazy," Tim said. "Especially since the financial crash, but even before. You'd be amazed at how many people, even people we grew up with—well, never mind. I really didn't bring you here to give you a fund-raising speech."

Kyle thought about it. "You could start a legal fund," he said. "You could explain the situation. It's not like you've been accused of diddling the choirboys. People know what you do here. If they've been giving you money, they almost certainly approve of it. Most of them probably hold the same views you do about abortion and the morning-after pill. That might not cover everything you need, but it would go a long way, I'd think."

"Except that if they're giving to the legal defense fund, they're not giving to the clinic," Tim said. "Money only goes so far. And the kind of people who give to the clinic tend not to be, how do I put it? In your financial position."

"You mean most of your donors are small donors."

"Exactly," Tim said. "And we don't take any government money—not Medicare, not Medicaid, nothing. We can't. As soon as you take their money, they think they have the right to tell you how to run your clinic."

"I don't think that's all that outrageous," Kyle said.

"I don't either," Tim said. "But it does bring us back to being in that same position."

Kyle picked up the letters again. He glanced through them again. He put them down again.

"Was Virginia like this when we were all growing up?" he asked. "This doctrinaire."

Tim was surprised. "You were married to her."

"I know I was married to her, but that doesn't tell me much, does it?" Kyle said. "I get along with Virginia. I always have. Married or divorced, it never made any difference. But lately, it's like she's turned into petrified wood."

"She'd say I've turned into petrified wood," Tim said.

"I know. She'd be right. You both have. I don't think either of you understands how completely alike you are."

"And now Chapin is dead," Tim said, "and there's a world-class detective consultant the town is paying God only knows what to do something about it."

"Have you met the Great Detective?"

"No," Tim said. "I have been keeping up on the gossip. He's apparently closeted himself in the records room of the police department and is reading through every scrap of paper he can find. The word is that our particular local police force isn't much good at collecting evidence and analyzing it."

"Have you had a call to go and talk to him?" Kyle asked.

"No, of course not," Tim said. "Why would I?"

"They're going to have to come along and talk to every-body who was involved in that other thing, even if 'involved' only means that they were part of the same deb party circuit as the principals. Didn't the local police come and talk to you after the murder?"

"For a couple of minutes," Tim said.

"They got me for a couple of minutes, too," Kyle said. "But it's all going to come back around. If I were you and I were going to worry about something happening to the clinic, I'd worry about the blowback from that."

Tim watched him stand up, moving carefully so that he didn't tip over books and papers and make something fall. Tim got the impression that Kyle was almost completely ex-hausted, that he'd had so little sleep for so long, he was about to fall over. For a moment, Tim was actually frightened.

"Are you all right?" he asked. "I know you've got perfect

health insurance and you don't come here, but if you need something—"

"I'm fine," Kyle said, looking even less fine. "Do you still give the same answer, when people ask you why you do what you do?"

"The same answer?" Tim asked.

"I remember it from the first interview I read," Kyle said. "Something in Latin, about—"

"Ad maiorem Dei gloriam," Tim said. " 'For the greater glory of God.' "

"That's it," Kyle said. "At least it's a reason."

"You really are sick," Tim said. "Do you have something I don't know about? Because you look like you're about to fall over."

"I am about to fall over," Kyle said. "I've been working late forever, and I've gotten to that age. I'm just overworked, and I don't think any good can come of this."

"Can good come of this thing with Chapin?" Tim asked. "She was murdered. Of course no good can come of it."

"Well, somebody thought some good could come of it," Kyle said. "It's the only reason why anybody ever murders anybody else."

"Oh," Tim said.

"Listen," Kyle said. "Why don't we go somewhere off the premises? Somewhere no one can hear us talking? I think I may have a solution to your problem."

"To the problem of the Health Care Access thing?"

"Exactly," Kyle said. "Let me just hit a restroom and we'll go somewhere and talk."

3

Hope Matlock had ridden the train into New York dozens of times when she was in high school and college. It was one of the things they did as a group, over and over again, because it annoyed the hell out of their parents. She could remember herself on those trains, looking out windows as Westport and Stamford and Greenwich rolled by, mentally counting up her money in her head. She'd never had as much money as the rest of them. She'd always been afraid that they would want to go somewhere where she couldn't handle the freight.

Today she had been worried about money, too, and she was right to worry. The trains were a lot more expensive than they had been thirty years ago. They were nicer, too, but Hope only cared about the expense. Everything in Manhattan had been more expensive, too, especially the buses and the subways. It hadn't taken her long to realize that if the day didn't work out, she wasn't going to have enough to get back to Grand Central Station.

As it turned out, the day had worked out fine. It was quarter past six, and she was sitting in a Metro-North car, watching the towns go by again in reverse order.

The outskirts of Alwych began rolling by, the big red barn that was now a farmers' market every Saturday afternoon in the spring and summer, the "smaller" houses with their postage stamp lawns where new people lived when they really couldn't afford to live in Alwych. Hope waited to see the facade of Lanyard's going by. Then she began to get up and move into the aisle, even though the conductor had yet to call the stop.

She knew better than to look into her pocketbook where people could see her. She was afraid that she'd held it much to close to her during the trip. The conductor came through and had to squeeze by her, which was embarrassing. The train began to slow and other people began to get up out of their seats. Hope shoved the embarrassment down her throat and made for the door.

When the train came to a stop, Hope got off onto the cement platform and then made her way to the stairs to the depot. She got to the depot waiting room and made for one of the benches at the front. She sat down and closed her eyes. She was still hugging her pocketbook. There was sweat on her forehead. She could feel it. She was having trouble breathing. This was all she needed. She'd pass out here and be hauled off to the emergency room or Tim's clinic, and somebody would steal her purse.

She was willing herself not to pass out when a familiar voice said, "Hope? Is that you? Are you feeling all right?"

"I'm fine," Hope said, opening her eyes and looking into Evaline Veer's. Evaline was bending over her.

Hope sat up a little straighter in her chair. "I'm exhausted," she said. "I was just getting myself psyched up for the long walk home."

"Walk?" Evaline said. "You walked all the way here from your place? Whatever for?"

"Parking around the depot is ridiculous," Hope said. She meant parking around the depot was expensive, and she didn't have one of those monthly parking passes. "And I knew I was going to be back before dark."

"Oh, you went in to the city," Evaline said.

"Just for lunch," Hope said. "I'd forgotten how tiring it was. And now I'm back and all I want to do is go to sleep."

"Well, go to sleep in your own bed," Evaline said. "I'll walk you out to your place and make sure you're settled. You really don't look all that well."

"I'm fine, really."

"Nonsense," Evaline said. "And the walk will do me good. I'm beyond agitated, I hate to tell you. Gregor Demarkian got here."

"I heard it on the news this morning," Hope said.

"Yes, well. I still haven't met the man, and he's already made my life one huge complication. I've had Jason Battlesea on the phone all day, reporting in when so much as a leaf falls in the forest, and then of course there had to be an *Incident*. There always has to be an *Incident*."

"What kind of incident?" Hope asked, stalling for time. She really didn't want to get up and get moving just yet.

"Oh, the alarm went off over at the Waring house," Evaline said. "I know we're all supposed to be on hyperalert since the murder, but that alarm goes off all the time and everybody knows it. The police had to go check it out anyway, of course, and then Caroline Holder came roaring in, being her usual Waring self. And then Caroline came to see me, right at the end of the day, as if I had nothing to do in the world except listen to her screech about how the police are complete idiots."

"I remember going off to college and then to graduate school and coming back, and almost nobody ever talked about Chapin," Hope said.

"Oh, of course they did," Evaline said. "They just didn't talk about it around us. I think they're all crazy, all the Warings. Holding on to that house all these years. What did they think was going to happen? Chapin was going to walk through the front doors one day and then—what? Go on trial for murdering two people in a bank robbery?"

"I don't think they did," Hope said. "Mr. and Mrs. Waring, I mean. I don't think they wanted her to come back."

"I always thought they wanted her dead," Evaline said, "I'd have wanted her dead if I was them. But you knew them better than I did."

"It wasn't the way everybody is always saying it was," Hope said. She was getting her wind back. She felt better. "Everybody talks about it as if we all knew about the robberies when they were going on. But we didn't. I didn't. And I don't think Tim did, either."

"And you think I knew?" Evaline said. "Is that it?"

Hope shook her head. "I think it was a secret, just between the two of them," she said. "I think they liked having a secret so they could laugh at the rest of us."

"Well, that would have been in character."

"Do you know what the very worst thing about the murder is?" Hope asked. "The very worst thing is that you can't stop thinking about it."

"And," Evaline said, "you're right, I can't stop thinking about it. Although mostly I remember what came just before we knew about the robberies. I remember the police coming to the door of the house to tell us about the accident, and that Marty was in the hospital. I remember thinking that the hospital was a good sign, because you didn't take someone to the hospital if he was dead. And then he was dead. It turned out that you did take somebody to the hospital if he was dead, because the morgue was in the hospital basement."

"Is it?" Hope said.

"Not the real morgue," Evaline said. "We've got a state facility for that. It's just the place we put bodies while we're waiting for a transfer. That's a terrible thing to think of, isn't it? A transfer. Like you're hauling meat. Marty was transferred to the funeral home that used to be next to the Congregational Church. I don't even remember what it was called anymore."

"They took all of us to the hospital that night," Hope said. "Chapin was in the backseat and she was barely even scratched. I remember Tim getting out from the back and walking around the car. Just walking around it and around it. And the car was all crumpled up. They made a big deal in the papers about how Marty had been drinking that night, but I didn't think it made any difference. We were always drinking in those days. Nobody thought anything of it. It wasn't like now."

"No," Evaline agreed. "It wasn't like now."

"Sometimes I look back on it and I realize that they must have been acting crazy because of the two people who were killed," Hope said. "Chapin and Marty, I mean. They were high as kites and we hadn't taken anything. We'd just had a few drinks, these pink cocktail things Chapin liked to make. But at the time, it just seemed like Chapin being Chapin."

"I know what you mean," Evaline said.

"I'm not surprised someone stabbed her in the back," Hope said. "She was always stabbing everybody else in the back."

"Well, I wouldn't say anything like that too loudly around here at the moment," Evaline said. "That Mr. Demarkian is here now. You could turn yourself into a prime suspect."

Hope was definitely feeling better now. Her lungs were full of air. Her muscles were willing to move on their own.

She got up off the bench very carefully, holding on to the armrest with one hand and praying to God she wouldn't tip the thing over. She had her other arm still clutching her pocketbook to her chest.

"There you go," Evaline said cheerfully. "Let's walk home, then. Maybe we can walk over to my house and get my car."

THREE

1

Gregor had his dinner out on the terrace. He brought his laptop and his phone and all the papers he had brought with him and spread himself out across two chairs, a chaise, and the round metal table.

He'd been staring at the black blank space that was the Waring house for half an hour before he decided that he was being an idiot. He picked up the phone and called Bennis. He listened to the ring and ring that went on long enough to make him wonder if she'd left her phone someplace, and then she picked up.

"I was wondering when you were going to call," she said.

"I've been calling," Gregor said. "I've been calling every chance I've gotten. I wish you were here."

"I thought you didn't like me interfering in your professional life."

"I didn't say I wanted you to interfere. I just said I wished you were here. And I do. And it's only partly because I miss you."

"Are all the people awful?" Bennis asked. "I thought about it after you went up there, and it occurred to me that you were probably headed for Connecticut's version of the Main Line. And all the people would be awful."

"The people are strange enough," Gregor said, "but that's not the big issue. The big issue is that I have nobody to talk to."

"I thought they always hired you drivers and you talked to them," Bennis said.

"I do sometimes," Gregor agreed, "but in this case, my driver does not seem to speak any English. His name is Juan Valdez—"

"Wait? Like the coffee guy? From the commercials?"

"I knew the name was familiar," Gregor said. "Well, that's his name. I don't know if he's legal or illegal. I don't know if he understands a word I say. He sits in the front of the car and gives me a lot of rapid-fire Spanish and I have no idea what it means, and then he drives me around. He must understand something, because we always get where we're going. But he's symptomatic of this whole thing, if you ask me."

"Symptomatic how?"

"Well," Gregor said, "let's just say that I've felt as if everybody I've met came from central casting. Juan Valdez seems less like a person than the worst kind of stereotype. It's been like that with a lot of these people. I met a woman named Caroline Waring Holder—"

"Is that the youngest sister?" Bennis asked. "I've heard about her. She's gotten all social consciency or something and sends her kids to the local public school."

"The local public school can out-Eton Eton," Gregor said. "And yes, she's the youngest sister. The other two sisters don't live in the area. I think one of them is in Chicago. Anyway, that's been checked out, by both the local police and the Bureau, so that's all right. But she felt like somebody from central casting, too."

"Do I feel like something from central casting?"

"No," Gregor said. "You're sui generis. And I always thought so. But I just feel up against a wall here. I've talked to two Bureau people, one retired and one very much on the case. I've talked to all the police officers locally who've had anything to do with the murder. And in all of that, I've only got one significant piece of information."

"What's that?"

"The uniform that went to the Waring house on the night of the murder is a woman named Angela Harkin. She says that when she was checking the place out, before she actually knew there was something wrong, she went around to the back and looked through a gap in the curtains and saw a single foot, wearing an espadrille."

"And espadrilles mean something important?"

"When she found the body of Chapin Waring, Chapin Waring was wearing tennis shoes."

"But that is interesting," Bennis said. "That must have been the murderer. And the murderer must have been a woman."

"Maybe," Gregor said.

"But if there was another person there while the officer was looking around, how did she get out? Wouldn't she have been seen?"

"Not necessarily," Gregor said. "The place isn't as big as Engine House, but it's big. There are lots of ways to get in and out. And the alarm wasn't tripped that night, so whoever got in knew how to turn it on and off. There was just the one officer there at the time. What bothers me the most is that that wasn't in the notes I got, and the officers on the case didn't seem to make anything of it. Everybody here is so wrapped up in discussing what happened thirty years ago, they lose sight of the obvious."

"They probably just think that if Chapin Waring was murdered in her own hometown, it probably had something to do with what happened thirty years ago. Don't you?"

"I don't know."

"That's interesting," Bennis said.

"Everybody loses sight of the fact that Chapin Waring may have been missing for thirty years, but that doesn't mean she'd ceased to exist for thirty years. She was doing something all that time. And there's really no reason to suppose that she'd been murdered now for something that old. From what I hear about her—in the notes and out—she was something of a juvenile delinquent all her life, except that she never was called that and she didn't end up in reform school, because her family had too much money. But the general feeling seems to be that she was never good for herself or for other people. She was the kind of person who got people wrapped up in things they couldn't really handle."

"Well, that seems true enough."

"I know," Gregor said. "I'm just saying there's no reason to suppose she stopped doing that when she left here. That leads me back to the other brick wall, and that's the question of what she was actually doing for those thirty years."

"And then you're the one who's bringing the whole thing back to what happened thirty years ago."

"I know," Gregor said. "This is why I need somebody to talk to. If I don't talk, I end up going around and around in circles in my head. Today, the alarm went off at the house. We all hauled ourselves out there, and I do mean all of us, and all we found was the front door, slightly open. The alarm had gone off, so either the person who opened the door didn't know how to disengage it or didn't want to. But there were no signs of forced entry anywhere in the place, which would seem to indicate that whoever opened the door had the key. And there was absolutely no reason for this that I could tell."

"Maybe somebody came to steal something?"

"If they did, it was nothing immediately discernible. Caroline Holder didn't look around and go, 'Oh, my God! The family credenza is missing!' "

"Maybe whoever it was took something not immediately evident," Bennis said. "Maybe they took something from upstairs, or in the kitchen."

"I've got every intention of asking Caroline Holder to make a revised inventory," Gregor said. "But if whoever broke in didn't know how to disarm the alarm, then she didn't have enough time to look much farther than the foyer. And if she did know how to disarm the alarm, then that means she had to have come into the house, disarmed the alarm, done whatever it was she had to do, reset the alarm, and then left and let it go off. Does that sequence of events sound plausible?"

"She could have made a mistake," Bennis said. "Although I don't think we should go on calling her 'she.' We'll get in the habit and then we won't see it when the murderer turns out to be some big guy with a mustache who likes to dress up in women's shoes."

"There is no such big guy that I know of," Gregor said. "There are only two guys in this case, and I haven't met either of them yet. One is Dr. Timothy Brand. The other is Kyle Westervan. They were two of the six."

"Two of the six?"

"There were six people in the group Chapin Waring ran around with in those days," Gregor said. "There was Chapin Waring herself. There was Martin Veer, the one who wrecked the car on the night of the fifth robbery and died in the crash. Then there was Timothy Brand, his sister Virginia Brand, a girl named Hope Matlock, and then Kyle Westervan. All local kids, all in their first year of college. And they'd all been hanging out together since grammar school."

"I see."

"The Bureau checked them all out at the time," Gregor said, "but the conclusion was that Chapin Waring and Martin Veer had committed the robberies together, and the rest of the group didn't know anything about them. You look at the case notes and start to wonder if it was ever really possible that anybody came to that conclusion."

"You couldn't change that conclusion?" Bennis asked in surprise.

"I could change the conclusion," Gregor said, "but I can't go back in time and ask the questions I'd want asked and do the checking I'd want checked. Like it or not, there's going to be a lot of evidence that has disappeared into the mists. And then we're left with all the same questions we had before, plus the new ones. I keep telling myself to concentrate on what's been happening here, right now. But not enough has been happening."

"Well, you do have a dead body."

"I do have that," Gregor said. "And that tells me even less than it usually does. I have a dead body and it was stabbed in the back—actually, in the left shoulder blade. The instrument used was a large kitchen knife, serrated, that probably came from the Waring house kitchen."

"Probably?"

"There's nothing to say that it did, and nothing to say that it didn't. It wasn't part of a set, although it was similar to the ones in the kitchen. That makes the police here think it must have come from outside, but I don't think so. The house is— the Warings have maintained that house like something in a Faulkner story. They didn't just not sell the place; they maintained it. They paid ground crews and maids to clean it and keep it up. All the furniture is there and dusted and in perfectly good repair. The kitchen still has all the kitchen equipment in it. The dining room has two large glass display cabinets with china in them. And that's what I saw without doing a search. I got the impression that if I'd started opening drawers or if I'd gone up to the bedrooms, there would be clothes and bedspreads and everything else all set out and ready to go."

"And Caroline Holder doesn't live there?"

"No, she definitely does not." Gregor sighed. "The knife had no fingerprints on it except those of Chapin Waring, but all that means is that somebody was wearing gloves. I keep trying to visualize the actual murder, and I get nowhere. How did that work, exactly? You have to get up close to stab somebody in the back. And if that person's back is to you, then he either didn't know you were there, or he wasn't expecting you to do anything, or he was running away from you. And if he was running away from you, you couldn't get too good a stab in anyway. It just goes around and around and around."

"And you're still left with thirty years ago," Bennis said.

"I'm not going back to that again," Gregor said.

"I don't blame you," Bennis said. "If it's any consolation,

I wish you were here. This house is remarkably cavernous and creepy when I'm here on my own."

"You could go stay with Donna," Gregor said.

"Donna's got enough going on without hearing from me," Bennis said. "Besides, I see her all the time. She decided to decorate this house for the Fourth, and she's only got until the day after tomorrow."

"What?" Gregor said.

"She's only got until the day after tomorrow," Bennis said. "She wants the whole street to look good for the parade. Then we get pictures in the paper and the Ararat gets more business. So she came over today and wrapped the entire house up in blue crepe paper, and she's got red and white to do tomorrow."

"The Fourth of July is the day after tomorrow."

"Last I checked," Bennis said. "Are you all right?"

"No," Gregor said. "I put it entirely out of my mind. I mean, I did and I didn't. Everybody has been talking about the Fourth, and I kept thinking it was somewhere in the distance."

"It is," Bennis said. "It's the day after tomorrow."

"That's not nearly distant enough."

2

Later, when Darlee Corn had been in to pick up the plates and bring him a glass of brandy, Gregor sat on the edge of the big old-fashioned bed and tried to get it all straight in his head. The Fourth of July meant a day of no real work, so he would have to revise his tentative schedule. It might even mean that he wouldn't be able to get out and look around. He had no idea what Alwych did on the Fourth. He didn't mind fireworks, if they were handled by professionals. He was generally in favor of celebrating the Fourth, but what he wanted for a celebration was a big barbecue out somewhere that also had a pavilion, and then he wanted it to rain so that everybody had to go indoors.

Gregor was not much in favor of eating outside.

He got up off the bed and began to pace. He expected a phone call any minute, telling him the people below him had complained. He stopped and looked at his laptop for a while. He scrolled through notes about the bank robberies, the money, the murder, everything that might be connected to this case.

He brooded a little about what he meant when he thought about "everything" that might be connected to this case. Did anybody at all know what "everything" meant here?

He got out Patrick's diaries and went through them, page after page, not knowing what he was looking for. He read through long passages of what was essentially angst, of Patrick not being able to figure it all out, of leads that went nowhere and ideas that turned out to have nothing to do with anything.

He got to the section with the pictures in it and went through those one after the other. He got to the ones that had been taken by the security cameras and started to go very slowly. The pictures were blurry. Too much was shot from over the tops of people's heads, so that you could see hats or caps but not faces.

He got to the ones he had found curious even the first time he saw them, and stopped. In these, he could see Chapin Waring clearly, and he understood completely why she had been identified from the photographs of Martin Veer's funeral. The way she held her head and shoulders was distinctive all on its own.

He moved the photographs around and tried to concentrate on the figure of Marty Veer. This was not so distinctive, and looking at the photographs he could see what everybody who had looked at them had seen, from the beginning until now. The figure of the accomplice was—distorted, sort of. It bulked in odd places, and flattened out in even odder ones.

Gregor set the photographs out in order: first robbery, second robbery, third robbery, fourth robbery, fifth robbery.

He looked at the figure of the accomplice over time. It was always bulky and distorted, but it was not always bulky and distorted in the same way. He didn't see why he should think the figure *was* Martin Veer, or anybody else. He didn't even see why he should think the figure was the same person each time. This was not a body type. Nobody on earth was built to look like that.

Surely, Gregor thought, the Bureau must have thought of this at the time. There had to be some reason why they had fixed on Martin Veer as the accomplice.

He went through Patrick's notes again, and found it: Once Chapin Waring had been identified as one of the robbers, there were search warrants issued for all six of the kids in that tight little group. In Martin Veer's house, police had found one of the bags from the Fairfield County Savings Bank—just the bag, not any money, and nothing else.

On the other hand, they had found nothing at all in the houses of any of the others.

Gregor looked around for more, but couldn't find it. They had found the bag with Martin Veer, and nothing else with any of the others, and they had decided on Martin Veer as the accomplice.

Gregor got up and walked around to where he had dumped his bags this morning when he checked in. The big picture book on the Waring case was lying on the floor near a wing chair. He picked it up and walked back to the other side of the bed to sit down.

The picture book, unlike the case notes from the Bureau, included a lot of photographs of Chapin Waring and her friends that were not in any way connected to the robberies.

Gregor found a caption that identified the group by name, and picked Martin Veer out from that. Then he went back over the rest of the pictures and checked out each one Martin was in. There was Martin at the beach in a bathing suit. There was Martin in tennis whites with a racket. There was Martin sitting at a table with all the rest of them, drinking something in a tall glass.

Gregor went back to the security pictures. He went back and forth.

The accomplice could have been Martin Veer. In fact,

faced with this same evidence, if he'd have been on the case at the time, that's the way he would have bet. There was still something about it he didn't like.

He went back to the picture book and paged through slowly, looking at photographs so wildly divergent, they might have had nothing to do with one another. Some of those photographs were of the principals as small children. In those, Martin Veer was freckled and awkward. There was another set that consisted of baby pictures. Gregor looked through the Bureau file and found that the agents had picked up on this the first time Ray Guy Pearce published them, and had discovered that these same photographs were genuine.

After that, the file contained a lot of references to Ray Guy Pearce and his publishing company, but in the end they had come to nothing. It was obvious somebody was feeding him material, but nobody had ever discovered who that was. The last note suggested that Ray Guy Pearce might be getting fed by more than one person, especially if he was paying them.

He paged through more photographs, one coming after the other with only the slightest nod to organization.

He put the book away and thought for a moment.

The day after tomorrow was the Fourth of July. If he was going to get something done, he would have to do it fast.

There were at least two things that would make sense if only you worked them right.

The first of those things he would have to deal with tomorrow.

FOUR

1

Evaline Veer hadn't been able to sleep all night. She'd finally given up trying at half past four, and at quarter to six she'd started into the center of town again. The walk was eerily quiet, as if lots of people were taking the day off before the Fourth.

Evaline was just coming around the corner at the depot when she saw a very tall, massively built man get out of the backseat of a car and come around to the depot's front door. She hesitated. There was no mistaking who the man was, even though she had never met him. In the natural order of things, she would be introduced to him by Jason Battlesea, or one of the detectives. She was a little miffed that Jason hadn't brought him over yesterday.

There was a lot to do yesterday, she told herself as Demarkian walked through the station's doors. Evaline went in after him. She looked for him at the single open ticket window, but he wasn't there. She spotted him at the newsstand. He was taking an absolute armload of books and putting them on the counter.

Evaline thought it over for a split second, and then walked

right over to him. The books he'd laid on the counter were all books about Chapin Waring.

She leaned close to him without touching and said, "Mr. Demarkian? We should be introduced. I'm Evaline Veer."

Gregor Demarkian looked up from his apparent attempt to buy one copy of every title of what the newsstand had of those books.

"Evaline Veer," he said.

"I'm the mayor," Evaline said helpfully. "I just thought I'd come over and introduce myself."

"It's very good to meet you," Demarkian said. "Give me a second here."

Evaline watched as he turned away from her and took out his wallet to pay for the books. The man behind the counter found a big bag and piled them all inside.

"Boy," the man said. "You must be taking the train to Hawaii."

Evaline waited until Gregor Demarkian turned back to her and tried a smile.

"Is that what you came in here for?" she asked. "I was worried you were taking the train back to Philadelphia. I know we must seem completely clueless out here. Jason indicated that you might be a little—annoyed."

"Not annoyed, exactly," Gregor said. "A little exasperated might be more like it."

"Because of the forensics, and all that kind of thing?" Evaline asked. "I do know that the state crime lab has lost its accreditation. Connecticut prides itself on being very sophisticated, but the truth is we're mostly suburbs with a few small urban spots that are going completely to hell. It's not New York out here, even if most of the people in town work in New York."

Gregor Demarkian tilted his head, as if he were trying to think something through. Then he straightened it again and said, "I don't mind the weakness of the forensics, or even the lack of acquaintance with serious crime. It's my job to help people out with just those things. No, what was getting me a little exasperated was the lack of interest in the crime at hand. All anybody seems to want to talk to me about is the crime that happened thirty years ago."

"Ah," Evaline said.

"It does look like a very interesting crime," Gregor said, "but contrary to what everybody seems to think, solving it will not necessarily solve this one."

"I didn't think it had to be solved," Evaline said. "Everybody already knows who committed those bank robberies. Martin Veer was my brother, do you know that?"

"I did know that," Gregor said.

"From the FBI?" Evaline said. "I suppose they thought it was some kind of conflict of interest."

"Something like that."

"Well," Evaline said, "I don't see it. I was very young when those robberies happened. I wasn't even out of grade school. And they don't stick in my mind at all. Every time somebody says something about the crime that happened thirty years ago, I have to stop myself. Because we're never thinking about the same crime."

"There was another crime that happened thirty years ago?" Gregor asked.

Evaline shrugged. "Not in that sense, no," she said. "But what sticks out in my mind after all this time is the accident. Maybe if Marty had lived, and there'd have been a massive manhunt like there was for Chapin—except if he'd lived, they might never have caught Chapin or Marty either. The only way anybody put two and two together was because somebody saw Chapin on television at Marty's funeral."

"They would have caught them eventually," Gregor said. "Once those two people were killed, there would have been a lot of scrutiny and enhanced security. If they had done any more robberies, they would have ended up getting caught."

"Oh, I suppose I know that," Evaline said. "I knew my brother fairly well, and when I heard about everything, it sounded plausible enough. I could see him doing those things. Things got out of hand and they did things they didn't expect to do. But Martin really wanted to be part of Chapin

Waring's crowd. And of course, it was very important to Hope."

"Hope," Gregor Demarkian said. It was not a question.

Evaline plunged ahead as if it had been. "Hope Matlock," she said. "She was Marty's girlfriend at the time. She's still in town, you know. I talked to her only yesterday. She's from an impossibly old New England family. They've been here—and I do mean here, in town or right around it—since somewhere in the 1690s. Hope still lives in the family place. It was built before the Revolutionary War. But there isn't any money. Hope's mother had to tie herself in knots just to send her to Alwych Country Day. I don't know how they managed Vassar. Hope wanted to be part of Chapin Waring's crowd, too. I used to think Chapin kept her around for a pet."

"That's a little harsh."

Evaline shrugged. "It's like I said. When I think of the crime that happened thirty years ago, the crime I think about is the accident. The six of them all piled into that car, and all at least partially drunk. Marty driving. And then there was the weirdness of it. The police came and talked to my parents after the funeral. They said the car had just veered off the road and into that tree as if Marty had been aiming at it. They didn't think he had, you know. They didn't think he'd done it on purpose or was trying to commit suicide or anything. He was just young and drunk and stupid. But still."

"I can see that," Gregor said.

"And then he was the only one who was really hurt," Evaline went on. "All the rest of them walked away from it with minor injuries at most. Oh, I think Kyle Westervan broke his wrist. He was the third person in the front seat. You couldn't even do that anymore. You can't get three people in a front seat."

"But they'd all been drinking," Gregor said.

"Oh, yes," Evaline said. "They found absolute buckets of stuff at the accident site. Bottles of scotch. Bottles of, of all things, rye whiskey. I tell myself that if Marty had lived, maybe he and Chapin would have been caught, and then he would have gone to jail and his life would have been ruined anyway. But I'd still rather have him alive to visit in jail than dead. And that probably makes me a fool."

"I don't think so," Gregor said.

Evaline looked down at the very full bag Gregor Demarkian was carrying.

"I don't think you're going to get very far with those," she said. "There's some idiot in New York that's been putting them out for years. The FBI itself investigated him. He seems to just make the stuff up. I can find you some more accurate accounts, if you want them. There was a time when I bought every account I could find."

"Maybe I'll take you up on it after the Fourth."

"Well," she said. "I think I'd better get to my office. I couldn't sleep last night, and now of course I'm a mess."

"I used to pull all-nighters on the job," Gregor said. "But it was a long time ago."

"And now you're busy," Evaline said, "and I've kept you. Have a good day, Mr. Demarkian. We'll probably see each other later."

"I'm sure we will."

They stood there, stock-still, looking at each other. Finally Gregor Demarkian nodded to her one last time and turned away, heading out of the station.

Evaline watched him go through the station doors. It was not just her tiredness talking. He really was a massive man.

2

Cordelia was the first one on the phone this morning. Caroline Waring Holder heard the sound of the Chopin funeral march before she saw the picture of Maleficent flash up on the caller ID.

Caroline considered just not picking up. She considered it just long enough to realize that Cordelia would just call back later, and not much later, complaining that Caroline was ignoring her.

"Yes," Caroline said into the cell phone. She knew she

sounded snappish. She didn't care. "I've just dropped off the kids, Cordelia, and I'm in the car and this red light isn't going to last forever. We can talk later."

"We need to talk now," Cordelia said. "I thought they'd bring in this Gregor Demarkian and it might calm things down some, but that's not what's happening. They had a whole segment on the thing out here just last night, and not just about the murder. They're bringing it all up again."

"Of course they're bringing it all up again," Caroline said.

"They said there was a break-in yesterday at the house."

"It wasn't exactly a break-in," Caroline said. The light turned green. She inched forward in the traffic.

"They said it was a break-in on the news," Cordelia said. "I would have called you last night, but then I remembered you go to bed practically before sundown and I wanted to be considerate."

"It wasn't a break-in," Caroline said, thinking that Cordelia had never been considerate a day in her life. "The alarm went off. When everybody got out there, the front door was open. That was it. Nothing had been taken that I could see, and the house hadn't been broken into—"

"What?"

"According to the police, the house hadn't been broken into," Caroline said. "Nobody forced a lock. Either somebody got in there with a key, or the police didn't lock up the last time they were there."

"But that's terrible," Cordelia said. "How many people can possibly have keys to that house? And isn't that a creepy idea, the cleaning lady or whoever it was going to look around when you're not there? When was the last time we changed those locks?"

"I changed them the day after Chapin's body was found," Caroline said, "and you should remember it. You were on the phone with me most of the day. And yes, they're being changed again as we speak. I'm on my way to meet the locksmith right now."

"Still, you have to wonder," Cordelia said. "Why would

anybody want to do something like that? Going into the house and—what? Just walking around? What could they possibly have expected to find?"

"Two hundred and fifty thousand dollars," Caroline said.

Cordelia snorted. "There's no money in that house, and you know it. I don't even believe there ever was that much money. It was just a lot of hype they put out to make people take it more seriously. You know what it's like when rich people are involved. It's always our fault."

"They didn't have to hype anything to make people take it seriously," Caroline said. "Two people died. And Chapin shot at least one of them. It's on tape."

"That's what the real problem is with this country," Cordelia said. "Half the population lives on jealousy and spite. And then, of course, when something like this comes along, they blow it all out of proportion."

"Two people died," Caroline said. "I don't think anything is out of proportion."

"It would be better if you went and lived in that house yourself," Cordelia said. "God only knows it's a better house than the one you're living in, and the children would be right there on the beach. And then we wouldn't have these problems with people breaking in."

"I have a perfectly adequate house, and what we ought to have done, years ago, is sell the one on Beach Drive."

"You never understand these things. You really don't. I suppose I ought to let you get on with getting the locks changed. Maybe we should hire a security guard until this thing blows over. If the police can't have somebody there even when the place is a crime scene—"

"Hire a security guard, then," Caroline said.

"Oh," Cordelia said. "I meant you should. You should hire a security guard."

"Yes, I know that's what you meant," Caroline said.

She snapped the phone closed. She tried to concentrate on her driving. She stopped at another traffic light and saw Gregor Demarkian in the backseat of a car. He didn't notice her, and she didn't make herself known.

One block up, the car with Demarkian in it went on and Caroline turned left, going the short way out to the start of Beach Drive. The houses got bigger and bigger. The haze in the air that was high humidity and evaporated seawater got heavier.

Beach Drive looked deserted, as always. Caroline pulled into the driveway of the house and cut her engine. There was no sign of the locksmith's van. She started to gather up her things, and then the phone went off again.

This time it was the song "Cruella de Vil," along with a picture of Glenn Close in a fright wig. Caroline put her forehead on the steering wheel and counted to ten.

The phone did not stop ringing. Caroline picked it up and said, "What do you want? I've already had Cordelia. I really can't take much more."

"Do you know you're always like this these days?" Charlotte said. "It's not healthy for you."

"I'm sitting in the driveway of the house on Beach Drive, waiting for a locksmith for the second time in two weeks. I've got a lot to do, and I've got no patience with any of this. Don't start."

"I'm not starting anything," Charlotte said. "I'm just very worried about what's going on out there. You never call me. You never tell me anything. Do you know a reporter ambushed me right after I got out of work yesterday?"

"Reporters ambush me all the time," Caroline said. "Honest to God, Charlotte, there's nothing I can do about any of this. Cordelia wants to hire a security guard for the house. I don't think it's a bad idea, but if somebody's going to do it, it's not going to be me—"

"But you're right *there*."

"I may be right here, but that is absolutely no justification for landing all this crap on me. And I do mean crap, Charlotte. First-rate, unrelieved crap."

"I don't understand why you don't live in the place," Charlotte said.

Caroline hit the steering wheel so hard, the horn blasted. It sounded like the muffled screech of somebody else dying.

"I don't want to talk about this now," she said. "We've talked about everything a hundred times over. I'm not going to move into this house. I never liked this house. I don't want to live on Beach Drive. I don't even want to live in Alwych. I thought, apparently futilely, that if I just lived my own life and minded my own business, I could just get on with—with being normal, for God's sake. What's wrong with the two of you?"

"We weren't the ones who stayed in Alwych," Charlotte said. "If you didn't want to live in Alwych, you should have gotten out."

"If I'd gotten out, you wouldn't have had anybody to run your errands on the house for you. What would you have done then?"

"Listen," Charlotte said. "Cor just called me. You got her so upset, she forgot to tell you what she wanted to tell you, and you were so grumpy, she didn't want to call back. You affect her energy charge. She doesn't want to be negative first thing in the morning."

"I don't see why not," Caroline said. "She's negative enough the rest of the time."

"It's about the funeral," Charlotte said.

"I'm not staging any funeral," Caroline said. "I told you that already."

"Yes, I know you did," Charlotte said, "but Cor and I didn't take it seriously. How could we? You can't just say you're not going to stage a funeral. You have to do something. If you don't—well, what's going to happen to the body?"

"I have no idea what's going to happen to the body," Caroline said. "And I don't care."

Charlotte let out a long stream of aggravatedly aggrieved air. "You have to care what's going to happen to the body," she said, "because something is going to have to happen to it. It's ready to be released. It's sitting there in the morgue, ready to be released."

"Yes, I know that."

"And the police called us after they talked to you," Charlotte said, "because they said you said you didn't care what happened to it, and you wouldn't do anything about it. Do you realize what's going to happen if that gets into the papers?"

"If you want to do something about it, you're welcome," Caroline said.

"Cor and I talked about it. We think you should call a funeral home and have the body sent there, and then set up for a service at the house. I don't mean a public service, of course. It would be a zoo. But you could have the casket there in the living room, it's big enough, and whoever is pastor at the Episcopal Church these days could come and do something, and then you could bury it with all the rest of the Warings. I mean, we've got a *huge* plot out there, and there would be room for it."

"At the house," Caroline said.

"Of course."

"And out near Mother and Daddy at the cemetery."

"That's where she would have been buried if none of this had happened. It would be perfectly natural. There wouldn't be anything odd about it. And you wouldn't have to announce it to the public. It could be just you and the reverend."

"While the two of you stay off wherever you are and pretend it isn't happening."

"We've been over this before," Charlotte said. "We really can't come out for a funeral. It would be too complicated."

"Then I don't see why my solution isn't the one that makes sense," Caroline said. "Let the police have her. Let them bury her wherever they want."

"At some point in this thing, you really have to start being reasonable. This is going to get out and then we're all going to look like monsters. Is that what you want?"

"What I want," Caroline said, "is to be left alone by all of you. And that includes the police."

"Well," Charlotte said, "I'm just trying to tell you to be careful. Of course, it didn't occur to me right away, because why would it, but now—well, with everything that's been happening. And people in the house and all of that. Well, I'm sure you get my drift. And it's not like it was the first time. They've got all this technology now. They've got cell phone records and security cameras and cell phone towers and I don't know what else."

"They can even pick up cell phone conversations while you're having them," Caroline said.

"Oh, God," Charlotte said. "I'd forgotten about that. I'd better get off the phone. All I'm saying is that you have to take care of yourself. Because even if you don't care about yourself, you've got children and a husband to worry about. Any kind of really adverse publicity will just kill you."

"And you," Caroline said. "And Cordelia."

"Well, of course, but I wasn't thinking of us. We're not there, so—"

"You know," Caroline said, "if I actually admitted to knowing what you were talking about, I'd have to stop talking to you. Not just now. Forever."

"Honestly," Charlotte said. "You're so melodramatic."

"I was eight when all that happened," Caroline said. "Try to remember that."

"How could I not remember that?"

"I'm going to hang up now," Caroline said.

Charlotte went on squawking. Caroline clicked the phone shut again. Her brain felt as if it were boiling inside her skull. *Honest to God*, she thought. *Honest to God. Honest to God. Honest to God.*

She put her forehead down on the steering wheel again and closed her eyes. When she looked up, the locksmith's van was just pulling into the driveway. She took a deep breath, counted to ten, and tried to drive everything out of her mind but the locks.

She didn't want to kill the locksmith just because he was handy, and she could no longer control herself.

3

Virginia didn't support the programs she supported because she was kinder or more nurturing. She supported those programs because they made sense, and because they were *moral.* You didn't leave people to die in the street, no matter what way they ran their lives, and you certainly didn't leave their children to die in the street. You treated people like people. You didn't consign them to little boxes with labels on them and say that their lives could never be more than the labels said they could.

She had always found The Right Thing To Do perfectly obvious. This morning, she was thinking about them because the newspapers that had been delivered to her front door were full of stories about Tim's clinic and the danger posed by the "assault" on it by the Office of Health Care Access and the Office of the Health Care Advocate. Virginia wanted to kick somebody. Then her phone rang.

She picked up the receiver and said, very cautiously, "Yes?"

There was a low chuckle on the other end of the line, and Kyle said, "Ah. Worried I'm going to be somebody from the *Stamford Advocate*?"

"Oh, God," Virginia said. "How did you know I was here?"

"I guessed. It's Fourth of July weekend coming up and you're running for the Senate. Even if you weren't, you'd have to be here."

"That's true," Virginia said. "Do you remember if people made a big fuss out of the Fourth of July when we were growing up? I was thinking about it in the shower this morning. I can't remember a single parade."

"The parade didn't go down Beach Drive," Kyle said, "and we didn't belong to the kind of organizations that participated in it. There were no Boy and Girl Scouts at Alwych Country Day."

"I think I always thought of that stuff as being part of the Midwest," Virginia said. "Little towns where nobody ever makes much of anything of their lives and all the men are trying to relive their youth as high school football stars. Did you play football in high school?"

"It was prep school, and I rowed crew."

"I didn't do anything. They made me play field hockey

and I spent all my time wanting to kill somebody. I never actually made a team. There's something nobody ever talks about. The way private schools make everyone run around doing sports as if they were going to make the Olympics."

"It's in the aid of physical fitness, and nobody talks about private schools. Have you or your people been in touch with Jason Battlesea?"

"No, of course not," Virginia said. "Why would I be?"

"Because there's about to be something of an issue, and if you're not aware of it, you should be."

"If you're talking about this thing with Tim's clinic, I am aware of it. And I'm staying out of it."

"I'm not talking about Tim's clinic."

"What is it, then?"

"The body of Chapin Waring."

"What," she asked, "do I have to do with the body of Chapin Waring?"

Kyle let out another of those enormous sighs. "Of course you don't have anything to do with it," he said, "but it's going to be an issue, and things being what they are, you're going to be asked about it. It doesn't matter if it has nothing to do with you anymore. It had something to do with you once."

"It had something to do with you, too."

"I'm not running for anything," Kyle said. "But yes, it had something to do with me once, too. Not the least of which being that it's a damned miracle that I'm not dead. Maybe it's a damned miracle that we're all not dead."

"I was in the backseat," Virginia said. "I was in no danger of being dead."

"Tim was in the backseat, too, and I broke my arm upfront," Kyle said. "But no, that's not the point. The point is that the police are ready to release Chapin Waring's body to her family, and her family is refusing to take it."

"Seriously?"

"Definitely seriously," Kyle said. "I'm working on sources here, you understand. I don't have a direct link into the Alwych Police Department. I never thought I'd need one. But from what I hear, the coroner's office called Caroline Waring Holder and she said that she didn't care if they left it out for carrion. Then they called the other two sisters, and they said that of course Caroline would be handling it. They don't live in the area anymore."

"What in the name of God is Caroline thinking of? She's got to know that everybody on the planet is going to hear about this. And the publicity is going to be awful."

"It is if it isn't handled. I thought you might like to get your people working to handle it."

"Handle it how?"

"The story doesn't have to be how awful the Waring family is," Kyle said. "It could be how awful Chapin was. It doesn't have to be about how the family was cold and heartless and turned Chapin into a criminal. It could be about how Chapin was always such a sociopath that even her family couldn't handle her. If it runs as how the family made Chapin a criminal, you know what's going to happen. They're going to start in on all our families, and we're going to sound, all of us, as a group—"

"Yes," Virginia said. "I know. Why won't Caroline take the body?"

"I don't know. I haven't talked to her in years. I wouldn't be surprised if Caroline thinks that Chapin ruined her entire life."

"She's a grown woman," Virginia said.

"Grown women have been known to harbor grudges. I'm just telling you that this could work out very badly. It could be exactly the kind of story we were all worried about when this started. You may be running for office, but it wouldn't be good publicity for me, either. Or for Tim. Or for Hope. Or even for Evaline. The papers like stories about psychopathic preppies way too much."

"I know," Virginia said.

She looked down at the paper again. There was a sudden silence between them. It was a deep and abiding silence, and it was the way they ended nearly all their conversations since they'd gotten their divorce. When they were married, there had been a different kind of silence that came between them. Virginia had liked that one better.

She started to look for something to say that would get them both off the hook when Kyle started up again.

"About that other thing," he said.

"What other thing?"

"Let me just say that I think you'd better have your ass completely and irrevocably covered on that one," Kyle said. "It doesn't matter what your rationale is. It doesn't even matter if you're right. It's going to look like hell, and it's going to kill you politically. Even in the state of Connecticut."

"I haven't got the faintest idea what you're talking about."

"I'm going to get off the line now," Kyle said. "There's no point in you and I playing that particular game. We know each other too well."

Kyle hung up. Virginia looked at the phone for a minute and then hung up herself.

It was true that she and Kyle knew each other too well, but there were a lot of people who knew her too well. And there wasn't a thing she could do about it.

FIVE

1

Gregor Demarkian had finally made up his mind about what he had to do next at about midnight. He started by putting in a call to Juan to pick him up at six o'clock in the morning. That much English, Juan seemed to understand. Then Gregor had looked up the address he wanted and gone in search of Darlee Corn and a printer.

As it turned out, Darlee Corn did have a printer, although she made it clear that she didn't usually make it available to guests.

Gregor took two copies of what he would need in the morning and headed off to bed. He set his alarm clock for four. He packed his attaché case with everything he could imagine he might need. Then he went to bed and tried to sleep against the drumming insistence in his mind that everybody who was ever involved in this case had been something worse than idiotic.

He got up at four o'clock in the morning and showered and shaved. He found the best suit Bennis had ever given him, then went down to the front door to wait for Juan. Darlee Corn was up and about, but nobody else seemed to be. The large dining room was empty, although hot serving stations were set up on a long table at the side. He grabbed a coffee in a paper cup.

Juan parked the car at the curb. Gregor got into it and handed over one copy of the detailed directions he had pulled off Google.

Juan took his time getting through Alwych, so that by the time they reached I-95 it was full-on rush hour, but he followed the directions he'd been given right to the quarter mile. Gregor began to relax. Somewhere around Greenwich, he decided he could stop monitoring their progress. He opened his attaché case and began going over what he had.

It was useless to tell himself that he had no more information than anybody else had had in all these years. The issue was never what you had, but how you interpreted it. He had gone over and over everything in everybody's set of notes, and he had ended with Sherlock Holmes. When you've eliminated the impossible, whatever is left, no matter how improbable, is the truth.

Gregor knew where Chapin Waring had been, and who had helped her stay out of sight, because there was only one possible answer. There was only one person who would have run interference for her all those years, and there was only one person who would have gone back to the house on Beach Drive after she was dead and let the security alarm ring.

They got to a neighborhood of row houses, each one of them two stories tall. The place reminded Gregor of the old Archie Bunker television show, except that the population was obviously neither white nor working class. It might be actually African, rather than African-American. It might be Caribbean. The people on the street looked relaxed and pleased with themselves. The corner markets were full of brightly colored vegetables.

Juan pulled the car up in front of one of the houses smack in the middle of a block. Gregor looked down at his own set of directions and double-checked the address was correct. Talk about the changes that had happened in the last thirty years. Gregor wondered how the man got out of his house to do his shopping. He wondered what happened to the house when it was empty because its occupant was away.

Gregor got out of the car. He stopped by Juan's window and said, "Wait here as long as it takes. If you have a problem with a meter reader, circle the block for a while and come back. I may be a long time."

Juan gave no indication that he'd heard or understood a thing. Gregor let it pass.

Gregor went up the short walk, and then onto the stoop. There was a bell on the left side.

Gregor tried leaning on the doorbell, but nothing happened. He couldn't hear a sound from inside. The doorbell might be broken, or disconnected. Gregor opened the rickety screen door and pounded on the thicker, more substantial door behind it. When his fist banged against it, he realized the door was metal—and not hollow metal, either.

Gregor pounded hard. Then he stopped and listened. A faint rustling sound came from inside, but it was not the sound of someone coming to open the door.

Gregor waited for a few seconds and pounded again. When he stopped, there was again a faint rustling, but it was faster now. It sounded agitated.

Gregor pounded a third time. Then he said, in as loud a voice as he could muster, "I'm not going away, Mr. Pearce. I'll stand here on this doorstep for the rest of the day if I have to, and I won't be quiet. I need you to open this door and talk to me, right this minute."

This time, there was no rustling sound from the other side of the door. Gregor could imagine Ray Guy Pearce somewhere inside there, holding his breath.

"Mr. Pearce," Gregor said, "not only can I stand here all day, but I've got no compunction about breaking in if I have to. Nothing I need from you is necessary in a trial. Nothing I get from you outside the law will do anything to compromise anyone's case in any way. Open up."

There was still no sound behind the door. Gregor waited just long enough to be sure that Ray Guy Pearce wasn't headed upstairs, and then he began pounding again.

The door opened when Gregor was in mid-pound. It swung inward so fast, Gregor almost stumbled across the threshhold.

The man on the other side of the door was not what Gregor had expected. He was not rabbity and small. He did not have eyes that darted from side to side as if they had a will of their own. Instead, he was large and hulking, as tall as Gregor himself and several times broader, but not with fat. He looked as if he spent several hours every day at the gym.

Ray Guy Pearce looked directly into Gregor Demarkian's eyes and didn't blink. "You can't pull your crap here," he said. "I'm not one of the civilians who don't know any better. Produce a search warrant or get out."

"I'm not going to produce a search warrant," Gregor said, "because I don't have one, and I wouldn't bother to get one, because you and I both know there would be no point. But you are going to let me in, and you are going to talk to me, and you are going to do one more thing. And I think you even know what that is."

"You're out of your mind," Ray Guy Pearce said.

"No," Gregor said. "I'm just in a position to get you arrested on suspicion of first-degree murder. I can even get you extradited to Connecticut. So first you're going to let me in, and then you're going to answer my questions, and then you're either going to hand over that two hundred and fifty thousand dollars, or you're going to tell me where I can get it."

2

The house was not only Ray Guy Pearce's home. It was the headquarters of Knight Sion Books, the "premier publisher of Truth on the planet." Gregor saw a sign that said just that as soon as he stepped over the threshold. The sign also had a picture of Saint George and the Dragon on it, with Saint George meant to symbolize either Knight Sion, or Ray Guy Pearce himself.

On second look, Gregor realized that the dragon was a little odd. It had seven heads, like a hydra, and seven eyes.

Ray Guy closed the door behind Gregor's back and then came around to glower. He did a very effective glower, but Gregor knew better than to take it seriously.

"You have no right to enter a private house," Ray Guy said. "If you think I'm one of the Sheeple, somebody who does not know my rights under the Constitution of the United States, you're going to find that you're very much mistaken."

Sheeple, Gregor thought.

There were tables and couches and chairs all around them, and all of them were covered with books and papers. It was as if somebody had exploded a library. Gregor went over to the largest of the tables and put his attaché case down. Then he opened the attaché case up and took out the book he'd bought in Greenwich Village.

"Let's start by discussing this," he said.

Ray Guy came over and looked at the book. "Everybody is in a mad race to publish e-books," he said, "but we know better. You can't trust e-books. They're wired into the central system. The authorities can reach right into them and delete anything they want. They can eliminate the book altogether. They can change passages. Once a hard copy is printed, though—well. It's almost impossible to get rid of a hard copy."

Gregor opened the book to a spread in the middle and pointed to it. It contained a dozen snapshots of the Waring sisters at the beach, on a picnic, on the back terrace of their own house. Many of the pictures were so old, there were only three of the four Waring sisters in them, and the three in the pictures were all under ten.

"See this?" Gregor said. "Do you know what this is?"

"It's the Waring family," Ray Guy said blandly. "It's a book about the Waring robbery case, so it's hardly surprising there are pictures of the Waring family in it. Have pictures of the Waring family been declared subversive?"

"This," Gregor said, pointing again to the picture spread,

"is a photo spread consisting of pictures that could have come from only one place: a Waring family photo album. There is no place else anybody could have gotten these. Somehow or the other, you got access to the Waring family photo albums."

"Maybe one of the sisters gave them to me," Ray Guy said.

"I'm sure one of the sisters did," Gregor said. "Chapin Waring did. I do think you know where Chapin Waring has been, and I do think you've been protecting her all this time. But I looked you up on the Internet—"

"The Internet is the tool of the authorities," Ray Guy Pearce said. "The Internet gives the Sheeple the illusion that they have choice, and access, and information—"

Gregor ran right over him. "I've looked you up on the Internet," he said again, "and from what I've been able to figure out, you started publishing pictures like these within weeks of Chapin Waring's disappearance. She couldn't have gotten back into the house in Alwych to get them that early. Everybody was being much too careful."

"The authorities are powerful, but they have flaws," Ray Guy Pearce said. "They're too sure of themselves. They're too convinced that they have everything under control. It's what's going to bring them down in the end."

"And that means," Gregor said, "that you've been in that house. And given the increase in the available pictures over time, you've been in it more than once. The last time, a couple of days ago."

"A couple of days ago, I was where I always am. I was here, making sure the truth gets out in spite of what you people do to try to stop it."

Gregor gave Ray Guy Pearce a long look. Now that he'd had time to observe the man close up and over a little time, he could see that he hadn't been so wrong in what he'd expected when he came here. The big, hulking, well-buffed physique was out of place, but the attitude was not. Behind the intimidating exterior was a man who was close to hysterical with fear and paranoia. Ray Guy kept his hands on his waist, but in the split seconds of the one or two times he removed them, Gregor could see that they were shaking. And physique or not, this was a relatively old man. He had to be at least sixty.

"Here's the thing," Gregor said. "You run around, telling yourself that you're some kind of genius at black ops, but the simple fact of the matter is that you've gotten away with what you've gotten away with for so long because nobody took you seriously. They would have if they'd known what you were actually doing, but they didn't. In a way, I can hardly blame them. There are dozens of you people across the country. The agencies watch you more or less, just in case one of you goes crazy. But mostly you don't, and mostly we don't have to worry about you. But I'm not like the other Bureau people you've had to deal with so far. I spent the first third of my career on kidnapping detail."

"So that's it," Ray Guy said triumphantly. "Kidnapping. You're going to try to frame me for kidnapping."

"Don't be any more of an ass than you already are."

"An ass? Really? That's what you've got? I know what you're up to, and it won't work. I know what you can do. I know what you can't do. And I'm not a Sheeple."

"No," Gregor said. "You're a man who goes around saying that the United States is secretly a police state that inflicted the 9/11 disaster on itself in order to tighten the screws against its own people, that it's being secretly run by the half-human descendants of Satan's demons and human women in aid of bringing the reign of the Antichrist about as quickly as possible, and that it still, for some reason, is absolutely required to observe your rights to freedom of speech and freedom of the press."

"They can't show their hand," Ray Guy said. "If they show their hand, the people will know what's going on and they'll rise up in rebellion."

"They will?" Gregor said. "The Sheeple?"

"The difference between the Sheeple and the Patriots is knowledge," Ray Guy said.

Gregor snapped the book shut. "You got those photographs by taking them out of photo albums in the Waring house yourself. It had to be you, because you act alone and Chapin Waring couldn't have gone for them herself. Not for the earliest ones. You had both a key and the code to the security system, because Chapin Waring herself gave them to you. And she kept giving them to you, because she always had them. You never took any of those albums outright. Somebody might have realized they were missing. You opened them up and took individual pictures out of them. You got lucky that the Waring family was what it was. Nobody was going to go looking through old picture albums."

"The old lady did," Ray Guy said. "Back in the first year or so. She told the FBI. The FBI came asking."

"And?"

Ray Guy shrugged. "I know my rights," he said. "I knew they couldn't search without a warrant. It takes time to get a warrant. And there was nothing here. Because I didn't take them."

"Of course you took them," Gregor said. "And you took something else the other day when you broke in—except you don't have to break in in the usual sense. My guess is that one of the things you do well is pick locks without leaving a trail. And I do take you seriously, Mr. Pearce. Unlike the rest of them, I know something about how people behave when they're trying to both be in contact and not be in contact at the same time, when they have to give out information even though it would be safer not to. And I also know that if I insist they take you seriously, both the local police and the Bureau, they will find a connection to you from that break-in a couple of days ago. They will find it, and I'll make sure they use it."

"I'm ready for persecution," Ray Guy said. "I've been ready for persecution for years."

"Where did you hide Chapin Waring?"

"I didn't hide Chapin Waring," Ray Guy said, "and don't tell me I should have turned her in. I'm a private citizen. I've got no legal obligation to do any such thing. And I wouldn't. I'm not going to make their work any easier for them."

"Where did you hide Chapin Waring?"

"I didn't hide her," Ray Guy said again. "She didn't even have to hide herself. She just moved into a neighborhood half a dozen blocks from here, dressed herself up in a *hijab*, and went about her business. A *hijab*, for Christ's sake. Thirty years ago. There couldn't have been more than five or ten thousand Muslims in all New York, and still all she needed to make herself invisible was a head scarf."

Gregor considered this. "It wouldn't have made her invisible after 9/11," he said.

"Sure it would have," Ray Guy said. "Everybody was running around so frantic that anything they did would look like some kind of anti-Muslim bigotry, she was safer after 9/11 than she was before it. Besides, your Bureau can't find clover in a country meadow. She lived a perfectly normal life. She even went back to that silly town half a dozen times. People reported seeing her. Oh, I've been watching all of it. I really have. And the authorities have been useless."

"Which explains why they're running the world and controlling the minds of the masses with such precision, nobody even notices," Gregor said. "Where's the money?"

"I don't have the money," Ray Guy said. "And if you want to know, she didn't have it, either. My best guess is that there never was any money. There never were any bank robberies. Those were frames, setups to prevent the public from believing anything she said. After all, she was one of their own. She was a child of the very people who are running this world conspiracy, and she was ready to testify to all of it—to the infant sacrifices, to the devil worship, to the systematic rape of children to make them pliable agents of the powers that be—"

"For God's sake," Gregor said.

"I knew as soon as she showed up here that she was the greatest victory for right and truth and reason since I started this publishing company," Ray Guy said. "I knew it and I knew that all the people at the top would know it, too. They got to her too early, though. If I'd been able to advise her, I could have kept her out of that kind of trouble. But even if she couldn't testify directly, she could give me the information and I could get it on the record. And I have. And I will."

"Information about child sacrifice and Satan worship."

"Information about the powers that be."

"Why did she go back to Alwych?" Gregor asked.

Ray Guy shrugged. "I'm not entirely sure. I didn't live with her. I didn't even see her all that often. It wasn't safe. I think there was somebody there who was having trouble, somebody who wanted to come out and tell the truth, but who was too afraid."

"And who was that?"

Ray Guy looked away, and in that instant, Gregor knew he was about to lie. "I never knew who it was," he said. "But she needed a lot of encouragement, and Chapin went back every once in a while to encourage her. But it didn't work. Chapin died without bringing her over."

Gregor filed this away in the back of his mind. It was not what he was here for, but there might be better ways of discovering what was going on with this than pounding at Ray Guy Pearce. Besides, it was impossible not to notice that Ray Guy was exhausted. He was much more exhausted than he should have been.

Suddenly, the big man turned away, walked to the couch, and sat down on top of papers and books as if there were nothing there but a seat cushion.

"You can't be here," he said, his voice coming out in a whine. "You have no right to enter my house without a warrant. Nothing you find here is going to be of any use to you. You can't use anything I've said. I don't know why you people keep trying this stuff when you know it will never work. I don't know why you people haven't figured out that you have to lose in the end. Evil always loses in the end."

It was an odd performance, distant and fluctuating. Gregor thought through his options, and then headed for the door.

"You'll probably have a few visitors in the next few days," he said. "You have to know that."

"I'm ready for persecution," Ray Guy Pearce said, his voice climbing almost to a scream. "I'm ready for persecution. I always have been."

3

Back in the car, having given Juan Valdez the information that he'd like to be taken back to Alwych, Gregor got out his cell phone and started making calls.

His first was the New York Bureau office, where he was threaded through a dozen offices before he found one that had some direct responsibility for the Waring case. He explained Ray Guy Pearce's declarations about where Chapin Waring had been for the last thirty years and why she hadn't been found, and he tried to do it in a way that didn't make any of the agents over the years sound like rank idiots.

"Hidden in plain sight is always the best way," he said, desperately trying to sound nonjudgmental. "He said a dozen blocks. That might have been an estimate. You guys should probably do concentric circles until you find where she was. I didn't get the name she was using, but there will be somebody who disappeared, and that will probably be the one. I don't think you'll get lucky enough to have an actual missing persons report. I doubt if she got close to anybody where she was living. It wouldn't have been safe. And she wasn't the kind of person who got close to people anyway."

"Yes, Mr. Demarkian," the agent on the line said. She sounded very young and very frightened. "Of course. We can probably get people out there today. You said she was living as a Muslim?"

"I said that Ray Guy Pearce reported that she was wearing a *hijab* when she went out. That doesn't mean that she was living as a Muslim. And I don't think it makes sense that she would have been doing that. There weren't many Muslims in New York thirty years ago. What Muslims there were almost certainly comprised a small community and that community was likely to have been enforcing at least some cultural standards. They would have recognized a stranger as a stranger."

"Oh," the agent said. "Yes, of course."

"He says he doesn't have the money, and he doesn't think she had it, either," Gregor said. "But you need to find where she was living and look. God only knows if it would still be there if she did have it, with whatever place she was living in being empty for weeks. You still have to look. But if she really didn't have it, and he really didn't have it, then that presents an interesting problem. Give me about a day, and I can get you probable cause for a warrant to search his house," Gregor said. "But you might want to put details up there to watch him. Whether that's going to be any good or not if he's got the money in the house, I don't know."

"Details," the agent said. "I'll get right on this. Does Mr. Fitzgerald have a number where he can call you?"

"He's got my cell number, yes," Gregor said. "Have him call me. It would help."

The agent fluttered and apologized and thanked until Gregor's eardrums felt as if they had been coated in goo. He hung up and called the Alwych Police Department.

Jason Battlesea was in his office, and apparently busy.

"What I need you to do," Gregor said, "is to make sure your people get all the fingerprints, every single one, in the Waring house. Send somebody back out there and go over the place with tweezers and microscopes. Get fibers. Get prints. Get anything and everything, even if it looks utterly irrelevant. Then I need you to find any DNA you can get off those, and any fingerprints, through every database in existence."

"We got everything," Jason Battlesea said.

"I don't mean at the crime scene, and I don't mean around the door where somebody got in," Gregor said. "I mean the whole house, upstairs and down. The attic. The basement. Every single inch of flooring and carpet and furniture. Everything."

"My God," Jason Battlesea said. "That will take months. And what for? We looked through the house both times. Nothing had been disturbed—"

"Nothing had been noticeably disturbed," Gregor said. "And it shouldn't take more than twenty-four to forty-eight hours if you put everybody you've got on it and start now."

"But it's the weekend of the Fourth! We've got ordinary policing to do—"

"Not with forensics people, you don't. Call the state police in to help if you have to. Oh, and one more thing. Look through drawers. We need to find photograph albums, or loose photographs, or wherever it is the Warings put their snapshots of things like family outings. My guess is that there will be formal photograph albums all done up with those little corner holders. We need to find those, and we need to start going through them. And be *very* careful. If we're going to find fingerprints or DNA, those are going to be the most likely places."

"In the photograph albums," Jason Battlesea said.

"In the photograph albums," Gregor said. "Just get it done, and I'll be back in a couple of hours."

"Where are you?" Jason Battlesea asked.

"I'm in New York," Gregor said. "And don't ask why now. I think I'm running out of cell phone battery."

SIX

1

It was the third of July and in spite of the legendary work ethic of Wall Street lawyers, men and women were clearing out of the office as fast as they could go. Kyle Westervan was sitting at his desk, wondering if there was something wrong with him. His briefcase was on the desk in front of him, locked. He had been staring at it for fifteen minutes. He had not been able to move.

"Cheesecake," he had said into the phone just fifteen minutes ago, after he listened to the usual opening.

"Cohen's Kosher Deli," was the way the phone had been answered when he called.

"It all sounds ridiculous," they'd told him when they started this.

At the time, he hadn't agreed. Cloak-and-dagger was cloak-and-dagger. You went with it or you didn't. It had taken all this time to feel that the entire situation was just stupid. At this point, looking out his open office door at the empty corridor, it didn't even seem real.

"No, I'll come down and pick it up," he'd told them.

That was standard, too. They asked if he wanted his food delivered. He told them he'd come down and pick it up.

He forced himself to his feet. He took the briefcase off the desk. It felt unbelievably heavy.

He went out into the corridor. There was nobody there. He looked into the few offices with their doors open. They were all shut down for the night. He went through what the assistants called CubicleLand, where the paralegals worked. The cubicles were all empty, too. Even the receptionist at the front desk was gone, her little clutch of photographs in silver frames all put away in a locked desk drawer for the night.

He went through the lobby and into the foyer. He went down in the elevator to the first floor. Kyle said good evening to the night guard and went out into the street. The street instantly made him feel better. It was not so empty, and it was very much the real world. Maybe he had begun to feel he no longer lived in the real world.

Maybe he had felt that way from the moment he started working on Wall Street.

Cohen's Kosher Deli was half deserted, which was good. Kyle went in through the front door and asked the woman at the register about his cheesecake. She found it in a little pile of bags behind the counter and handed it to him. He paid for it and looked around. The man he had never known as anything but "Andy" was sitting in the last booth but one against the back, the ones without the windows.

"Well?" Andy said as Kyle sat down across from him.

Kyle shrugged. "I don't think you want me to take ten stacks of five-hundred-dollar bills out right here in the restaurant."

"Of course I don't," Andy said. "I wasn't happy that night when you had to take them home."

"They're all counted, Andy. I'm not going to rip you off."

"I didn't say you were. But things happen. Traffic accidents. Traffic stops. You could have been pulled over by a policeman. Then what would you have done?"

"I'd have had a very hard time explaining why all that money was in the glove compartment without blowing your cover."

"Your problem is that you always want to be funny,"

Andy said. "This kind of thing isn't funny. And it isn't safe. Our marks don't routinely kill off our informants, but they have been known to do it once or twice. You might at least try to consider that."

"I have considered it," Kyle said. Then he looked around him and felt instantly depressed. "Everything is in the brief-case. And I do mean everything. Including the tape of the two of us talking. And he didn't send an aide."

"Really?" Andy looked impressed.

Kyle shrugged. "It's not the Nixon administration," he said. "Aides don't fall on their swords and go to jail for their bosses these days. They write tell-all books. So he came himself. The great Senator Durham of South Carolina."

"You hear about this kind of thing, but you don't ever really believe it," Andy said. "There's still something in my head that says these guys are too smart, too successful, too clued in to the way the world works to get involved in this kind of thing. How much did the senator give you?"

"Ten stacks of five-hundred-dollar bills. Twenty bills to the stack. You do the math."

"A hundred thousand dollars? In cash? In your brief-case?"

"Exactly. And the tape. And it was an easy tape to get. I hate it when I have to wear that buttonhole thing."

"And the tape says?"

"It's explicit enough, Andy, trust me. There's no doubt about what he's trying to do. And I'm going to need a receipt for this money, so you'd better find a way to check it discreetly."

Andy looked around the deli. There were a few people sitting along the counter, but they were all up near the cash register. Kyle felt the briefcase slide past his leg under the table. A moment later, Andy had it up and open and his head down over it.

Andy snapped the briefcase shut. He put it back down on the floor again, but near his own leg instead of Kyle's. Kyle felt the other briefcase being slid toward him. Andy reached into the breast pocket of his suit jacket and took out a pad and pen.

"You'd think they'd have at least a modicum of common sense," Andy said, "and they never do."

"It's the time and the place," Kyle said. "It's tax-free money. And the money is all that matters."

"The money was always all that mattered," Andy said.

"Maybe," Kyle said.

"No maybe about it," Andy said. "Can you imagine Steve Durham pulling a stunt like this for anything but money? Bringing some guy a hundred thousand dollars in cash, in the middle of the day, coming all the way up here from Washington, the whole bit—can you imagine him doing it for any other reason?"

"No," Kyle said. "But it wasn't Senator Durham I was thinking about."

"Who were you thinking about? Mother Teresa? She did a lot for money, too, even if it wasn't to buy herself Mercedes convertibles. The whole world runs on money."

Andy wrote a long note on the top page of the pad, signed it at the bottom, and handed it across the table to Kyle. Kyle read it through very carefully and then folded it up and put it in his pocket.

"Have you ever heard of Dr. Jonas Salk?" he asked Andy.

Andy had ordered himself a cheesecake of his own. Now that business had been concluded, he was happily eating it.

"Not a clue," he said.

"He was a guy back in the forties and fifties who discovered one of the first really effective vaccines for polio," Kyle said. "There was another guy around the same time who discovered one, too, but the guy you hear about is always Salk. He was a doctor at a time when doctors didn't get rich, and he discovered the vaccine in a back room. He wasn't part of a big research staff. Anyway, he discovered this vaccine, and the offers came pouring in to have him lease the rights to it to drug companies. He could have gotten hugely rich. People were willing to pay anything to make sure their children didn't get polio, and there were polio epidemics almost every summer."

"So?" Andy asked. "Did he end his days living in the Caribbean with native girls?"

"There are no native girls in the Caribbean," Kyle said. "And he ended his days in a modest two-story house where he'd lived for most of his adult life. He didn't make a dime out of the polio vaccine. He gave the formula away for free on condition that the people who made the stuff also give it away or free. He thought making sure no child ever again got polio was more important than the money."

Andy shook his head. "If you think I'm going to admire that, I don't. It's a stupid Hollywood gesture. You need money to survive in this world, and there's no point in scraping by if you don't have to. I don't see you scraping by. You had a job with Legal Aid. You didn't stay there."

"No," Kyle admitted. "I didn't."

"And that friend of yours out in Alwych," Andy said. "Tim what's his name, that runs the clinic."

"Brand," Kyle said.

"He may spend his time running a free clinic, but he's got trust fund money out the wazoo. He isn't putting himself in any danger of going broke."

"No, he isn't."

"Life's a bitch and then you die," Andy said. "There isn't anything that would make me sit still with scraping by if I didn't have to. And the only reason why I don't go for the kind of thing the senator did is that I know I wouldn't get away with it."

"I've got to go," Kyle said. "I'm supposed to be doing something with fireworks for a party tonight. Tomorrow's the Fourth of July."

"Don't I know it."

"Do you think it was all about the money for them, too?" Kyle asked. "John Adams. George Washington. Thomas Jefferson."

"Sure it was," Andy said. "They were a bunch of rich guys who didn't want to pay taxes to Great Britain. I can't believe you're having this fit. You never struck me as that kind of guy."

"I never struck me as that kind of guy, either," Kyle said.

He got out of the booth and reached under the table for the briefcase that was identical to the one he'd brought, but much lighter. Then he walked down the length of the deli and out into the bright hot air.

2

By eight o'clock, Tim Brand was willing to admit that there was not going to be much business at the clinic for the night. He went out the back door to sit on the low stone wall next to the stairs that led up to Main Street. It was usually quiet back there, except for the nurses taking cigarette breaks.

He took his cell phone out of his pocket and checked for messages, but there were none of any importance. He took out a package of Altoids peppermints and opened it. He stuck three of the things in his mouth and felt his tongue burn.

There was a noise at the top of the cement stairs and he looked up. A woman was coming down toward him, wearing a longish skirt and a T-shirt and espadrilles. He knew who she was immediately, but what his mind told him was: *She's still eighteen.*

The woman got to the bottom of the stairs, and the face became—well, not eighteen anymore.

We're both forty-eight, Tim thought.

Virginia came the rest of the way down the stairs and took a seat a little ways from him on the stone wall. Then she took a pack of cigarettes out of the pocket of her skirt and lit up.

"I can't do this in public anymore," she said. "Put a picture of this in the paper and I'm probably done. I love cigarettes, though. I think it's one of the great injustices of the world that they aren't good for you."

"They are good for you in some ways," Tim said. "It's just that, in other ways, they kill you. I thought you'd quit."

"I thought I'd quit, too. I smoke about five of the things a day now. It's better than the old three packs."

Tim watched as Virginia studied her cigarette. People rarely noticed it, but they looked remarkably alike. It wasn't that common in fraternal twins.

"Is there a reason for the visit?" he asked. "It can't be just because you're in town. You're in town a lot without coming to see me."

"I could say I came because there are things I wanted to know, but you wouldn't believe me."

"What do you want to know?"

"Well," Virginia said, "I'd like to know why it's all right for you to do what you do and at the same time deny women common ordinary things men would expect to have without issue, but when I fight for women to have those things, I'm just advancing a selfish agenda. I'd like to know why denying and depriving and restricting women is an acceptable foible in someone doing Good Works, when it wouldn't be an acceptable foible to treat anybody else that way. Why is it, Tim, that what women need is always a side issue?"

"I'm not depriving or denying anyone anything," Tim said. "I am living according to the dictates of my conscience, just as you're living according to the dictates of yours."

"And the dictates of your conscience say what? That what women need, what they want, what they hope, what they dream—that all that doesn't matter? That they're nothing but broodmares for the social order? That nothing about them is really human except the content of their wombs?"

"We're not going to get anywhere with this, Virginia. We've done it before."

"I know," Virginia said.

The cigarette had burned down to the stub. She threw it on the ground and stubbed it out. She was, Tim thought, a very beautiful woman.

"I thought we ought to talk about something else," Virginia said, sounding more than a little abrupt. "That man is here. Gregor Demarkian."

"I know," Tim said.

"I'm not worried about him, exactly," Virginia said. "I know I didn't kill Chapin. I'm pretty sure you didn't, either. And I don't know who did. If you want to know the truth, it astonishes me that anybody would after all this time."

"Evaline Veer?" Tim suggested. "That's the best I've been able to come up with."

"Hope called me," Virginia said.

"She came here, too," Tim said.

"She was out of her mind frantic," Virginia said. "I mean completely out of her mind. She doesn't—handle things well."

"No," Tim agreed.

"I kept thinking she was going to make people think she was guilty of something whether she was or not."

"She did go and talk to that man," Tim said. "You know, the one with the books. Knight Sion Publishing, or whatever that was."

"I can't see what she had to tell him that he didn't already know," Virginia said.

"He paid her a few hundred dollars," Tim said. "She came and talked to me about it this morning. She said she was feeling guilty about betraying us, and I said I didn't think it was much of a betrayal. You're right. There isn't much the man didn't already know, and not much he hadn't published, either. I was glad she had the money. There isn't much teaching available in the summers. I don't think she eats right."

"There wasn't any need for it to ruin any of us. It didn't ruin you. Or me. Or Kyle."

"It ruined Marty and Chapin."

"Marty is dead," Virginia said. Then she shivered. "Chapin is dead, too, but it doesn't feel real to me. I think I've been assuming she's been dead all these years. But Marty—well, I don't think about the robberies much. I didn't take part in them, and I didn't suspect Chapin and Marty did until there was all that fuss on the news. But I do remember that damned accident."

"I don't think it would be possible to forget, either," Tim

said. "I remember the screeching noise and then being slammed into the back of the front seat and then being twisted around like a pretzel. I wasn't wearing a seat belt."

Virginia took out her cigarettes again, looked at them for a moment, and put them back into her pocket.

"I'd better go," she said. "They're probably looking for me."

"You know I'm not praying that you win your election."

"I do know," Virginia said. "And I don't pray, but I'm not hoping you get out from under the laws of the State of Connecticut. I'm not hoping that you have to close, mind you. I do hope you're going to see the light."

"I have seen the light," Tim said, "and if the state prevails and demands that I hand out the morning-after pill, I will close. I will shut the place down cold and I'll make it entirely clear why."

"And everybody will call you a hero for doing it," Virginia said. "I do have to go, Tim. I have to get back to the fight to make the world safe for selfish, shallow feminists."

"Your words, not mine."

"I don't understand why it's always all right to short-change and restrict and disadvantage women," Virginia said. "Except, on some level, mostly I do. I'll see you later."

"Probably sometime next year," Tim said.

Virginia gave him a little smile and then ran up the concrete steps as quickly and as smoothly as if she really had been still eighteen. Tim watched her go with a feeling that was a lot like pain.

SEVEN

1

Gregor Demarkian's instructions to the Alwych Police Department did just what he'd expected them to do. They'd made the entire population of the APD headquarters start running around in circles. By the time he arrived back in Alwych, officers and technicians had been dispatched to the Waring house to "fingerprint everything in sight," as Jason Battlesea put it, and a couple of people had been called in from the state police to help. Gregor had an almost irresistible urge to ask if the state police forensics people had lost their accreditation along with their lab, but he managed to choke it back and then to go over, once more, what he needed them all to do. He had no idea if he would actually be able to get Ray Guy Pearce arrested for something, but he did know he was going to try.

"We got the FBI on the phone," Jason Battlesea said, "and some guy named Fitzgerald said to tell you that this man you're interested in has never been fingerprinted. So if you're going to check for his fingerprints, you're going to have to have some reason to bring him in. He's some kind of lawyer."

Gregor considered this. Ray Guy Pearce a lawyer? There was nothing impossible about it, and given the man's mental state on every level, it had probably been a smart move. Lawyer or not, though, there were ways to get a man fingerprinted.

"I'm surprised somebody hasn't insisted over the years," Gregor said, "but it doesn't matter. We'll get him finger-printed. And then I'm going to break his head."

"But I don't understand," Jason Battlesea said. "Is this the person who killed Chapin Waring? He came in from outside and killed her? But why would he do that? If he knew her in Queens, why didn't he kill her in Queens?"

"He didn't know her like that," Gregor said. "He thought he was shielding her from the agents of the worldwide rep-tilian conspiracy."

"What?"

Gregor shook his head. "Mr. Pearce believes," he said, "that the entire world is run by thirteen families, the richest thirteen families on the planet. The members of these fami-lies are not human. They are the descendants of the union of human women with Satan's demons. And these thirteen families have been the same families since the beginning of time. They just pretend to be other people in order to fool the public about the true nature of the world. So, you see, they'll create the illusion that someone like Bill Clinton was born and grew up in poverty, when in reality he was the son of one of these families, and being groomed to take power."

Jason Battlesea looked bewildered. "I'm sorry," he said, "but that sounds like gibberish. Are you trying to tell me that this Pearce guy is crazy?"

"Not in the way you mean, no," Gregor said. "There are a lot of people in the world—in the world, mind you, not just in the United States—who believe versions of that story. And there are a lot of versions. There are Catholic and Prot-estant versions, atheist versions, Muslim versions. A little twist here and there, and the story works for anybody. Ray Guy Pearce thought Chapin Waring was a member of one of those thirteen families, and that she had escaped from that family and now wanted to tell the truth to the world. But she couldn't poke her head above the radar, or they would find her, capture her, and destroy her."

"She was wanted for a double homicide," Jason Battlesea said. "Of course we wanted to find her and capture her."

"Mr. Pearce believes that was all just a cover story for the forces of evil who were afraid she'd blow their cover. So, he covered for her when she needed covering, he taught her how to live underground and without being noticed—"

"He published books. He wasn't trying not to be noticed."

"Some of the books he published were manuals on how not to be noticed," Gregor said. "And I have to admit, he was smarter than most of these guys. The usual thing in trying to hide is to take yourself off to some remote area and do what's called 'going sovereign.' That means trying to stay off the grid entirely. No hooking up to the electrical system. No buying oil for the furnace. No going to the grocery store. You build yourself a place out in the middle of nowhere. You hunt and grow your food and use firewood to heat your house in winter. You don't use money and you don't let yourself get seen. And it fails every time."

"It sounds like the Unabomber," Battlesea said.

"It is like the Unabomber," Gregor said, "and like a half dozen other people you've heard of. The Weavers at Ruby Ridge, for instance. Do you know what the two big problems with going sovereign are?"

"Is one of them that it's crazy?"

"No," Gregor said. "The first thing is that it's really hard to hide out in areas with sparse populations. We're talking about really small towns here. There's not much to do. There's not much to see. And there's nowhere to go. That means that people watch other people. They see somebody new, they notice him. They check out the new guy's behavior. They try to figure out what he's doing. Of course, they know about going sovereign. They've seen these guys before, and they know a lot of them aren't stable, and a lot of them are wanted by somebody or other. So they watch, and they watch television, and when the guy's picture shows up on *America's Most Wanted,* they pick up the phone and give the authorities all the necessary directions."

"Okay," Battlesea said.

"The second problem," Gregor said, "is that these guys almost always want guns. And, by the way, I think we're going to find that was true of Chapin Waring, too, as soon as we find the apartment she was living in. The gun she used to shoot up the mirrors while she was dying is going to be one she brought with her. Not that we'll necessarily be able to prove it, but I think that's a pretty good bet. But that's the thing. They're running, they feel hunted, and they want guns. Even if they're smart enough to have given up modern transportation. Even if they've gotten themselves to the point where they don't need to buy gas or tires or spare parts because they're relying on horse and mule power. They want guns, they want a lot of them, and they want good ones. They've got to hunt, and guns are better for hunting game than traps or bows and arrows. But the big reason is that they're convinced they're under siege and have to protect themselves from the forces of the United States government. That means they want an arsenal. And if there's one thing the United States government pays a lot of attention to, it's indications that some guy or group of guys somewhere is stockpiling a lot of firepower."

"Didn't you just say Chapin Waring was stockpiling firepower? Why didn't they pick up on that?"

"I don't think she was buying bazookas and Uzis," Gregor said. "She probably picked up a few Saturday night specials, the kind of thing you can get off the street. And she didn't need to have bought anything herself. Ray Guy Pearce could have gotten a couple of hand guns for her without raising too much of a profile. The Bureau has been looking into him, on and off, for years, but the general opinion is that the man is a flake and a crank and not particularly dangerous to anything but your sanity. He hasn't been buying bazookas and Uzis either."

"But he was out here, right? He was in the Waring house?"

"On and off the whole thirty years," Gregor agreed. "Chapin Waring gave him a key and the security codes. Which means she had them, at least at the very beginning. I don't think anybody would have noticed he was there. All he wanted was the photographs. He wouldn't have stolen the silver or anything obvious that would have triggered a police investigation. And he didn't take the photograph albums, just in case they might be missed. I think Chapin Waring told him where the albums were in the house. He went in and took whatever photographs he wanted and then put the albums back in place. He got out as quickly as he could. As long as he wasn't stupid, as long as he was careful to time it, he would have been fine. Just take off down the beach."

"But how did he get into the house without leaving signs of forced entry?" Jason Battlesea said. "I get you about the first time. Chapin Waring could have given him a key. But after a while, the locks were changed. And they were changed a lot."

"There are plenty of lock-picking tools that won't leave much if anything of a trace," Gregor said. "They're not very popular, because they take a long time to work. You have to have about half an hour or so to go at it without being afraid of being caught."

"Well, he couldn't have used something like that," Jason Battlesea said. "He couldn't just hang around, picking a lock for half an hour. Somebody would have seen him."

"Would they have? If he'd tried to pick a lock on the beach side, then yes, I think there's a good chance he would have been seen, at least at certain seasons of the year. But the front door is shielded from the road by hedges, and so is the side door that leads to the kitchen. He could have spent all the time he wanted at either of those two without having to worry about being interrupted. He would have parked somewhere on the beach, walked down and come around to the side door or the front door. Beach Drive is as closed off and isolated as any residential road I've ever seen. People don't look out their windows. They don't spy on their neighbors. They take privacy to an extreme. Did you get one notification that Chapin Waring was anywhere near her house the day she died? Because there's none in the notes. People saw her all over the place, including on the parts of Beach

Drive that are closest to town, but nobody seems to have seen her in the strictly residential area where the house was."

"Right," Battlesea said. "But you still don't think he killed her."

"No," Gregor said. "He had no reason to. In fact, he had good reason to want to keep her alive. Technically, he wasn't harboring a fugitive, and they'd done all the right things to make sure she'd be very hard to find. She'd stayed in a major city, with lots of people around, and in a very diverse area, so that nobody stood out no matter what they were like unless they started behaving outrageously and dangerously. He said she was wearing a *hijab*, which would have been an excellent way for her not to get seen, even before there was a significant Muslim population in the area. As long as there was something of a population, a *hijab* would have turned her into somebody nobody really looked at. Most people, when they see a woman in a *hijab*, look at the *hijab*, not the woman."

"Right," Jason Battlesea said.

"I've got to take a walk," Gregor said. "There's somebody I want to talk to."

Jason Battlesea looked mulish. "I don't understand why we shouldn't think this guy killed her," he said. "Then we could arrest him."

2

Sometimes, near the middle of consulting cases, Gregor Demarkian felt as if he were going to explode. The local police who called him in were often either incompetent or unwilling to be competent. More often the latter. A friend of Bennis's had once told him that that was what being a management consultant was. Nine times out of ten, you went into a business and found—although nobody ever told you—that it was desperate to fire some idiot and just couldn't bring itself to the point.

With Alwych, the problem wasn't incompetence or unwillingness to be competent so much as it was an ingrained sense of what was and wasn't "done" here. The Alwych police didn't have a suspect they weren't afraid to name or nervous to arrest. They didn't have any idea at all of what might have happened here. They only knew that they were suddenly famous, and they had to do something about it.

Juan Valdez was sitting in the car in the parking lot behind the station, but Gregor didn't go to him. He walked out the front door of the police station instead and looked around on Main Street. The clinic was next to the hospital, up on a hill and easy to spot.

Gregor started walking in that direction. Twilight had begun, and it was sliding inexorably into darkness. Some of the stores were open, selling little American flags and American flag pins and American flag hats and even American flag bikinis.

After Gregor had gone about three blocks, there was a little square sign with a large H on it, and a smaller sign under that that said HOSPITAL with an arrow to the left. He followed the arrow and found himself on a wide road with a sidewalk only on one side. It curved around to the right in a wide sweep. Halfway up the sweep, there was another sign with another arrow.

He had gotten nearly to the top of the curve when he saw them: the hospital, modern and shiny and a little farther up the incline, and the clinic, also modern, also shiny, but very much smaller. He went through the little parking lot to the front door.

He saw the man he had come to see almost immediately. He looked just like all the pictures of him in newspapers and magazines. And he would have been a noticeable person even if he hadn't been semifamous. He was very tall and very dark and very—*there*. Bennis would have called him one of those people who glowed in the dark.

The tall man was leaning up against the reception counter, talking to one of the nurses. He did not seem to be in a hurry, or in the middle of an emergency. Gregor walked up to him and held out his hand.

"Dr. Brand?" he said. "My name is Gregor Demarkian."

Tim Brand looked up, looked puzzled for a moment, and

then smiled. The smile was wide and broad and completely unaffected.

"Excellent," he said. "I knew you were going to come and talk to all of us, but I thought it was going to be with Jason Battlesea or one of those detectives. Come right in. We're having a very slow night."

"It's the Fourth of July eve," the woman behind the counter said. "Of course it's a very slow night. You watch what happens tomorrow. We'll be full up and frantic."

"Some of the guys who drink seriously don't like to go to the emergency room to get dried out," Tim Brand said. "The emergency room people tend to feel like they have to refer these guys to alcohol programs or get them to talk to social workers. We try to do what the earliest Christians did. You need help, we give it to you, no questions asked. If you want to talk to us, we'll listen."

"We listen to too much, if you ask me," the woman behind the counter said.

Tim Brand gestured to the corridor behind the desk. "Come with me. I have an office of sorts, if you want to be private."

Gregor let the doctor lead him first down the corridor that had been visible, then around a corner, then to an open door. The office inside was very small, and there was so much stuff strewn around that Gregor wasn't sure he'd have a seat.

Tim Brand leaned over a chair and took a huge wad of papers off it. "You're in luck," he said. "Kyle was here not too long ago, and I had to clear a chair for him. I expect you'll be talking to Kyle, too, eventually. You'll be talking to everybody that hung around with Chapin Waring thirty years ago."

Gregor thought about the notes. "Westervan," he said finally. "Kyle Westervan. There were six of you. You were linked to Chapin Waring. Kyle Westervan was linked to—"

"To Virginia Brand, now Virginia Brand Westervan," Tim said. "She's my sister. My fraternal twin sister, if you want to know. After that, there was Hope Matlock and poor Marty Veer. The absolutely coolest crowd at Alwych Country Day, all home from college for the summer and causing more trouble than any of us were worth. Jason Battlesea thinks Chapin was murdered over all that stuff that happened thirty years ago. Do you?"

"I don't know," Gregor said. "Right now I'm interested in something else. Have you ever heard of a man named Ray Guy Pearce?"

"Sure," Tim said. "He publishes all those conspiracy books. He's published two or three dozen about Chapin and the robberies. Just after all those things happened, I used to read those books and wonder where he was getting all his information. I even went into Queens one day and threatened to punch him out."

"Did you?"

"No," Tim admitted. "I was never really any good with physical violence. I just came home and fumed some more."

"He was getting all the information from Chapin Waring," Gregor said carefully. "He knew where she was, and he was in contact with her for all of those thirty years. Someday when I have more time, I'll tell you all about it, if you'd like. Right now, I need to know something, and you seem to me the most likely person to have the information."

"Sure. What do you need to know?"

"One of the things Ray Guy Pearce said to me when I talked to him earlier today was that Chapin Waring used to come into Alwych every once in a while, and that she came here because, she said, there was somebody here she wanted to talk to. And that she was making these trips fairly recently. It seems logical to me to think that the person she was meeting was either one of you four remaining from thirty years ago, or a member of her family."

"Why wouldn't a member of the family be the most logical choice?"

"I've met the only member of the family still living here," Gregor said, "and that's possible. There are two other sisters, but there's no reason why Chapin Waring would have met them in Alwych. They don't live anywhere near Alwych, and they would have been putting themselves in danger of being caught if they kept coming here. If Chapin Waring was coming to Alwych to meet someone, it would most likely have been someone who lives in Alwych and has to do nothing unnatural to be here. That includes the four of you. I'll admit that I don't know anything much about this Hope Matlock. I do think, though, that it's implausible that Chapin would have been coming here to meet your sister. Your sister is a United States congresswoman. She's much too high profile. That leaves you, Hope Matlock, and Kyle Westervan. Kyle Westervan works in the city. Chapin could have met him there more safely than she could have here. That leaves you and Hope Matlock."

"Not bad," Tim said. "But it could have been Evaline, you know. Marty's sister. If there's anybody in town who has a reason to want to talk to Chapin Waring, it's Evaline. I don't think she's ever gotten over the accident. None of us have, of course, in some ways, but for Evaline it's been very painful for a very long time. When I first heard that Chapin had been stabbed in the back, the first person who came to mind was Evaline."

"And you weren't meeting Chapin Waring in town on and off over the years?"

"No," Tim said. "Not even once. I had no idea that anybody was. I'll admit I think I'd be the last person in the world she would want to see."

"Why?" Gregor asked. "You were her boyfriend at the time of the robberies, weren't you? That's in my notes, too."

"I was her boyfriend," Tim agreed, "in the sense that we'd been going around together all through high school and, yes, we slept together on and off when Chapin found it convenient. She didn't always find it convenient. But being boyfriend and girlfriend at that age isn't usually a matter of affection. I never did think Chapin liked me very much. I never very much liked her. We were the perfect match on paper—families, education, background, all of that—and a complete mismatch when it came to personality."

"Were you surprised when you heard about the robberies?"

"Yes and no," Tim said. "It shocked me that she'd killed someone, or participated in the killings, or whatever it was.

I would never have thought Chapin capable of murder. But Chapin liked pushing the envelope. She liked causing trouble. And she loved an adrenaline rush."

"I see," Gregor said, "you'd have been in the backseat because you'd have been sitting next to her as—her boyfriend."

"That's right," Tim said. "As it was, I was in the backseat. Hope and Kyle were lucky that they didn't end up dead or worse."

Gregor nodded. "Were you shocked to find that Martin Veer had participated in the robberies?"

"Not really," Tim said. "Marty and Hope were both eager to please. They wanted to keep Chapin happy, because Chapin was what kept them as part of the Popular Crowd. Sorry if I seem to be verbally capitalizing, but it was that kind of thing. Chapin had the power in high school to determine who was in and who was out. And she kept that power when we were all at home that summer after the first year in college. I have no idea why we give people that kind of power over us at those ages, but we do. And Marty and Hope— especially Hope—would never have been considered anybody important at Alwych Country Day if Chapin hadn't taken them up."

"Have you seen them since?" Gregor asked. "Did the five of you keep up with each other?"

"I didn't see Chapin, if you're asking that again," Tim said, "but I do see the others. Kyle and I have remained reasonably good friends, in spite of the fact that he spends his time worshiping Mammon. I saw Virginia less than an hour ago. She came down by the back stairs by herself. It gets a little touch and go, our relationship. She says it's because we both have constituencies."

"I can see that," Gregor said.

"As for Hope," Tim said. He looked away for a moment. Gregor was sure he saw a flash of pain in the man's eyes.

"As for Hope," Tim said again. "Well, let's just say that she drops by the clinic every once in a while, too. She's had the hardest time of all of us. Her family never did have any money, but that isn't really it. She got a doctorate. She could have had a decent teaching career. There were a lot of jobs open for English professors when she finished graduate school. And she started out to do that, I think, and then she came back here and—nothing. Maybe she has posttraumatic stress syndrome, and we're all too stupid to notice it."

"What were you doing on the night Chapin Waring died?" Gregor asked.

"Good question," Tim said. "I don't think I have what you'd call an alibi. For most of the evening and night I was here. We had a big crowd that night. Earlier, though—well. I got up around noon. I did some errands. I attended the Vigil Mass at Our Lady of Perpetual Help at five. It was a perfectly ordinary day. And that was surprising."

"Surprising?" Gregor asked. "Why?"

"Because I thought, unconsciously, that if Chapin ever came back into my life, there'd be something spectacular about it. After all, she represented the most spectacular thing that had ever happened to me except for my conversion, and my conversion wasn't a public event. Maybe I thought she'd come into town followed by a posse of FBI agents firing machine guns."

"The Bureau hasn't indulged itself in machine guns in some decades," Gregor said.

"You know what I mean," Tim said. "I thought it would fit in with the rest of it, the robberies, the crash, the insane manhunt after the police had figured out that it was Chapin who'd masterminded the robberies."

There was something of a commotion in the hallway. Tim Brand crossed the small office and opened the door. He stuck his head out and said, "Marcie? Jennifer? Somebody? What's going on?"

Gregor went to the door, too. Tim stepped out into the corridor. The woman who had been at the reception desk came around the corner, hurrying.

"What's going on?" Tim Brand asked again. "Marcie, what are you—?"

"Something happened on the terrace," the woman said,

picking up the pace a little and sounding winded. She came
to an abrupt stop in front of Tim Brand's office door. "Maartje
was out there taking a break and she called in and was incoherent, so I sent Juliette out to see what was going on. Then
Juliette called and she was even more incoherent."

"Maybe we ought to go back there and look."

Gregor thought the two of them had forgotten he was
there. They took off down the corridor to the back, and he
followed them.

The corridor turned again at the very back, and then
there was a small vestibule. Outside, Gregor could see two
very young women huddled together near a low stone wall,
and cement steps going up the hill behind them toward the
hospital above.

Tim and Marcie went outside, and Gregor went after
them. The first thing he noticed was that one of the young
girls was very, very pregnant.

Marcie went up to the girls and then past them, almost to
the wall. Then she stepped back quickly and said, "Oh, my
God."

Tim Brand moved in swiftly. He stopped and stared at
something on the ground. Then he stepped back, too.

"Bloody hell," he said, and all three of the women looked
at him, shocked.

Marcie started to move forward again. Tim Brand
grabbed her by the sleeve and pulled her back.

"Don't touch anything," he said. "The most important
thing right now is that you don't touch anything. Has anybody touched anything?"

The two young girls shook their heads. The one who
wasn't pregnant started to cry.

Gregor moved up, past the girls, past Marcie and Tim,
and right up to the low stone wall.

Lying right next to it on the ground was the body of a
man in what Gregor could recognize even in the half darkness was a very good suit.

He was lying on his face.

He had been stabbed in the back.

PART THREE

"Why the hell don't you sit in your office and let people come to you fully clothed?"
— Paul Drake to Perry Mason in Erle Stanley Gardner's *Case of the Half-Wakened Wife*

ONE

1

It was an hour later when yet another high-voiced, much-too-young special agent returned Gregor's call, and the too-young special agent was obviously bewildered.

"He's giving a speech," the special agent said. Gregor decided that it was a he, although the evidence was ambiguous.

"He's been here since six o'clock," the special agent said. "And he couldn't have left, not even for a moment. There are hundreds of people here. He walked in at six, he went up onto the platform, and they've been staring at him ever since. According to the people here, he hasn't so much as taken a bathroom break."

"All right," Gregor said. "Good. That was better than I expected."

"He's also signing books," the special agent said. "Do you mind if I ask you something?"

"Go right ahead."

"Are all these people crazy? Because I've been listening to this stuff, and I've been looking at some of the books, and this stuff is—"

"'Crazy' is as good a word as any," Gregor said.

Over near the wall, a state police forensics officer was

guiding two uniformed Alwych police officers through collecting the fibers and the fingerprints and the fluids. On the other side of the open space, Tim Brand was leaning against the door to the clinic, where Marcie and the two young women had gone with another uniformed police officer. Jason Battlesea, Mike Held, and Jack Mann were standing in the middle of everything, looking useless.

"What was that?" Jason Battlesea asked when Gregor put his cell phone away.

"I asked the Bureau to do us a favor and check on the whereabouts of Ray Guy Pearce."

"You did? That's great. Is he in town?"

"He's in a Midtown Manhattan hotel giving a talk and signing books in front of a couple of hundred people," Gregor said. "He's been there since at least six o'clock, and he hasn't left the stage even once."

Jason Battlesea looked confused. "But that's not good, is it?" he asked. "I mean, how could he have been here committing a murder—"

"He wasn't."

"Are you trying to tell me that this Pearce guy killed Chapin Waring and then somebody else came in and killed Mr. Westervan here? Because—"

"No," Gregor said. "I told you before. Pearce was responsible for the break-ins, but he wasn't the person who murdered Chapin Waring, and he has what most people would call an airtight alibi for the murder of—Mr. Westervan."

"Kyle," Tim Brand said from his place at the door. "His first name was Kyle. And he was here, in this clinic, yesterday. And he was fine."

Gregor turned to face Tim. "He didn't die of a heart attack," he said. "He was stabbed in the back."

"And how did he get here?" Tim demanded. "I was out here just as it was getting dark, and Virginia—oh, crap. Virginia was here, too. She came down those stairs and we talked for a couple of minutes and then she left. And no, there wasn't a body here when she was here. I was sitting right on that wall. I'd have seen it. And it couldn't have been more than an hour before Maartje and Juliette came out here. What did he do? Come down the stairs and then what? Why would he come down the stairs? Why wouldn't he just come right into the clinic by the front door? It's what he usually did."

"Oh, my God," Jason Battlesea said. "The congresswoman was here? Right here? In back here?"

"And I was here with her," Tim Brand said. "I was sitting right over there when she came down the steps and I was sitting right there when she went back up."

"Did she have anybody with her?" Jason Battlesea asked. "Don't politicians usually travel around with lots of people with them?"

"No, she didn't have anybody with her," Tim said. "There might have been somebody waiting for her up there, but she didn't say anything."

"Were you expecting her?" Gregor asked.

Tim shook his head. "I'm never expecting her. She drops in on me about once a year. She's my twin sister. There's really nothing sinister in all this."

"Why would she have come by the route here," Gregor asked, "instead of by the front door?"

"Because unlike Kyle, she does have to be careful about who sees her going where," Tim said, and shook his head. "She gets a lot of bad publicity when she comes to the clinic. So mostly she goes to my house. She's in town for the Fourth. She's doing something public tomorrow, I think. She decided to stop in and not direct attention to herself by going through the front door. If I hadn't been down here, she would have come through this door and found me in my office."

Gregor nodded, and walked over toward the wall where the forensics people were working. There was no access for cars or vans out here. It was an enclosed back space, used mostly for people who worked at the clinic to have somewhere to go when they wanted to take a break. Now there was crime scene tape across the top of the stairs and too many people in the small space.

Gregor went back to Tim Brand.

"I think you're going to find," he said, "that Mr. Westervan was killed up there and the body tipped down here. Tipped or pushed. If he hadn't fallen all that way, he might still be alive. Would most people here have known that tipping a body over that wall up there would land it here, behind the clinic?"

"I don't know," Tim said. "A lot of people would have known it, probably."

"What's up there, exactly?"

"That's the overflow parking lot for the hospital," Tim said. "They've got a regular parking lot in the front, and then they've got that one if it gets full up. I don't think it does, very much. They put it in about ten years ago when there was a school bus accident and the place went crazy, with parents coming in and that kind of thing. I doubt if they've used it much since."

"So there's not likely to be any cars parked there?" Gregor asked.

"Not many," Tim said.

"Is it well lit?"

"There are security lights around the perimeter," Tim Brand said. "You can see them if you look up. I don't know how well lit that makes it. I don't know if I've ever been up there in the dark."

"You told me before that Mr. Westervan had given you some legal advice recently," Gregor said. "Would you mind telling us what it was about?"

Tim stared at the sky above him. "If you really think that is why he was murdered, you're out of your mind," he said. "We got letters recently from the Office of Health Care Access and the Office of the Health Care Advocate that said we were operating as an emergency room and that as an emergency room, we would have to follow Connecticut law as regards emergency rooms."

"And?" It was Gregor's turn to be puzzled.

"And," Tim said, "in the state of Connecticut, emergency rooms are required by law to provide rape victims with the morning-after pill if they want it. The morning-after pill is an abortifacient. That means it essentially causes an abortion, although a very early abortion. This is a Catholic clinic. We will not provide abortions or abortifacients for any reason. If the state changes our classification from that of a clinic to that of an emergency room, we'll have to shut down. And yes, Mr. Demarkian, we will shut down under those circumstances. I will not compromise on that."

Gregor nodded. "The advice that Mr. Westervan gave you, was it workable advice?"

Tim Brand shrugged. "It was what I expected," he said. "The state really doesn't have a leg to stand on in reclassifying us. If the case goes to court, they will not win it. But if the case goes to court, it will cost us a lot of money we'd be better off spending on the things we do."

"And Mr. Westervan was going to act as your attorney for this case?" Gregor asked.

"No," Tim said. "I think he would have, if I'd asked, but it's not the kind of law he does. I don't even know if he's passed the bar in Connecticut. He works in a Wall Street firm. He deals with financial people."

"Do you have any idea why somebody would want to kill Mr. Westervan?"

"No," Tim said. "At least, not anybody in Alwych. I've got no idea what he was doing on Wall Street, but then, why would somebody from Wall Street come all the way out here to kill him?"

"They probably wouldn't," Gregor said.

"I know he seems to have been killed just the way Chapin was, but you can't tell me he had anything to do with those robberies. The surveillance pictures were everywhere at the time, and the two people responsible were Chapin and Marty. Kyle and I were both much too tall, by half a foot at least. Even Virginia was too tall."

"Yes," Gregor said. "I agree with you."

"Never mind what you agree with," Jason Battlesea said. "The congresswoman was here. Do you know what a can of worms that's going to be?"

Gregor turned and gave Jason Battlesea a long look. He was what he had always been, a reasonably competent man as long as his skills were not subjected to serious stress, and a man who thought politically before he thought forensically or morally. He was obviously scared to death.

"Do you think Congresswoman Westervan murdered her ex-husband?"

"Of course I don't," Jason Battlesea said. The words nearly exploded out of him.

"She wouldn't have," Tim Brand said. "They liked each other, Kyle and Virginia. They liked each other in high school and they liked each other in college and they got along ever since. He contributed to her campaigns. And the divorce was years ago. It's not like there are unresolved issues. And she'd be very easily recognized. No matter how discreet she was being, she could never be sure that somebody wouldn't spot her. I don't think you stab somebody and then push a body over a wall under those conditions."

"No," Gregor said. "I agree with you."

"It would be a lot better if it was this guy you were all talking about, this Ray Guy Pearce," Jason Battlesea said. "It would clear the whole thing up, both murders, and we wouldn't have to bother the congresswoman with questions or get ourselves in the paper being accused of deliberately ruining her campaign for the Senate. Particularly when it turns out she didn't do it anyway."

"I could probably get Mr. Demarkian in to see Virginia without too much of a fuss," Tim Brand said, "as long as he didn't come accompanied by two patrol cars and a lot of screaming sirens. There's no reason to make everything a lot of drama if you don't want to."

"I'm not making anything a lot of drama," Jason Battlesea said. "I'm just being realistic here. And realistically—"

"Realistically," Gregor said, "we should talk to the two young women who found the body. They're inside the clinic?"

"Yes," Tim Brand said. "I sent them into the conference

room. Marcie will be with them, and so will the police-woman who went with them."

"Angela Harkin," Gregor said.

"I just hope she's empathetic," Tim said. "Maartje is in her ninth month and stress could bring on labor any minute. I do not want a premature delivery."

2

Tim Brand led the way back into the clinic and down the corridor to the conference room where he had asked Maartje, Juliette, and Marcie to stay. As soon as they came through the doors, Gregor could hear the hum and bustle of the clinic farther along toward the front. It was not the hum and bustle of work, but of panic and more than a little excitement. Tim Brand heard it, too, and turned to look back at Gregor and Jason Battlesea.

"It really is a light night," he said. "We have about a third our usual appointments, and I didn't see a huge line when I came in. They've got nothing to do but worry about this."

"The line's going to be longer as soon as this gets out," Jason Battlesea said, "and my guess is that it already is out."

"That's my guess, too," Tim Brand said, looking uneasily up the corridor. He stopped at a door and turned back to Gregor and Battlesea. "Listen," he said. "Maartje is very pregnant. We're not entirely, one hundred percent sure, because, like many people who come here, she's got inadequate medical records, but I think she's in her ninth month. And the child already has issues. Which means that if you get her too worked up—"

"She could go into labor," Gregor said. "I'll try to be careful. But I'd think finding a body would get her more worked up than answering questions."

Tim shrugged. "You can never tell with pregnant women. I'm Catholic, not fundamentalist. I have no problem accepting the theory of evolution. But I've met a lot of pregnant women in my time, and if there's an evolutionary advantage to the way they behave, I'll eat dust."

Tim opened the door, and Gregor looked through it to see the three women sitting around a medium-sized conference table, each with a cup of something in front of her.

"What have you got?" Tim demanded.

The one Gregor supposed was Maartje—because she was so obviously in a late stage of pregnancy—blushed. "Lemon Ginger herb tea," she said. "And I have in it some honey, which is the kind you told Marcie I should have."

"Pasteurized," Tim explained. "You can get some bad forms of food poisoning from honey. You gentlemen want to come in here and sit down?"

"You aren't going to do anything about what's happening up front?" Gregor asked him.

"I've already been up to look once," Marcie said. "The line's getting longer but there's nothing we can really do anything about yet. When I'm done here, I'll go ahead and get it organized."

"And you are?" Gregor asked.

"Marcie Connors. I'm a nurse and the assistant director here."

"Marcie's been with me since we opened," Tim Brand said.

"Were you one of the people who found the body?" Gregor asked.

"Oh, goodness no," the other young woman said. She would have to be Juliette. "Maartje and I found that thing. I mean, we didn't actually go out there looking for something. We were going to just sit there and have something with ice in it. Maartje was feeling a little rocky."

"It was the being pregnant," Maartje said, looking embarrassed.

Gregor looked the two of them over. "So," he said. "The two of you went out to the terrace to get some air, and—that was it? You just saw a body?"

"We were going to sit on the wall," Juliette said. "Everybody does. You don't have to worry about anything because nobody uses that parking lot up there. And nobody ever comes down the stairs."

"Of course they do," Tim said. "I had someone come down the stairs to talk to me not an hour before the two of you went out."

"Let's get that straight," Gregor said. "You came out here—when?"

"Eight o'clock," Tim said. "Almost exactly."

"And your visitor came?"

"Right away," Tim said. "I'd barely had a chance to sit down before I heard the footsteps on the stairs. We talked for maybe ten minutes, if that. Then she left, and I went back inside."

"Do you know if anybody went out to the back between that time and the time when Maartje and Juliette went out?"

"No," Tim said.

"I was in and out of the back corridor quite a bit," Marcie said, "and I didn't see anybody go out. And Tim was with you, Mr. Demarkian, his office is on the route—"

"We had the door closed," Tim said.

"Oh," Marcie said. "That's too bad."

"So that was eight to no more than eight fifteen, probably closer to eight ten," Gregor said. "And Maartje and Juliette went out—"

"It was exactly quarter to nine," Juliette said. "I checked."

"Fine," Gregor said. "So we had half an hour to thirty-five minutes. You went right out and headed for the wall?"

"Absolutely," Juliette said.

"And then what?" Gregor asked.

Juliette looked confused. "Then nothing," she said. "We went out and we were walking over to the wall and there it was. He was. I mean, it was just lying there."

"And nobody else was there. In the bushes, or going up the stairs," Gregor said.

"No, of course not," Juliette said. "If someone was hanging around, I would have seen him."

"What about the top of the stairs?" Gregor asked. "Or the space above it? Did you see anybody up there? Did you sense any movement, or hear anything?"

"Not a thing," Juliette said.

Maartje was shaking her head. "It was very quiet," she said. "There wasn't even wind."

"I think it's frightening," Juliette said. "That somebody could have come down into our terrace and stabbed Mr. Westervan like that and nobody even heard anything."

"It's more probable that Mr. Westervan was knifed up top, in the parking lot," Gregor said, "and that he then fell over the wall up there or was pushed. There were what looked like signs of impact on the body and around it."

"My God," Juliette said.

"We'll check it out," Jason Battlesea said.

"Still, we're looking at thirty-five minutes," Gregor said. "That's not a lot of time."

They all sat around and looked at each other. A figure from a chair in the corner that Gregor had not noticed before suddenly stirred, and stood up. It was Angela Harkin, in full uniform.

"Maybe it would be a good idea if I went out front and checked on what's going on," she said. "I've got a uniform, I've got a badge, I could probably calm things down."

"Oh, what a wonderful idea," Marcie said. She gave Jason Battlesea a look. "You can't really be thinking of holding these two girls here all night. One of them's pregnant and the other needs to get home sooner rather than later. She can't be out all night."

"I want to go up to the parking lot," Gregor said. "And we ought to have tech people up there. If he was pushed over the wall, there will be evidence to find."

"Of course," Jason Battlesea said. "Of course. Let me go out and check with Held and Mann—"

He rushed out of the room, as if he'd been dying to escape the entire time he was in it.

Gregor and Tim Brand both watched him go.

Then Tim turned to Gregor and said, "Why don't I go up the stairs to the other parking lot with you? I've got something I want to talk to you about."

3

Outside felt like barely controlled chaos. Jason Battlesea had given orders for officers to search the hospital's overflow parking lot. The crime scene tape had been pulled off the cement stairs. Men were going rapidly up and down.

Gregor surveyed the scene and turned to Tim. "Well?" he said.

Tim nodded. "You're going to want to talk to Virginia," he said. "And she's not going to want to talk to you, but she's not stupid. She's going to see the advantage in it. I think I can arrange it."

"When?"

"Now," Tim Brand said.

Gregor was surprised. "It's after ten o'clock," he said. "In fact, it's nearly eleven. Does your sister take meetings this late?"

"I'm pretty sure she'll take this one," Tim said. "The primary consideration here is discretion. Her best bet is to talk to you when nobody knows she's talked to you."

Gregor looked at the stairs. They were empty. Tim started off and Gregor followed him.

He got to the top and stepped off into the large, dark parking lot. There were many more people up here than Gregor had expected from what he had been able to see from below. There were the tech people Jason Battlesea had sent up, but there were also spectators, drawn by the police lights and the clutch of law enforcement officers.

Gregor shook his head. "There is going to be nothing discreet about this," he said.

"You need to go into the hospital and through the emergency room to the emergency room entrance," Tim said. "I'll arrange to have you picked up by somebody who nobody will be looking at, and I'll arrange to have Virginia let you in when you get to her place. But it's got to be right now."

"Yes," Gregor said.

Tim Brand walked off to a completely empty part of the overflow lot and took out his cell phone.

Gregor watched a state police van pull up with its sirens blaring and its lights whirling. These would be the state forsenics experts.

The tech crew worked as if they knew what they were doing, and Gregor was grateful for that. He moved in a little closer and saw one of the Alwych uniforms tell a statie that he was not to be stopped. He got close to the wall and looked over. There were still a lot of people down there, measuring, testing, talking too loudly.

The back door of the clinic opened and two men came out carrying a gurney. It was obviously time for the body to be gone.

Gregor saw Tim Brand walking back across the parking lot and started in his direction. Tim stopped not halfway to him and beckoned him to come on.

Gregor came. When he got to Tim, they were mostly in the dark, and mostly out of earshot of everybody else, official and unofficial.

"Here's what you're going to do," Tim said. "You're going to walk around to the front of the hospital. There's no other way for you to get in. If you try the back door, about a hundred alarms are going to go off. You're going to go in through the hospital's ordinary front door, and then you're going to go down the wide corridor to your left. At the end of that corridor there will be another door, actually a set of swinging doors. That's the side entrance to the emergency room. You're going to go through there, and your ride will be waiting for you in the waiting room."

"My ride?" Gregor asked.

"Her name is Hope Matlock," Tim said. "Hope is probably on your list of people to talk to. She was part of Chapin's group, and she was in the car on the night of the accident. Maybe you could kill two birds with one stone."

"How will I know who she is? Or will she know me?"

"She'll probably recognize you on sight," Tim said. "But

you'll have no trouble recognizing her. She weighs nearly five hundred pounds."

"Ah," Gregor said.

"She's got an absolute crap of an old car. It's reasonably reliable, but it's not the kind of thing for Alwych. But nobody will pay attention to it tonight, and nobody who knows her will pay attention to it at any time. She'll drive you to Virginia's. She'll go park somewhere that doesn't look connected. Then you just text her when you're done and she'll come get you. Virginia is waiting for you, and she is more than ready to talk."

"And you think nobody will know I was there?"

"I think nobody will have a clue," Tim Brand said. "Trust me. I know Alwych. And I know Alwych on the Fourth of July."

TWO

1

From the moment Tim had called her to arrange for Gregor Demarkian to visit, Virginia Brand Westervan felt as if she had been shot through with methamphetamine. Everything inside her was speeded up, so speeded up that the fact that Kyle was dead was almost like a dream. The fact of it was there, and it was a raw pain that would not stop aching. But the pain felt old. The ache felt familiar. It was as if all this had happened years and years ago, and hurting had become as natural to her as eating breakfast.

Virginia heard the car out in the parking lot, the edgy humming of it that announced an old and not very well cared for vehicle. She went to the window and looked out. Nobody was out there. There were no paparazzi in the bushes.

She heard a step outside the front door and went to it immediately. She flung it back without bothering to double-check through the peephole. The man who stood in front of her once the door was open was very tall, taller even than Tim and Kyle, and they'd both been six foot three. Virginia stepped back and let him come in. She closed the door behind him and watched him look around the room. She wondered what, if anything, the room said about her.

"Sit down," she said, gesturing at the living room with its deeply cushioned couch and even more deeply cushioned club chairs. "I don't think I ever thought about the way I furnished this room before. It's not a place I entertain. It's usually only me here, or staffers. Sometimes it's Tim or Kyle. I can't really picture Kyle dead. He isn't the sort of person who dies."

"Everyone dies," Gregor Demarkian said.

"I know that." Virginia thought her voice was too sharp. She tried to soften it. "Maybe I just meant to say that he isn't the kind of person who dies young."

Gregor Demarkian took a seat on one of the chairs. He sank into its cushion like a lead weight sinking in pond water. He looked a little disconcerted.

Virginia took her seat on the edge of the couch. "Do me a favor," she said. "Before we start getting into things, tell me how he died."

"It's a little too early to know exactly how he died," Gregor said. "There will have to be an autopsy. He *apparently* died by being stabbed in the back with a kitchen carving knife."

"Like Chapin," Virginia said.

"Possibly," Gregor Demarkian said. "Or possibly somebody was just hoping to make it look like Chapin Waring's death. Killers do tend to be creatures of habit. They do the same thing over and over again if they kill more than once. On the other hand, copycats are common, if for no other reason than because a copycat killing often throws the police off the real scent. We'll have to see."

"Tim said he'd been pushed off the wall at the back of the overflow parking lot at the hospital."

"Again," Gregor Demarkian said. "Apparently."

"I know," Virginia said. "Apparently. For God's sake, who would want to do something like that? If it wasn't for Chapin, you'd assume this was a random mugging. Except we don't have muggings in Alwych. Not even on the Fourth of July." She walked away. "You want to know about my visit to Tim. Well, we do visit every once in a while. Sometimes he comes to see me, and sometimes I go to see him. It's a little complicated. You'd be amazed at how many people—my supporters and his—think we shouldn't speak, because we're on different sides of the abortion issue. We're supposed to hate each other. Except I don't hate him. I've known him, quite literally, all my life."

"What made you decide to visit him tonight?"

Virginia shrugged. "I've been thinking about him. I'm running for Senate. There were the inevitable clashes because the Saint of Alwych who is my own twin brother wouldn't endorse my run. I didn't expect him to, of course, but the press make a big deal of it. It annoys both of us. Anyway, I was there, and my night was mostly free—"

"Just a minute," Gregor said. "When you say you were there, where were you?"

"Oh," Virginia said. "I was at the hospital. I'm doing nearly wall-to-wall campaign events these days. About five o'clock I gave a talk to the staff at the hospital about the importance of ensuring universal health insurance."

"Is that what you talked to your brother about?"

"No," Virginia said. "Did he tell you that's what we talked about?"

"He said you talked about politics, and morality."

Virginia smiled. "That's about right. He thinks morality resides in denying women their full humanity, and I think he's wrong."

"And *that's* what you talked about? Denying women their full humanity?"

"Something like that," Virginia said. "He'd put it differently."

"Do you know when you got there?"

"No," Virginia said. "Not exactly. I finished the talk, and then I was on my way out and Evaline was there."

"Evaline Veer? The mayor."

"She's the mayor now, yes," Virginia said. "She was there, and she was agitated, so I stopped to talk. And then the talk sort of went on for a while, so I told my people to go on to dinner, and they did. They know when I want to be left alone."

"What did Miss Veer want to talk about?"

"She wanted to talk about Chapin being murdered. You coming. The publicity. Evaline's always been the jumpy sort, but this thing has hit her hard. She's called me at least five times in Washington, as if I could do something about it."

"So you talked to Miss Veer," Gregor said. "Then what?"

"Then nothing, really. I got her calmed down, more or less, and then I started to walk over to the restaurant where my people were having dinner. Except I didn't really feel like going. And I knew the stairs were there and Tim's place was there. So I called my assistant, told her what I was going to do, and went down to see Tim. It worked out better than I expected. He was right there. Sitting on the wall."

"And Kyle Westervan was not there? Lying in the shrubbery right against the wall?"

"Is that where he was found? Right next to the retaining wall?" Virginia almost laughed. "Mr. Demarkian, Tim was *sitting on the wall.* He'd have seen a body. I'd have seen a body. It's not like there's much there to hide something in, even something small."

Gregor Demarkian nodded. Virginia could not decide if she liked him or not.

"Tell me something," he said. "Can you think of any reason why somebody would kill Kyle Westervan?"

"Not a one," Virginia said. "But I haven't seen him all that often in recent years. He has a whole life I know nothing about."

"What about a reason connected to the events of thirty years ago?"

"The robberies? Mr. Demarkian, I can't even think of a good reason connected to those that would make anybody want to kill Chapin Waring. I know that's the most fashionable theory at the moment, but all of that happened thirty years ago. I don't know if I would have known Chapin if I'd run into her on the street. And it wasn't like she took off and left an accomplice behind. Marty was her accomplice, and he was already dead. There was nobody left holding the bag."

"Did you know anything about the robberies when they were occurring?"

"No," Virginia said. "And neither did Kyle. The two of us were completely out of it. Tim was dating Chapin, and Hope was dating Marty—so they at least had some connection to the crimes, even if it was secondhand. But Kyle and I had no connection at all."

"Do you think your brother knew about the robberies while they were going on?"

"He's always said he didn't," Virginia said. "And I believe him. Hope always said she didn't, too. I never knew her as well as I knew the rest of them, but I've got no reason to think she was lying, either. This was Chapin Waring's baby. Except for roping Marty in and taking him for a ride, she never breathed a word of it to the rest of us."

"She never asked you to participate?"

"No," Virginia said. "I think she knew better. She knew I wouldn't go along with it."

"And she didn't ask any of the others?"

"It's as I've said," Virginia said. "They always said not, and I've got no reason not to believe them. It's not like this wasn't all checked out at the time. They questioned all of us, endlessly, for months. They got search warrants and searched our houses. It was a very bad and frightening time, made worse by the fact that it all took place right after the accident, and Marty was dead and Kyle had fractures and I don't know what else. It's incredible that Marty was the only one who died. And it was years before I could get into a car without panicking. I stopped driving for half a decade. But neither the police nor the FBI ever found anything to connect any of the rest of us to those robberies, and I still think that was because there was nothing to find."

"Can you guess at all what time you got to the clinic? Did you stay long?"

"I stayed about ten minutes," Virginia said. "Say seven to seven ten. It couldn't have been much past seven ten, because after I left I did go to the restaurant, and most of my people were still there."

Virginia felt ready for more questions, but it appeared there would be no more. Gregor Demarkian was getting to his feet. Virginia made herself rise, too, and hold out her hand to him. He took it.

"Thank you," he said. "I'm supposed to send a text message, and then my ride is supposed to appear outside and pick me up. Your brother thought having me go in my own car would be too conspicuous."

"My brother is a very cautious human being."

"I suppose that's one way of putting it," Gregor Demarkian said.

2

Hope Matlock had spent the entire time waiting for Gregor Demarkian wishing she had something to fend off the cold, and then worrying, because it was July, and it was not cold. The truth was that she hated this idea of Tim's. She hated the idea of taking Gregor Demarkian anywhere. All the way over here from the hospital, he had sat beside her in the front seat and stared through the windshield as if he had X-ray vision. Then he'd made a few comments that made no sense at all. Then he'd thanked her, and she had said "You're welcome," without knowing what she was welcome to.

When the text message came saying Hope could pick him up again, she turned on the engine of her car and left it in park for a minute or two. Then she inched carefully out into the street and around the corner. She was so enormously stressed, she could barely breathe.

She saw the tall man coming down the walk toward her and sped up just a little. There was no reason to crawl down the road as if she were casing the condominiums.

Gregor Demarkian was almost at the car. Hope looked up and down his incredibly tall body and shivered a little. Then she pulled the car to a stop. Demarkian opened the passenger side door and got in.

"Thank you," he said. "This was very good of you."

There it was again, the thank-you. Hope drove carefully

through the streets of the complex and then out onto the
two-lane blacktop that she knew would swing around and
end up near Beach Drive. There shouldn't be many people
on Beach Drive tonight.

Hope slid a look at Demarkian. He was staring straight
ahead out the windshield. It was unnerving.

"You're at Darlee Corn's place, aren't you?" Hope said,
because she really couldn't stand the silence any longer.

Demarkian nodded. "The Switch and Shingle," he said.
"I still don't know what that means."

"I don't know that it's supposed to mean anything," Hope
said.

"I hope I haven't gotten you at a bad time," Demarkian
said. "He was a friend of yours, wasn't he? The man who
died tonight?"

"We grew up together," she said. "We used to hang
around together in high school. It was a long time ago."

"You didn't see him recently?"

"Well, I did see him," Hope said. "I mean, we lived here,
you know, and he was around. And sometimes we ran into
each other."

"Did I take you out of your way?" Demarkian asked her.
"Did you have to come out and pick me up?"

"Oh, no," Hope said. "I was at the emergency room. I
didn't used to go to the emergency room when my heart
didn't feel right, but Tim says it's important now that if we
have emergency room problems we go to the one at the
hospital. It's very expensive. And it isn't true what they say
about how you go to the emergency room and you never
get charged. You get bills, and big ones. And they don't go
away."

"Are you feeling all right now?" Demarkian asked. "Should
we get you someplace?"

"No, no," Hope said. "I'm fine. It was just stress. And,
you know, I'm confused."

"Confused about what?"

Hope took in enough air to power a sailboat and had at it.
"The rumors around town say you already know who killed

Chapin. That it was that man, Ray Guy Pearce, the one who publishes all the conspiracy books. But why would Ray Guy Pearce want to kill Kyle?"

"I don't think he did kill Kyle Westervan," Demarkian said. "In fact, I know he didn't. And for what it's worth, I don't think he killed Chapin Waring, either."

"Really?" Hope said. "Because I've been worried about it ever since I heard."

"Why?"

Hope felt her body squirming against the wheel, and tried to make it stop. "It was just," she said, and then decided she was going after it the wrong way. "I know Ray Guy Pearce," she said finally. "I mean, I've met him. I went in to see him just this week."

"Did you? Why would you do that?"

The squirming now felt like some kind of fit. Hope didn't know what she was going to do if she didn't learn to keep herself in check.

"I needed the money," she said finally. "And he would pay for things. If you told him things. If you gave him an interview about the robberies, you know, and knowing Chapin and that kind of thing. And if you had pictures."

"And you'd been going to see him for quite some time?"

Hope blushed. "No, no," she said. "He asked me right after it all happened, of course. He asked all of us, but none of us agreed to it. After a while he stopped asking. Then after Chapin was murdered, he started asking again. And I— well, I didn't get any summer teaching, and summer is always really bad, so this time I said yes. And I went into the city, you know, and talked to him."

"What did you talk to him about?"

"About what you'd expect," Hope said. "Growing up with Chapin. What Chapin was like. What I knew about the robberies. Except I didn't know anything about the robberies. I think I was disappointing all around. He wanted to know what it was like to grow up in one of the 'thirteen richest families,' but I hadn't grown up in a rich family at all. My family had lots of history, you know, but we never had very much money. I got to do everything because my mother really worked at it, that's all. And I was only part of Chapin's group because of Marty. She just put up with me."

They had reached Beach Drive. They were all the way on the wrong end of it, but just being here made Hope feel better.

"When I heard Kyle was dead, I thought—well, I thought there might be some connection. You know, that something I said, when I talked to him, might have set something off. I couldn't think of what it could be. We just talked a bit about all the old stuff. I didn't tell him anything he didn't already know. It felt strange that he'd give me money for it."

"Did you give him any pictures?"

"I brought some with me," she said, "but they weren't the kind of thing he was looking for. He wanted pictures of people in their deb dresses and people riding horses and all that kind of thing. My mother did the best she could, and I even came out, but mostly we couldn't manage it. I spent four years in boarding school as the only person in my house who wasn't boarding her horse."

The Switch and Shingle was right up ahead. Hope felt so relieved, she almost cried. She turned into the drive and slowed to a crawl again. The hedges went by her on either side, looking dark and blank, like the trees that lined the drive at Manderley.

The house came into view, lit up at the front door and in several of the windows on the second floor. Hope cut the engine.

"I was just worried," she said again, "that it was something I said, something I did, going to see Ray Guy Pearce. I thought, you know, that I may have said something I didn't realize, and now—now Kyle is dead—and—"

"I can absolutely assure you that Ray Guy Pearce did not kill Kyle Westervan," Gregor Demarkian said. "It would have been entirely impossible. I can't be exactly that positive with the murder of Chapin Waring, but I'd give you odds that he wasn't in any way involved. I don't think you have to worry about the kind of information Ray Guy Pearce was looking for."

"Really?" Hope said.

"Really," Gregor Demarkian said.

He opened the passenger side door and got out onto the gravel driveway. "Thank you for chauffeuring me around," he said.

"You're welcome," Hope said automatically.

Gregor Demarkian slammed the passenger side door shut and walked away without looking back.

Hope took a few moments, and then she turned the car around very carefully.

She drove slowly back down the drive, trying to ignore the hulking darkness all around her. She got out onto Beach Drive and found that it was a little more crowded now. There were people on foot on their way out to see the fireworks.

She wondered what time it was.

What felt like a few moments later, but must have been longer, she began to wonder where she was. She was back on the two-lane blacktop. She didn't remember getting there.

She pulled off to the side of the road and cut the engine.

She put her head down on the steering wheel and closed her eyes. She had forgotten to turn the headlights off. They were gleaming into the distance, like lighthouse beacons. She kept her eyes closed and her head down.

Then she started to cry.

3

Jason Battlesea called Evaline Veer and from the moment Evaline hung up the phone until the moment the midnight fireworks began to go off, she brooded.

When she knew she wasn't getting to sleep, she got a cotton sweater and went out.

She walked across the center of town, all the way to the Green, and sat down on one of the polished wooden benches near the War Memorial. She got her cell phone out. There was nobody else on the Green within hearing distance.

Evaline flicked through her address book and found

Caroline Holder's number. Then she pressed the Call button and waited.

The phone was picked up by Caroline herself, and Evaline relaxed a little.

"I'm sorry to call you so late," she said, "but I thought—well, I thought you'd like to know. And I didn't know if anybody would tell you."

"If you mean did anybody tell me that Kyle Westervan is dead," Caroline said, "I'd say you're about the twentieth call I've had."

"Demarkian was right there, on the scene, when it happened," Evaline said. "He was talking to Tim Brand, and then two of the girls from the clinic went out back, and there was Kyle on the ground. Jason Battlesea says Demarkian thinks that Kyle was killed in the overflow parking lot at the hospital and then pushed over the retaining wall, and that the ME's people thought that seemed likely, too, on first look. But we won't really know for days."

"I don't understand why they still run my life," Caroline said. "It's been thirty years, for God's sake."

"It keeps feeling to me as if I should have done something about all this long ago, but I don't know what," Evaline said. "I felt that way when Marty died, too. I remember sitting in the pew at the church during the funeral and wondering what I was supposed to do next. I never came up with anything."

"I remember sitting in California while the entire world was looking for my oldest sister and wondering if I'd ever be able to have a normal life again," Caroline said. "And do you know what the answer to that is? The answer is that I never was able to, and I'm still not. And now there's this, and earlier—did you hear about earlier? That man was sneaking into our house and taking our photographs? And of course we never noticed, because we don't like looking at photographs. We've got too much we don't want to be reminded of. My whole childhood is a big wash of stuff we don't want to be reminded of."

"Mine just stopped when Marty died," Evaline said. "Did

you ever wonder if they all knew about it? Not just Marty and Chapin, but all of them. Kyle and Virginia and Tim and Hope Matlock."

"Of course I never wondered," Caroline said. "I just assumed. Didn't you?"

"I never understood how she got caught for those robberies," Evaline said. "I remember my mother explaining it. She was at the funeral, and for some reason the press paid more attention to her than they did to the rest of us—"

"It wasn't 'for some reason.' They did because she was Chapin," Caroline said.

"Well, that time it meant that she was on the news a lot and somebody spotted her, because she wasn't really well disguised."

"And then she lived in obscurity for thirty years," Caroline said. "I couldn't sit still all night. I even drove into town and tried to do some shopping, but it wasn't any use. I finally just sat down on a bench in front of the hospital and let myself go limp. There was some kind of event going on. It was a pain in the ass."

"It was a talk Virginia Westervan was giving," Evaline said. "I was there. I wonder how she feels. I never got the impression that she and Kyle were on bad terms."

"I think they were annoyed with each other a lot," Caroline said. "It was like they were still married."

"I can't imagine she killed him, though, can you?" Evaline said. "I don't think she gets a lot of time to herself, for one thing, and what would they be doing meeting in the parking lot anyway? They'd go out to dinner together or he'd come to her place, or they'd meet in New York."

Evaline wondered why she'd called Caroline. Caroline was an angry woman. She'd been angry almost all the time Evaline had known her.

"Well," Evaline said.

There was nothing at all from the other end of the line.

"Well," Evaline said again. "I suppose I'd better go do something. There must be something to do."

"It's damn near midnight," Caroline said, hanging up.

Evaline put her cell phone away, and stayed put. She didn't want to go home. She didn't want to go anywhere she knew people.

She thought of Kyle Westervan, dead, with a knife in his back. She saw the knife rise up from the shoulder blade, just as it had when Chapin Waring died.

Then she leaned over the side of the bench and threw up.

THREE

1

When the phone rang at two o'clock in the morning, Gregor Demarkian almost didn't answer it. He was lying flat on his back on the big bed in his suite at the Switch and Shingle. The idea that anybody would call him at this hour and after the day he'd had was somehow seriously offensive.

The ringtone and the name in the photo ID belonged to Bennis, however, and his marriage was still too new for him to feel all right about not picking up for her.

Of course, his friendship with Bennis had lasted longer than any other relationship in his life except for his first marriage, so there was something to be said for the idea that he'd earned the right to a little slacking off.

He picked up and said, "Hello?"

Bennis chuckled and said, "I knew you wouldn't want me calling in the middle of the night, but I did call you at least twice before and you didn't return, and then there's this news on the CNN Web page about another murder out in Alwych. I just wanted to make sure it wasn't you."

"It wasn't me," Gregor said, yawning. "If it had been me, CNN would probably have said so."

"Only if they knew," Bennis said. "I don't understand

how we got along before the Internet and cable news and all the rest of it. Think of all the things that happened before we had all that. The *Challenger* disaster. The Kennedy assassination."

"You weren't alive for the Kennedy assassination."

"I know, but think about it. Three broadcast television networks and maybe PBS. And that was it. How did anybody ever get any information?"

"There were newspapers."

"Newspapers come out a couple of times a day and then you have to wait for the next day," Bennis said. "I got this in real time. Who got murdered?"

"A man named Kyle Westervan. He worked as a lawyer on Wall Street. He was on my interview list, but I never got a chance to talk to him."

"And is it all part of the Chapin Waring thing?"

Gregor moved a little on the bed. It was a very good bed, and he could feel himself beginning to sink into sleepiness.

"I don't know," he said finally. "It was a stabbing, like the Chapin Waring murder. I got a look at the knife in the body, and at the knife wound later. If you look at the pictures from the Waring murder, you see the knife in the victim's back and it's going slightly downward, if that makes sense. This wound was going slightly upward."

"I know what that is," Bennis said. "That's height. Was Kyle Westervan very tall?"

"Yes," Gregor said. "I thought of that, too. Kyle Westervan was tall. Chapin Waring was a little short. And both of the knifings were done from up close—"

"How could they not be done from up close?" Bennis asked.

"A knife can be thrown," Gregor said. "I'll admit, I've never seen a murder done with a thrown knife. But these weren't thrown. Whoever it was came right up to the back of both the victims and stabbed. And that's an interesting point."

"Is it? Why?"

"Because the murderer would have to be very close up to

make it work," Gregor said. "Whoever this was got right up to the bodies of the victims and then stabbed. Can you imagine letting somebody get that close to you from the back?"

"You do it all the time."

"We're married," Gregor said. "And I can see you allowing it with, say, Tibor, or Donna, or maybe even Linda. But even with people you know on Cavanaugh Street, I think you'd mostly get uncomfortable if they got that close. And that leaves me back where I was. The victims have to know the murderer very well. And the murderer has to be someone who would not cause fear or suspicion in any way, at least for those two people. Has to not cause suspicion in Kyle Westervan even after Chapin Waring's murder."

"In other words, someone Kyle Westervan has known forever."

"Yes," Gregor said. "I suppose so. But almost everybody involved in this has known almost everybody else 'forever.' Let's say someone Kyle Westervan wouldn't suspect of killing Chapin Waring. Or somebody who, even if he did suspect, he wouldn't feel threatened by."

"I take it Ray Guy Pearce isn't the kind of person Kyle Westervan would allow to come right up behind him," Bennis said.

"I think squirrels would be opposed to Ray Guy Pearce coming up behind them," Gregor said, "but in this case, it doesn't matter, because he has an ironclad alibi for Kyle Westervan's murder. He was spouting conspiracy delusions to several hundred people in a hotel. I never liked him for the Waring murder either, though. It was all wrong. Chapin Waring was his one and only live zoo exhibit, a member of the thirteen richest families willing to tell him that everything he'd ever believed was true."

"The Warings are hardly one of the thirteen richest families in the country," Bennis said. "I mean, they're members of the club, so to speak, but they're not—"

"I'll have to get up tomorrow morning and do a good job sorting through it all," Gregor said. "The problem with this one is that I can't make the thirty-year thing fit. With Chapin Waring, there were plenty of people who might want to kill her, including all the people who were involved in the robberies or affected by the robberies. But I'm positive that none of the pictures in the security tapes were of Kyle Westervan. He was much too tall. So if he wasn't involved in the robberies, and everybody is telling me the truth when they say that Chapin Waring didn't inform anybody but her accomplice of what was going on—"

"Well, that might just be self-protection," Bennis said. "Nobody would want to admit to knowing. They could probably get arrested as an accessory."

"The statute of limitations would have run out," Gregor said. "But even if he knew about the robberies at the time they happened, it wouldn't necessarily help. It *has* been thirty years. Why would anybody want to kill him over any of that now? And why him in particular? Other people who were part of all that are still in town."

"Have you talked to them?"

"Most of them, by now," Gregor said. "I haven't always had proper interviews. I've run into them and just asked whatever came into my head. One of them drove me home from Virginia Westervan's house a few hours ago."

"Congresswoman Virginia Westervan?"

"She was part of the original group. And she was in the place the murder happened only a half hour or so before it did happen."

"That would put an interesting spin on her Senate campaign."

"She was worried about the same thing. With her, I did do a proper interview. With Hope Matlock, I just talked a little in the car. Hope Matlock is the one who drove me home. She's very depressed, and very fat, and very squirrely. I don't know if I found out anything at all. But maybe I'm just too tired to check. And I want to go over the security tapes again, because something is bugging me, but I'm just too out of it to do it now."

"I should let you get to sleep."

"You may not have to. I'm sinking into this bed like a rock in the ocean."

"I just wanted to make sure you were all right."

"I'm not all right," Gregor said. "I'm exhausted, and every time I figure out one thing, it makes everything else sound absurd. And then there's the question of the money. I thought I knew where it was, but then I didn't, and now I have no idea where it's gone. And the reason that's frustrating is that it should have been obvious, and now it isn't. Two hundred and fifty thousand dollars. The reason you steal two hundred and fifty thousand dollars is because you want money. And even if you steal it because you want the thrill of stealing it, there it is, in cash. You don't just leave it lying around for thirty years. I can't think of anyplace it would have been stashed that the FBI and the police haven't searched a dozen times over. It's just out there, somewhere, sitting around."

"Gregor?"

"What is it?"

"You're falling asleep."

"I am, a little. I think I am. What's happening to the cat?"

"The cat?"

"I'm not dreaming that, am I? You and Donna rescued a cat. A kitten. It looked like a mess and you took it to the vet."

"You really are falling asleep," Bennis said. "Yes, we rescued the cat. It's staying with Hannah Krekorian on a trial basis. Hannah's checking out how she feels about living with a pet. Donna and I are paying for all the vet stuff and we've promised to pay for spaying or neutering. We'll see."

"I'm glad you didn't want to keep the cat," Gregor said. "I like cats all right, but I just couldn't imagine you as a cat person."

"Go to sleep, Gregor."

"I will. I'm going to dream about how when I get back from here, I'm going to have a real bedroom and a real master bath. If the kitchen isn't done, we can just go to the Ararat."

2

Gregor Demarkian was woken in the morning by another phone call, and the phone call came only seconds before his door was opened and Darlee Corn looked inside.

"Demarkian," Gregor said into the phone.

Darlee Corn fluttered her fingers at him and said, "Oh, of course, you must be exhausted. Sorry for intruding. I'm going to bring you breakfast."

"Sorry," he said. "This is—"

"This is Fitzgerald at the New York office," Fitzgerald said. "I'm sorry I woke you up. It is eight o'clock in the morning."

"I was out late last night," Gregor said.

"Chasing after a dead body," Fitzgerald said. "We heard about it. That's why I'm calling. We take it that the dead man is named Kyle Westervan?"

"Yes," Gregor said. "Why are you calling me? Shouldn't you be calling Jason Battlesea or one of the detectives?"

"We did," Fitzgerald said. "We called, we asked questions, we got less-than-coherent answers. I don't know what's wrong with the people in that place, but I've had the same experience Andy has—"

"Andy?"

"Andrew Corben. I don't remember what name he uses for cover, but it's still Andrew. Never mind. He's not doing anything connected with the Chapin Waring case."

"So why are we talking about him?"

"Because he is doing something on a major case involving securities fraud," Fitzgerald said, "and his main contact, the guy who informed the Bureau of the problem to begin with—"

"Was Kyle Westervan."

"Exactly," Fitzgerald said. "Excuse us for going for the obvious, but a number of us out here are wondering if the man might be dead because of something connected to the securities case. There's a lot of money involved. A lot. In the ten- and eleven-figures range."

"That is a lot," Gregor said.

"You mind talking to Andy directly?" Fitzgerald said.

"Not at all."

Gregor got out of bed and found his robe where he'd left it, over a chair near the table near the sliding doors. "Just a minute," he said. Then he put the phone down and put the robe on. The last thing he wanted was for Darlee Corn to come in and find him in his boxer shorts.

He picked up the phone again and headed out onto the deck. The town was fully decorated for the Fourth of July and there was band music, all of it at various stages of the national anthem, coming from all directions.

He sat down at the table on the deck and said, "Okay. I'm here. Is this Mr. Corben?"

"Andy," a strange voice said. It sounded young. "I am absolutely losing it. You have no idea."

"I think I do," Gregor said. "If it helps any, I don't think you have to worry that Kyle Wetervan was killed over any of the work he was doing for you. Would you mind telling me, if you can, what that was?"

"It's practically impossible to catch these guys if we don't have anything on tape. He was running tapes for us. Westervan was wearing wires sometimes, but usually it was just something he had in his briefcase. Oh, and he was picking up cash. A lot of it, sometimes. Mostly it was six or seven thousand here or there, but once it was over fifty. And we had participation."

"What kind of participation?"

"The CEO and the CFO both of two of the largest U.S. banks, the CEO and CFO of a huge international brokerage based in Switzerland, and several politicians, including a U.S. senator from a Southern state."

"That's a mess."

"Yeah, it really is. It's a very big deal. Big enough for somebody to hire an assassin."

"And Kyle Westervan was what? Participating in this fraud? And you caught him?"

"No, no," Andy said. "That's the weird part. He wasn't participating at all. He was clean as a whistle. We checked.

He just walked into the office one day, opened the briefcase, and took out an absolute mountain of paper. Then he sat down and explained it all to us. It was the oddest thing. I think the guy was downright, rank furious."

"Furious?"

"Yeah. It made him angry that the people he was working with were doing the things they were doing," Andy said. "He did agree to wire himself up, get hold of all the papers he could—he was collecting copies of papers before they were shredded. I don't know what else he was doing. If anyone had known he was feeding us information, it would be a very good motive for murder."

"Just a minute," Gregor said as Darlee Corn burst into the room with a tray full of just about everything—hash browns, sausages, bacon, orange juice, coffee, and what looked like three scrambled eggs.

"You didn't look to me like the fruit cup type," she said.

Gregor waved her a thank-you.

She sailed out again, and Gregor heard the snap of his door as she passed through it into the hall.

He took a long sip of coffee and said, "You were saying it was a good motive for murder. And I agree with you. But I don't think it was the motive for this murder."

"You've got something better?"

"There are facts here," Gregor said, "and I don't think the facts fit a hired assassin. For one thing, he was stabbed."

"A knife in the back," Andy said. "The symbolism is incredible."

"I agree with that, too," Gregor said, "but you see what kind of problem it makes for a theory like yours. The person who killed him had to be somebody he neither feared nor mistrusted. He wasn't in a crowded room when he was killed, or in a crowd of people. He was in a deserted overflow parking lot at the local hospital. He'd have heard virtually anybody coming up behind him, and he wouldn't have allowed somebody to come up behind him if he thought he had any reason for fear."

"Okay," Andy said. "But—"

"No buts," Gregor said. "I didn't say I was dismissing your idea outright. I think we ought to look into it, and so should you. I'm just saying that, right now, my best guess is that this isn't going to be your problem, but Alwych's. That whatever happened, to both Kyle Westervan and Chapin Waring, is personal."

"Personal? You mean not even connected to the robberies?"

"I don't know," Gregor said. "I think I dreamed my way through several possible solutions, and then lost them all when I woke up. And it's the Fourth of July."

"So?"

"Nobody's really working," Gregor said. "My guess is that the ME's office is off at the same parades as everybody else, on the assumption that there isn't anything that can't wait for twenty-four hours. And I don't know if I can get hold of anybody on the police force here. The uniforms are going to be out directing traffic and conducting the parades."

"Yeah," Andy said. "I see that."

"Just be patient and let us sort this out," Gregor said. "I suppose you're going to want to come down here eventually—"

"Yes, I definitely will."

"So come down and get it over with," Gregor said. "You might want to wait, but that's up to you. I'm sure once you explain it to local law enforcement, they'll give you what you need."

"Yeah," Andy said. "There's that. All right. We'll do it that way."

"Then I'll talk to you later."

"There's just one thing," Andy said.

Gregor looked at the hash browns. They were real hash browns.

"What is it?" he asked.

"It's about Kyle Westervan," Andy said. "He was like Joan of Arc. In that old movie, you know it? It starred Ingrid Bergman, and she played Joan of Arc. And right from the beginning, that was who Kyle Westervan reminded me of.

As if he'd seen God, or talked to God and God talked back, and now he was on some kind of a crusade. He didn't ever say that, you know. He didn't go around talking about visions or giving speeches about justice and truth and right, but there was something about him that made me think he was thinking all those things. And that's part of the reason why I'm so unnerved about this. Because those kinds of people, the people who are acting for justice and truth and right, well, in operations like the one we've been running here, those people tend to get killed. And there's Kyle, dead."

"Yes," Gregor said. "That's what he is. Dead."

3

It took a good ten minutes to convince Jason Battlesea that he was going to have to stop whatever he was doing and get to the Alwych Police Department. It took another five to get Juan Valdez to bring around the car.

By then, Gregor was dressed and carrying his attaché case. He had his laptop and his first headache of the morning. He stepped out of the Switch and Shingle and saw his next headache gearing up. Down at the end of the driveway, there were people. There were lots of people. Some of them were a band.

Gregor gave Juan Valdez directions and sat back to see how bad the problems would be. The people at the end of the drive were gearing up for a parade, but the parade wasn't due to start for an hour. The police keeping the road clear all knew who Gregor Demarkian was and what he was doing in Alwych. They passed him on from one watch post to the next as if he were visiting royalty.

The arrangement was worse when they got into the middle of town. The parade would be coming right down the middle of Main Street, and although that meant the police were more or less keeping Main Street clear, it really was only more or less. There were hundreds of people milling around, waiting for the parade to start. Some of these people were children, who didn't care at all that cars needed to move or that the barriers had been put up to keep the marchers safe. Some of these people were vendors, who only wanted to sell as much red, white, and blue cotton candy and little flags as they possibly could.

They got to the Alwych Police Department, but literally at a crawl. When they got there, Gregor found most of the police force that wasn't out dealing with the streets lined up in formation to march, too. At the head of that contingent was Jason Battlesea.

"For God's sake," Battlesea said after Juan Valdez got the car into an uninhabited part of the parking lot and Gregor got out. "What do you think you're doing? We're supposed to march in an hour and we're supposed to be lined up to march in half an hour. You can't tell me that this is something that couldn't have waited until after noon."

"Are Mike Held and Jack Mann marching?"

"They're right over there. Are you saying you want them, too? Want them for what?"

"To look at something," Gregor said.

"It's the goddamned Fourth of July."

Gregor took his attaché and laptop and marched himself into police headquarters. He did not bother to go looking for the interrogation room they had used before or for Jason Battlesea's office. He put his things down on one of the countertops and began to plug things in. He not only had the laptop up and working, but the three files he wanted them to see already running before they came in.

They landed at his side like a comedy group from a 1930s movie. They were all flustered, and Jason Battlesea was angry.

"This had better be important," he said. "This had better be the goddamned Second Coming, because we are all due somewhere or the other practically immediately."

Gregor pointed to the screen of his laptop. "Look at that," he said. "Those are three of the security tape sequences from the robberies. The thin figure is Chapin Waring. The lumpy figure is Martin Veer."

"We already knew that," Jason Battlesea said.

"Why is the lumpy figure lumpy?" Gregor asked.

"To make a disguise," Jason Battlesea said. "What the hell. We already knew that, too. They knew that back when the robberies happened."

"But there are lots of ways to make a disguise," Gregor said. "Why use that one? Why make Martin Veer look lumpy?"

"Because that was what they thought of?" Jason Battlesea asked. "Because they had some padding handy and they could use it? Who the hell knows? Who the hell knows why Chapin Waring and Martin Veer did anything? They were crazy as loons, if you ask me, and from what you've told me about what Chapin Waring was doing for the thirty years since, I'd say she got crazier as time went on."

"It doesn't remind you of anything?" Gregor asked, pointing at the lumpy figure on all three parts of the screen. The figure skittered and lumbered and almost lost its balance. It righted itself, and then the loop brought it back to the beginning. It skittered again.

"For God's sake," Jack Mann said. "We really do have to go."

"If there's something here that's urgent," Jason Battlesea said, "then get it out and we'll do something about it. If there's going to be another murder—"

"No," Gregor said, "I think I can guarantee that there isn't going to be another murder."

"Then there's no point in going into this now," Jason Battlesea said. "So if you would excuse us—"

"It doesn't matter to you that that film provides the last link that explains the reason for two murders and tells you who committed them?"

"It will still explain it after noon," Jason Battlesea said. "We're going to go now. I'll just point out that we were right after all. The murder of Chapin Waring was committed because of something having to do with those robberies."

"Oh," Gregor said. "In a way."

FOUR

1

Caroline Waring Holder had gotten the first of the telephone calls about the death of Kyle Westervan barely an hour after the police arrived to take possession of the crime scene, and she'd gotten telephone call after telephone call after that. It was well into the small hours of the night before she decided that she had to do something or go crazy. What she'd done was to go from place to place, turning off all possible connections to the outside world. She turned off the ringers on all the landline extensions. She turned off the cell phones. She shut down the computers. She didn't want to hear from anybody about anything.

Caroline had always liked Kyle Westervan. He was old enough to be entirely off her radar when she was a child, but she had run into him since, and he was one of the better ones. Since coming back to Alwych, Caroline had always tended to judge people by the way they approached the Waring case. Most people didn't bring it up at all. They gave her long, "significant" looks when they talked to her, and waited too long before answering her questions or responding to her comments to see if she would do something "inappropriate." The idea seemed to be that she must be traumatized by All

That, and as a traumatized person she would have to show signs of wear and tear.

It was just after five thirty in the morning when Caroline's alarm went off. Caroline got the children up and dressed. Then she got Dan up and dressed. She saw Dan pick up his cell phone and realize it was off.

"I couldn't take it anymore," she told him. "There were people calling all night, on your phone as well as mine, on the landlines, everywhere. So I turned everything off."

Dan got his phone up and running again. "Well," he said, "there's nothing on here that looks at all important. I do have about forty missed calls, but they all seem to be from people we know socially."

"Socially," Caroline said. "They'll all be about Kyle."

"Why do people think we'll know what happened to Kyle Westervan?"

"It's the Waring case," Caroline said. "He was in the car the night Martin Veer died. He was part of Chapin's clique at school. I suppose they think we live in each other's pockets."

"You weren't part of Chapin's clique at school," Dan pointed out. "You were eight. People are very, very odd sometimes."

Caroline agreed that people were very, very odd sometimes, and then went back to getting packed up for the day.

Then she turned on her own cell phone and found a total of 114 missed calls. She was staring at the phone when it vibrated to let her know another call was coming in. The number belonged to Reverend Harper at the church.

She answered the call, on the off chance that it had something to do with the picnic. She stood in the open front door of her house and looked at the Cross Country packed with children and gear. As soon as Chapin's body had been found, she should have packed up the entire family and taken them to California.

"Yes," she said into the phone. It was rude. She didn't care.

Reverend Harper cleared his throat.

"Good morning, Caroline," he said. "I do know that you're very busy right now. I hope you're not taking this call while driving."

"I haven't even gotten into the car yet."

"Ah, yes, good, I suppose, although I suppose it means you're running behind. Let me be quick about this, then, and we can talk it through at the picnic, when the rush is over and we have some time. Your sister Cordelia called me yesterday."

"Did she," Caroline said.

"Oh, yes," the Reverend Harper said. "She made a point of telling me how concerned she was about you, and how concerned your other sister was about you. I know you don't like people to fuss over you. And I think it's admirable. But I do think you may not realize just how deeply you've been affected by your sister's dying. So deeply that you may not realize that you are having a difficult time thinking clearly. And now, of course, with this other murder. I believe he was a friend of the family—"

"He was somebody I barely knew," Caroline said. "He was a friend of my sister's, the one who recently died. Who was recently murdered. Who was stabbed in the back with a kitchen knife."

"Yes," the Reverend Harper said. "Yes, of course. I do know the circumstances. It's difficult to know how to proceed in cases like this. One doesn't want to be too forward, of course, but on the other hand—"

"Is there a point to this phone call, Reverend Harper? Or did you just call because Cor decided to make a nuisance of herself?"

"Oh, oh no! Cordelia didn't make a nuisance of herself at all. Listening to people in their time of darkness is what I'm here for."

"Cordelia has never had a time of darkness in her life."

"I do understand how you might think that, Caroline, but I believe you're wrong. Of course, Cordelia, being an older sister, worked very hard to appear calm and unfrightened in the wake of all that tragedy, but that's not to say that she was unaffected. I'm sure this whole situation has been very difficult for all of you. And she's really only concerned, you understand, that your other sister, that your sister Chapin, be given a Christian burial. It would bring closure to you all."

Dan was standing up next to the driver's side door of the car, trying not to be too obvious about rushing her. Caroline wished he'd be a lot more obvious.

"Did you know my sister Chapin?" she asked the Reverend Harper.

"Well, no—of course, I didn't come to Alwych until many years later—"

"If you'd known my sister Chapin, you'd know that she wouldn't have wanted a Christian anything. She wasn't a believer. And don't tell me that a lot could have happened in thirty years. I've got nothing to show that she ever changed her mind about religion, or God, or anything else. And if what Cordelia called you about was seeing to Chapin's funeral, then as far as I'm concerned, we've got nothing to talk about. There will be no funeral. There will be no memorial service. There will be nothing that could bring down a hurricane of photographers and reporters to make yet another circus out of all of this. I've told Cordelia this several times. If she wants Chapin to have a funeral, then she can come out here herself and give Chapin a funeral. I will not attend."

"Oh," the Reverend Harper said. "I know that's how you feel about it *now*—"

"That's how I've felt about it since the beginning. It's how I'm going to feel about it ten years from now and twenty years from now and thirty years from now. And if you try to bring this up at the picnic, I will walk right out on it."

"Yes," the Reverend Harper said. "I can see—I'm sure the death of Mr. Westervan has upset you—maybe I'll just—"

"Don't just anything," Caroline said. "This is the way I feel about this, and it is none of your business."

She snapped the cell phone shut. Then she looked at it, lying dead and black in her hand.

The problem was that Caroline didn't want to get on with

things. She didn't want to go to the parade. She didn't want to go to the picnic. She didn't want to talk to anybody she knew.

2

Kyle Westervan was dead. It was the first thing Tim Brand thought of when he woke up on the Fourth of July, and the only thing he could make himself think about as he started his day.

He showered and shaved and dressed and drank a glass of orange juice, and then he headed out across town. With all the road blockages and the crowds, it was easier, and he didn't really want to drive when he was this distracted.

He got to the clinic feeling bone tired and looked inside to see if anybody was around. The reception desk was unmanned. The corridors were sparkling clean and uninhabited. Tim went out to the back and stopped when he saw the yellow crime scene tape over the back door.

He went back out to the reception area and found Marcie standing there, holding an enormous straw tote bag and wearing an enormous straw hat.

She looked up from something she'd been writing on a pad and smiled. "I thought I could find you here," she said. "I tried calling your house. Are you going to go up to the parade? I know you must feel like hell, but virtually every one of the kids from the children's clinic is marching in one capacity or the other, and it would mean a lot to them for you to be there."

"I know," Tim said. "I did intend to be there. And there's still time. I've just been wandering around a little aimlessly."

"Because of Kyle." It was not a question.

Tim sat down in one of the molded plastic chairs meant for people waiting to be called for clinic and winced, for the hundredth time, at just how hard they were.

"Tim?" Marcie said.

"I've just been wandering around thinking it was odd," he said. "Alwych without Kyle in it. I've known Kyle all my life, almost. Almost as long as I've known Virginia. We were in a nursery school play group together when we were two."

"It's not odd," Marcie said. "It's horrible. The whole thing is horrible, from start to finish."

"I agree. But it's also odd. Just before my father died, he told me that he'd outlived all his brothers and sisters and his aunts and uncles and even the two people he was closest to as friends, and that he felt as if he were adrift in a sea of forgetfulness. He was the only one left who remembered, and so he couldn't know if he was really remembering at all."

"There's Virginia," Marcie said. "She remembers. And there's Hope Matlock."

"It's different for women and men."

"Is it really?"

"Don't start that," Tim said. "I was never all that close to Hope, and Virginia—well, Virginia is Virginia. And she's my sister."

"I'll admit I never did understand the thing with Hope," Marcie said. "I know I didn't know her when she was younger—but still. She seems to me the most unlikely person in the world to belong to the popular crowd in a place like Alwych Country Day. She seems like an unlikely person to have gone to Alwych Country Day."

Tim shrugged. "Her family is one of the oldest in New England," he said. "They were here before the Revolutionary War. They've had members fight in every war the United States has ever been in. When I was growing up, all that was more important than the things you're thinking of. It was starting to change even then, but it was still more important."

"And then it changed to just being about money," Marcie said.

"Something like that," Tim agreed. "But there's a scholarship at Alwych Country Day that's named after her great-grandfather, and there's a scholarship at Miss Porter's that was named after her grandmother, and she got both of those because there were stipulations in the endowments that said she would. Not her specifically, you understand, but—"

"I know. Somebody in the family."

"Exactly."

"I still say I can't see it," Marcie said. "She's so mousy. It's all well and good to have an old money name, but she doesn't seem to have any money and she's got almost no personality at all. Even in fancy private schools, I'll bet you have to have personality to be part of the popular crowd. And now you'll tell me that she was the life of the party back then, and it was all that stuff that changed her."

"No," Tim said. "Hope was always Hope. Not just mousy but almost morbidly self-conscious. But Marty was part of Chapin's crowd, and Hope was Marty's girlfriend."

"And you were Chapin Waring's boyfriend. I can't see that, either."

"I can't see it myself at this late date," Tim said, "but at the time, it felt almost inevitable. I get surprised sometimes at how much seemed inevitable then that doesn't seem inevitable anymore. I don't think Chapin and I even liked each other much. Everybody knew from dancing school that I'd be her escort at her debut, and it just went from there. I think I was a little relieved not to have to go looking for a girlfriend."

Tim got out of the chair.

"Maybe I should take you to the parade," Marcie said. "You're beginning to look a little out of it."

"I'm tired," Tim said. "You were right. I didn't get any sleep last night."

"Let's go," Marcie said.

Instead, Tim headed on back again. When he got to the crime scene tape over the door, he reached past it and opened up so that he could see the little area outside. He could see a lot. There was crime scene tape over the stairs, at the bottom, right in front of him. He couldn't quite get a look at the top, but he was sure there would be crime scene tape there, too. There was a white chalk outline of a body near the wall. Other than that, the little outside space looked dead.

Tim felt Marcie come up behind him, and withdrew. He had no idea what it was he had wanted to see.

"Tim," she said, more than a little urgently.

Tim closed the door. "Sorry," he said.

"We ought to go to the parade."

Tim was still looking at the door. It reminded him of that part of a Harry Potter movie where there was a veil, and when you passed Beyond the Veil, you were dead. But that was not how Kyle had died. He had not passed beyond a veil. He had been knifed in the back and pushed off a retaining wall.

And he would be forever dead.

FIVE

1

Gregor Demarkian went up to Main Street to see the end of the parade, feeling restless and a little annoyed.

He stood for a while on Main Street and watched the parade come in. There were floats and marching bands and, of course, virtually the entirety of the Alwych Police Department, pounding away like soldiers on parade. Gregor spotted Jason Battlesea in a uniform so bedecked by medals and ribbons, it might as well have belonged to an Admiral of the Fleet.

The end of the parade reached the War Memorial in a little rush, the rear being brought up by a group of women in more or less Revolutionary Period costume, all playing flutes. Their music died out only fitfully, and then Evaline Veer, waiting on the podium, cleared her throat.

She had a sheaf of papers in her hands, and there was a microphone in front of her. Gregor thought she looked like bloody hell.

He backed away from the crowds and headed back to the police department. There wouldn't be much of anybody there, but it would be more peaceful than this. He took out his cell phone. Evaline's voice was booming out over the crowd, but he couldn't catch any of the words she was saying. He supposed it was one of those speeches every mayor in every town gave at the end of every Fourth of July parade.

He got to the point where the sound of Evaline Veer's voice was only thunder in the distance. He punched the speed dial for Bennis and listened to the phone ring. Then the annoying robo voice came on, telling him he was being sent to voice mail.

By that time, he was almost all the way back at the police department. He waited until he got back to the front doors and then punched the speed dial for Father Tibor. The phone rang and rang again. He went through the sliding glass doors and into the police department's lobby. The phone sent him to voice mail again. He closed it up and put it back in his pocket.

At the moment, the entire active police presence in the town of Alwych seemed to consist of a young woman behind the reception counter and a man in plain clothes talking to her. The man was very young and very tense. When Gregor walked in, he straightened up immediately.

"Mr. Demarkian? It is Mr. Demarkian? I'm Andy—"

"Okay," Gregor said. "Did you really come all the way out from New York on the Fourth of July?"

"I had to," Andy said. "I know we've talked on the phone, but the Bureau is going completely crazy over everything that's going on in Connecticut. That thing about the crime lab losing its accreditation—that was bad enough."

Gregor looked at the young woman behind the desk. "Is anybody here?" he asked. "I was just at the War Memorial—"

"They'll be another hour or about that," the young woman said. "I've got everybody's cell phone numbers if there's an emergency, but mostly they're supposed to be in the crowd, listening to the speeches."

"I feel like I went down the rabbit hole," Andy said. "They've got a murder, for God's sake, and the whole police force is listening to speeches and marching in a parade."

"It was the other way around," Gregor said. He turned to the young woman again. "Is there somewhere Andy and I can sit and talk in private?" he asked. "We can talk while we wait for the chief to come back."

"There's an entire building for you to sit and be private in," the young woman said. "Why don't you go back down that way and use the third room on the right."

Gregor led Andy down the hall as if he knew what he was doing.

He opened the third door on the right when he got to it and found a small conference room with a round table and six chairs. Andy had a large, bulky briefcase. He put it on the table and opened it.

"In a way, it's good I found you by yourself," he said. "You understand that I can't tell you very much about the operation we've been running."

"Of course," Gregor said. "I don't expect you to blow your operation."

"Well, blowing the operation may be moot. We got a judge out of bed at five o'clock this morning and we should be moving right this minute. I know you think it's certain that Kyle wasn't murdered by somebody connected to our case, but we can't take any chances. If his cover was blown, we could lose a lot of valuable evidence. And we need the evidence. This is the largest case of its kind since the founding of the Bureau. The publicity is going to be insane."

"I know what that's like," Gregor said. "What I don't know is what you need from us."

"I need to talk to everybody who was at the scene last night—all the professionals, I mean. I need to go back to the office with a clearer idea of what happened and of whether or not it could be part of what we're doing."

"Let me ask you something," Gregor said. "Is anybody under investigation in your operation a resident of Alwych, Connecticut?"

"Half a dozen people are," Andy said. "This is a bedroom

community for New York City. Half the Financial District lives in Alwych or Westport or Darien."

"What about people who are not part of the bedroom community? What about the people who live and work here full-time?"

Andy looked uncomfortable.

"I'm not asking you for names. It's just that I'm about ninety-nine percent sure I know what happened here, and why, and the only person the narrative fits is someone who lives and works here."

"So," Andy said. "You think this is all about the robberies."

"No," Gregor said. "I don't think it's all about the robberies. The robberies come into it, but only peripherally, only because they provided a catalyst for something considerably less sane. But it's the only explanation that takes in both murders, and the only one that explains where the money is."

"The robbery money?"

"Yes."

"But I thought you said this wasn't about the robberies."

"It's complicated," Gregor said.

"I've got to tell you," Andy said, "I never expected it to be like this. This is my first really big operation. I've been champing at the bit to get one. Now I feel like I just ate glass."

"It won't be that bad on your third big operation," Gregor said. "Take it from somebody with experience. As soon as Jason Battlesea gets back, we'll see if we can hook you up with the ME. You may not have any joy, though. The body wasn't shipped out until late last night. It's entirely possible that nobody has gotten to it yet."

"God, I hate these small towns," Andy said. "Give me a big city any day, where everybody works twenty-four/seven and you don't have to factor in parades when you need some forensic answers."

Gregor thought that there wasn't much Andy was going to get in the way of answers even if he waited for midnight. But he wasn't going to tell him that.

2

It took so long for Jason Battlesea to get back to the police station, Gregor Demarkian began to worry that he'd gone off to eat at one of the picnics. Andy was not in good shape waiting, and Gregor had no idea how to contact the state medical examiner, or even if the state medical examiner would be willing to talk to him. Andy paced. Gregor got out the big picture book on the Waring case that he'd bought in Greenwich Village and leafed through it.

It was one o'clock by the time Jason Battlesea came sailing through the door, and he was alone.

"We've deployed everybody we've got to keep watch on the crowds," he said. He unbuttoned his uniform jacket and took it off, leaving all the medals and ribbons in place. He took off his tie. "If you'll give me a minute, I'm going to go into my office and change."

"This is Andy—"

"The FBI guy," Battlesea said. "I can smell it on him. Give me a second."

Battlesea disappeared into his office, and Gregor and Andy gave each other the kind of look that said "This idiot is practically an amateur." When he came out, he was wearing khakis and a bright orange T-shirt.

Jason Battlesea tried to look authoritative. It was difficult for him to do under any circumstances. It was impossible dressed in all that orange.

"Well," Battlesea said. "What is it? What's so important on the Fourth of July?"

"Solving a murder might be nice," Gregor said. "Solving two might be even better."

"Right now, we just need to be reassured that the murder of Kyle Westervan had nothing to do with one of our cases," Andy hurried in.

"Do you have identification?" Battlesea demanded.

Andy reached into his jacket pocket and pulled out his badge. He handed it over and waited.

Jason Battlesea took the badge in its folder and looked at it. He turned it upside down. He turned it right side up again. Gregor was sure he had no idea what he was looking at. Battlesea closed the folder and handed it back.

"Okay," he said. "What is it exactly you think we can tell you?"

"I suggested that the two medical examiners' reports might show a resemblance between the two murders," Gregor said, "and a resemblance would prove to me the two murders were most likely connected, and most likely committed by the same person. And since Andy's case has nothing to do with the Waring robberies—"

"Yeah?" Jason Battlesea said. "How do I know it has nothing to do with the Waring robberies?"

"I don't work for that division," Andy said quickly. "I work with the task force on Financial Fraud."

"Which doesn't mean you couldn't be interested in the Waring robberies," Jason Battlesea said. "Those were financial."

"Those were bank robberies," Andy said, looking pained. "Robbery isn't the same thing as fraud."

"And how am I supposed to know that Chapin Waring wasn't involved in financial fraud in this other life she had for the last thirty years? Mr. Demarkian here says she was in New York all that time. New York is where the Financial District is."

"Oh, for God's sake," Gregor said.

"I'm not being stupid," Jason Battlesea said. "I've got two murders. They look to be connected. Then, the next thing I know, I've got the FBI on my tail, wanting to know everything there is to know, and nobody is telling me why."

"I can't tell you why," Andy said. "I can only tell you that Mr. Westervan was connected with an ongoing operation—"

"To hell with that," Jason Battlesea said.

Gregor closed his eyes for a moment. This was Bennis's idea, her best way to calm down when you wanted to strangle someone. It didn't really work, but it gave him a minute or two to breathe before he had to deal with the craziness again.

"If we could just have a copy of the ME's report on the Chapin Waring murder," Gregor said as calmly as he could, "just the summary. And if we could just rouse the ME or his assistant or whoever is working on the Westervan case—"

"Rouse him? On the Fourth of July?" Jason Battlesea snorted. "You've got to be out of your mind. Why isn't the preliminary report enough?"

"You have a preliminary report from the ME's office on the death of Kyle Westervan?" Gregor asked.

"Of course I do. It came in overnight. I've got it on the computer and in a fax," Jason Battlesea said. "I can find it in a minute if you let me."

"You didn't tell me anything about it," Gregor said.

"There wasn't time to tell you," Jason Battlesea said. "Let me see what I can find. Mike or Jack will have to have a copy around here somewhere."

Battlesea disappeared down the corridor again, and Gregor and Andy looked at each other.

"Jesus Christ," Andy said.

"I think this latest one blew all his corks," Gregor said. "He wasn't this bad when I got here."

"I don't want his blood type and his Social Security number," Andy said. "I just want to see if there's reasonable cause for me to back off for a bit and let you handle it. If the two murders are really as alike as you say, I can hold off a bit and see what happens. But if there's any indication—"

"I've got them," Jason Battlesea said, coming back down the corridor again with a sheaf of papers in his hand. "It's just like I thought it was. Of course, the preliminary is the preliminary. Anything could happen when the autopsy comes back. Maybe the guy didn't die of the stabbing at all. Maybe somebody poisoned him. But I'm not expecting that, and neither are you."

Jason Battlesea took the papers and held them out.

"I don't know who I'm supposed to be giving these to," he said.

Andy took the papers out of Battlesea's hand and looked at them blankly for a moment. Then he sat down in one of the plastic-covered chairs and spread them out on the seat of the chair next to him.

After another moment, he looked up and shook his head. "You can't tell, can you?" he said. "I mean, there's a lot of stuff here, a lot of detail, and it certainly looks like the two would have to be connected. But."

Gregor held his hand out. "Can I look at those?"

"Sure." Andy handed the papers over.

Jason Battlesea laughed. "You're not going to get anything out of those that you don't already know," he said. "Kyle Westervan was stabbed in the back with a kitchen knife. Chapin Waring was stabbed in the back with a kitchen knife. Not the same kind of kitchen knife. Westervan got a chopper thin and three times as long. We've got the knives in evidence bags."

Gregor nodded absently. "The angle-of-entry thing is interesting," he said.

"I thought that, too," Andy said. "What's all that about?"

"Angle of entry?" Jason Battlesea asked.

Gregor waved the papers in the air. "Chapin Waring was murdered by being stabbed in the back by a knife that was going downward when it entered the body," he said. "That's in the ME's final report summary, so I suppose that is a true finding and we can count on it. In the summary of the preliminary on the murder of Kyle Westervan, he was stabbed in the back by a knife going upward as it entered the body."

"It could be a lot of things," Andy said. "You can't just assume that it was two different murderers—"

"I don't assume it was two different murderers," Gregor said. "I assume it was a result of the fact that Chapin Waring was a small woman and Kyle Westervan was a tall man."

"So," Andy said, "you think the issue is that Chapin Waring was a lot shorter than the person who killed her, and Kyle Westervan was a lot taller."

"Chapin Waring didn't have to be a lot shorter," Gregor said, "but she did have to be shorter by at least a couple of inches. Kyle Westervan was, I think somebody said, about six-three. He was a lot taller than most people."

"You could still have had a situation where the murderer was standing on something at one point and not standing on it at another point. There are ways to do things about height," Andy said.

"I agree," Gregor said. "But you've also got to account for the fact that nobody could have made that kind of stab wound—either of these kinds of stab wounds—without behind able to get right up behind the victim. It's hard to see how that would have been possible if the murderer was carrying around a stepladder or standing on a bucket. And the murderer wasn't going to get that close from behind unless the victim either didn't know he was there, or didn't think he had any reason for distrust."

"You keep saying that," Jason Battlesea said, "but people come up behind each other all the time."

"Not like this, they don't," Gregor said. "It's a natural instinct to feel the presence of somebody coming up *right* behind you, close enough to press against you. And if you look at the ME's report on Chapin Waring, the murderer would have had to do just that. Come up behind Chapin Waring so that they were practically close enough to spoon. The murderer couldn't have been more than half a step away. And I think we're going to find that the same thing is true in the murder of Kyle Westervan. Whoever the murderer is, it's somebody both Chapin Waring and Kyle Westervan knew, and somebody they both thought they had nothing to fear from."

"Which gets us absolutely nowhere," Jason Battlesea said. "It's not like that didn't occur to us before you got here, Mr. Demarkian."

"Possibly," Gregor said. "But Kyle Westervan and Tim Brand knew each other forever in a different way than, say, Kyle Westervan and Caroline Holder."

"Why in the name of God would Caroline Holder want to kill Kyle Westervan?"

"I could think of a number of reasons," Gregor said, "starting with the fact that those robberies ruined her life—"

"But as far as we know," Jason Battlesea said, "Kyle Westervan wasn't involved in those robberies."

"As far as we know," Gregor agreed. "But as far as we know doesn't go all that far, does it? So maybe Kyle Westervan was involved. Or maybe Caroline Holder is looking for revenge, and she intends to get every member of her sister's little clique—"

"Now you're in psychopath territory," Andy said.

"I know," Gregor said.

"We don't know anything," Jason Battlesea said. "I could have killed them."

"No," Gregor said. "I don't think you could have. The angle of the wound in Chapin Waring's body is wrong. She was killed by somebody taller than she was, I think, but not so much taller as you."

"I'm not that tall."

"Chapin Waring was very short," Gregor said.

"I think I'm where I need to be," Andy said suddenly. "I think I can go back to New York and tell them it's not likely that this has anything to do with us. I do need you to keep us informed, just in case—"

"We will," Gregor said. "But I don't think it's going to be much longer now. I think we'll probably have a definitive answer for you in the next day or two, if not sooner."

Andy looked curious. "Do you mean you think you know who killed these people?"

"I do think so," Gregor said. "At least, I've got an explanation that I think is the only one that's likely to fit."

"Are you always this fast?" Andy asked.

"I haven't been all that fast," Gregor said. "I've been here for days, and I've been looking at the case files for longer than that. It took me a while to get past the miasma thrown up by that robbery case, in spite of the fact that I knew that wasn't where I should be focusing my attention. But I got there, eventually."

· "Got where?" Jason Battlesea demanded.

"I'm going to go," Andy said. "Thank you both for all your help. I'll have someone call in and give you our fax numbers and you can send the final autopsy report when it's ready. Happy Fourth of July."

"Damned idiot," Jason Battlesea said.

Andy walked out the door as if he hadn't heard.

3

The door had barely closed behind the retreating FBI agent when Jason Battlesea turned on Gregor Demarkian.

"You can't do this," he protested. "You can't. You're here as a consultant. The point is to consult. You're supposed to let us know what's going on."

"I am letting you know what's going on," Gregor said. "I tried to explain it to you before you went rushing off to the parade."

"You tried to show me pictures of the robberies."

"I did," Gregor said. "Security footage from two of the robberies. In both of which, Chapin Waring's accomplice, who was almost certainly Martin Veer, was dressed up in stretchy clothes and then padded out in a way that made him move awkwardly and that entirely distorted his body type."

"Yeah, he had a better disguise than she did," Jason Battlesea said. "So what?"

"He wasn't wearing a disguise," Gregor said. "He was wearing a costume, and that's the point. Chapin Waring wasn't murdered because of the robberies. She was murdered over a crime that was committed thirty years ago, but not that crime. The key to this is the fact that the robberies weren't the only crime, and Chapin Waring and Marty Veer weren't the only criminals."

Gregor packed up his attaché case and put it under his arm.

"Let's go," he said. "We've got people we need to talk to. And get Mike Held and Jack Mann. This is supposed to be their case."

SIX

1

Evaline Veer felt awful, and the only thing that made her feel even a little bit better was that Virginia Brand Westervan looked even more awful still. It had been an awful morning for the both of them. Evaline was not so obtuse as not to realize that Virginia had never really stopped loving Kyle, even if she'd stopped being able to live with him. Kyle and Virginia were, after all, the only two of that group who had stayed together many long years after the Waring case, and they were the two Evaline had never suspected of lying to her. She had even suspected Tim of lying to her. When Tim was younger, he lied as naturally as other people breathed. When he got older and got religion, he lied to save other people from hurt feelings—some of the time. It was always hard for Evaline to tell when he was trying to be good to her and when he was letting her know what was on his mind.

Evaline had expected to see Tim somewhere here at this largest of the official picnics, but he was nowhere to be found. She didn't know why she so desperately wanted to see Tim. She just knew that the sight of him would have been reassuring.

Virginia was over at the bandstand, talking to constituents and signing autographs.

Evaline tried to wave discreetly when Virginia looked in her direction, but of course it was useless. Evaline was so short, and almost everybody else was taller. Even some of the Girl Scouts were taller.

Evaline finally managed to catch Virginia's eye. When she was sure Virginia understood, she started drifting away toward the edges of the crowd. She ran into a few people who wanted to shake her hand and congratulate her on her speech. She avoided another—a man named Michael Kerr—who would certainly want to tell her what was wrong with it. She got all the way to the west end food tables, picked up a corn on the cob and put it on a plate, and waited.

It took Virginia a little time, but she got there.

"I'm exhausted," she said, picking up corn on the cob herself. "I didn't get any sleep last night, which I suppose was inevitable, but it hasn't been much good this morning. I keep waiting for the thing to explode."

"For what to explode?" Evaline asked.

Virginia shrugged. When she shrugged, it was a monumental event. She was, after all, nearly six feet tall. She got a skewer of peppers and chicken and said, "It's the usual thing to suspect the wife, or the ex-wife, first. And here I am. The ex-wife."

"Oh, for God's sake," Evaline said, a little shocked. "You can't really think they're going to do that. You wouldn't have killed Kyle. And you couldn't have. You were doing that thing at the hospital and then you were doing campaign things."

"Even if it's true that my alibi is absolutely ironclad, it won't matter. Do you remember the Chandra Levy thing? Do you honestly think anybody cared whether that congressman was actually guilty or not? Of course not. It was a much better story to hammer it home as 'Representative Implicated in Intern's Murder.'"

"Maybe Mr. Demarkian will find the murderer today," Evaline said, "and the police will arrest somebody. And you'll be out of it."

"I don't know if I would actually be out of it, even then," Virginia said. "I suppose it wouldn't hurt. And then, you know, it's Kyle. We were married. We got along, more or less, even after we weren't married anymore. We saw each other several times a year. There was no harm in him at all, you know. He was a thoroughly nice man. He was nicer than I am. That's why we could never stay married."

"I'd think it would be easier if he was a very nice man," Evaline said. "But then, I've never been married. So I don't know."

"I think it's odd how many women I know in my generation who never married," Virginia said. "And yes, I'm including you loosely, even if you are a bit younger. And it's not just women. Tim never married either."

"I suppose Chapin never married," Evaline said. "Although I don't really know that. Aren't a lot of them married, the ones who disappear for a long time? There was that woman who had something to do with a revolutionary group, or something."

"There was nothing revolutionary about Chapin Waring," Virginia said. "When we were in high school, and even when we were in our first year of college, we all thought she was a force of nature. But she wasn't, really. She was just a mildly charismatic teenager with very little impulse control and a wild streak a mile wide. And she was a lightweight. If she hadn't committed those robberies, she would have flunked out of college in her junior year, married some stockbroker, and gone crazy about exercise so she wouldn't get fat."

"Maybe," Evaline said. She felt a little uncomfortable. Other people were coming up to the buffet table now. Evaline began to drift a little toward a line of benches near the swing sets, hoping Virginia would go with her.

"I always blamed Chapin for Marty's dying," Evaline said. " I blamed all of you, really. Not for all of it. Not for the robberies. I assumed that you all had to know about it and you all had to have participated in it. And then later I thought that that couldn't have been right."

"I wouldn't worry yourself about it," Virginia said. "You weren't the only person who thought we must all have known. The FBI probably still thinks we must all have known."

"But I did blame you all for the accident," Evaline said. "I know it was Marty himself driving, and I know he was drunk, but you must have known he was drunk, too. And nobody tried to stop him."

"It wasn't the kind of thing you did in those days," Virginia said. "And he was drunk, yes, but he wasn't sloppy, falling-down drunk. It was a very odd night. Tense. One of those times when there's obviously going to be a fight somewhere but you're not sure about what yet and you're not sure who's going to be in it."

"He must have been upset because of those two people dying," Evaline said. "I've never been able to get my head around that, you know. That he was partially responsible for the murders of two people who hadn't done anything but be in the wrong place at the wrong time. I blame Chapin for that. I know he wouldn't have done it if it hadn't been in him. I know it had to be partially his fault. But that's the way things are, isn't it? You have the potential to do harm, but if you're never put into the right circumstance, you don't do it."

"Marty's been dead a long time," Virginia said.

"Would it be wrong to say I want Marty back?"

"It wouldn't be wrong to say it, but I don't see where it would do much good," Virginia said. "Chapin's dead, too, now. I'm sure that the families of the people they killed still find it impossible to accept, and they should. But it's over, Evaline. It was over the moment Chapin hit the floor."

Evaline shook her head. "I spent all night thinking about it. It can't be over. If it was, Kyle wouldn't be dead."

"It depends on why Kyle is dead," Virginia said.

Evaline looked away. She had had a reason for coming to see Virginia. She had had something she wanted to say, or something she wanted to learn. Now she couldn't remember what it was she had wanted, and she could feel Virginia looking at her with both puzzlement and interest. It wasn't a good feeling.

"I need to go somewhere and behave like the mayor," she said. "Maybe I should set a good example and pick up trash."

"Evaline, is there something going on here? Is there something I should know about? Because you're behaving—"

"I'm behaving like myself," Evaline said. "I was like this after Marty died, only I was worse. I'm a little upset, that's all."

"*I'm* a little upset," Virginia said. "I was married to him."

"Yes," Evaline said. There was a piece of trash on the ground right in front of her. Somebody had dropped a wrapper from a Fudgsicle and just let it lie. Evaline picked it up and folded it in her hands. "I just don't think it's over," she said finally. "I don't think it will ever be over. I think it will be part of all of us always. If it isn't, then it would be as if it had never happened at all. It would be as if Marty had never been alive at all."

2

At first, Hope Matlock wasn't entirely sure of what she was doing. She had walked a long way this morning to get to where the people were. She had started out from her own house at just after six. Then she had walked and walked through streets that were already cleared for the parade and other streets that were empty of everything but parked cars. Her feet hurt before she'd gone three full blocks. The rest of her hurt soon after, and still hurt. She was so heavy these days that she found it hard to move under the best of circumstances. Having to stop and go and turn and twist every few seconds made her feel as if she'd been run over by a truck.

She walked all the way out to Beach Drive. She felt winded the way she had when she was a child and fell off the low slides at Waldham Park.

"Got the breath knocked out of you," her mother used to say, making it sound like something so vilely stupid that no decent person would admit to it.

After a while, she had hated those slides so much, she refused to go on them.

"That's why you're always too fat," her mother had said. "And you're going to be as fat as a pig when you get older. You don't take any exercise. Decent people take exercise."

But it wasn't true she had been fat then. She had been a little chunky. She couldn't help that. That was her genes. Her mother was a little chunky, too, and her father was downright squat.

The day was hot. Hope found a place on the parade route where there was a bench she could sit on. She thought she should have brought a folding chair, but she was pretty sure she would not have been able to carry it all that distance. She sat down and folded her hands in her lap and looked into the empty road.

When she was younger, she used to come down here with Chapin and Virginia and Marty and Tim and Kyle. They would use Chapin's house, or Tim and Virginia's, and sit at the end of the driveway to watch the parade come by. The smaller children would stay on the lawn and come to the edge of the driveway only when there was something to see. You always had to worry about them darting out into traffic. On the last Fourth of July before everything fell apart . . .

But no, Hope didn't remember that. Everything fell apart in June that year, she was sure of it. The robberies. The accident. Marty's funeral out at the New Hope Cemetery where the reporters all wanted to take pictures of Chapin instead of Marty's parents. She could remember standing at the edge of the grave with that big hole dug into the ground and somebody droning on and on about an eternal life nobody really believed in. She had a bandaged arm. She had bruises all over her face. She looked a mess, and her mother told her so, even as she was making everything ready for a decent funeral appearance.

"You don't see Chapin all battered up like that," her mother had said. "You don't see Virginia all battered up, either."

"They were in the backseat," Hope had said.

This was true. Virginia and Tim and Chapin were in the backseat. Marty and Kyle and Hope herself were in the front. It was an old car, which her mother called "vintage," because she didn't want to admit that Marty could barely afford anything else. There was a long front seat without any buckets. None of them ever wore seat belts.

"I don't care where you were," her mother had said. "What will the Warings think of us?"

It was years before Hope understood how odd that sentence had been—how odd it was for everybody to worry about the Warings, and the Brands, but not about the Veers, who had lost a child. She remembered Evaline at the funeral, standing close to the casket with a furious, mulish scowl on her face, not looking at anybody. It was years afterwards before Evaline would talk to any of the people who had been her brother's friends. The first person she talked to was Hope—because, she said, Hope was the only one of them who had ever cared if Marty lived or died.

The parade was over, and Hope didn't remember any of it. She didn't remember the marching bands. She hadn't even heard them. She didn't remember the floats or the Girl Scouts or anything else. The road all around her was nearly devoid of people. Everyone was going on to one of the picnics. Or maybe it was earlier than that. Maybe the speeches were still going on at the War Memorial.

She waited for a while and then stood up. She had to. She couldn't sit all day on this bench, with nobody else around. She started up Beach Drive and back toward town. It was very hot, and she felt very dizzy.

If she was honest with herself, she had to admit that everything had started to fall apart long before Marty died, and long before the robberies became a public issue. Only Chapin looked as if she didn't care one way or the other.

Hope looked around. She had reached a street she didn't recognize. It was a "nice" street, with houses set back from the sidewalks. The houses were smaller than the ones on Beach Drive, but most houses anywhere were smaller than those. The houses were also newer than the ones in Hope's own part of town, but that wasn't strange either. The houses in Hope's part of town were some of the oldest ever built on the Continent.

Hope wished she knew more or less where she was. There had been so much construction in Alwych in these last thirty years. The lots were smaller and the houses were bigger, and the houses were full of people nobody had ever known.

It was so hot, the air felt thick and patterned. It would be better if there were a bench somewhere along here, but Alwych didn't have benches except in the middle of town. Why had she come out here to begin with? She wasn't sure.

It was really very hot. It was very, very hot. Hope's head hurt, but it felt as if it were floating about her neck, way into the stratosphere, so that it had nothing to do with her. She was nauseated, but the nausea was halfway up her chest, not in her stomach. She needed to stop moving and sit down. If she didn't do that, she was going to fall down. She felt enormously stupid. She hadn't had to walk all the way to Beach Drive. She could have walked to the train station. The War Memorial was only a little ways from there. She could have stayed home. That would have been an even better idea.

Hope stopped still and closed her eyes and took a deep breath. She was swaying. She could feel it. She didn't know what would happen if she fell down. She didn't know if anybody in any of these houses was at home. She had her cell phone, but she wasn't sure if it was working or not.

On the day of Marty's funeral, Hope had thought she was going to pass out right there in the church. She had stood in the pew for the singing and Chapin had been there right beside her, with that horrible smirk on her face, that horrible smirk that said she knew everything that had happened, and that nothing she didn't know mattered at all.

There was a sound of a car, and Hope thought she was hallucinating it.

Then she turned and saw a sedan parked at the curb, with its motor idling.

SEVEN

1

In the beginning, Gregor Demarkian was sure that Hope Matlock was going to fall down dead on the sidewalk. She was swaying the way people did when their hearts were giving out and their heads were like balloons and just as stable. Jason Battlesea thought something was wrong, too. He stuck his head out toward the passenger side window as soon as he pulled to the curb.

"What's wrong with her?" he asked. "Should we be getting her to a hospital?"

"I don't know," Gregor said.

He pushed the button that rolled down the window and stuck his head into the thick, humid air. Hope Matlock had come to a stop, if she could be said to have been walking before that. She looked at him with puzzlement.

"Are you all right?" Gregor asked her. "Do you need medical attention?"

The look on Hope Matlock's face said he might as well have been speaking in Mandarin. She stood swaying where she was and looking. She answered nothing.

Gregor made a decision. He looked around behind him to

make sure the back passenger door was unlocked. Then he twisted his arm around and popped it open.

"Why don't you get in," he said. "We were headed over to your house in any event. We can drive you home."

There was more swaying, and more of that faraway vacant look. Gregor came close to deciding that she hadn't heard him. Then Hope shuddered, and moved.

She was, Gregor thought, a very lumbering person. She walked by swaying back and forth and sort of pitching herself forward.

Hope got into the backseat, folding herself up very carefully. She had a small purse. She put it on the floor. Then she closed the door behind her and waited.

"We can take you to the hospital, Miss Matlock," Jason Battlesea said. "Gregor Demarkian here has a few questions he wants to ask you, he says it will sort of clear things up, but we can take you to the hospital instead if you need to go. You don't look well."

"I'm fine," Hope said, rasping a little.

Gregor thought "not looking well" was something of an understatement. The woman's face was both flushed and gray. Gregor hadn't even known that was possible. There were large round beads of sweat on her forehead.

"I'm fine," she said again.

Jason Battlesea got the car into drive and pulled away from the curb. "You'll be better in the air-conditioning," he said. "Do you have air-conditioning in that house of yours?"

"I'm fine," Hope Matlock said yet again.

This time, Gregor thought she was approaching telling the truth. Sitting down and the cold air were doing her good. The gray was leaving her complexion, even if the flush was not. She took a great deep gulp of air that sounded as if she hadn't had oxygen for hours.

"We were surprised to see you," Jason Battlesea said, moving through the side streets and the neat little neighborhoods of neat little houses. "We came this way because we wanted to avoid all the fuss left over from the parade. I never would have thought anybody was crazy enough to walk this way. I mean, it's out of your way, isn't it? And you're on foot."

Hope looked out the window. "I just started walking," she said. "The parade was over and I wanted to go home. I don't think I was paying attention to the way I was going."

"Well, you must not have been," Jason Battlesea said. "You could have killed yourself. Even a young person who was relatively healthy—I'm not saying you're not healthy, Miss Matlock—could get heat stroke in this weather."

She was looking out the car window as the streets went by. They were going by very quickly.

"When we get home, I want you to put your feet up," Jason Battlesea said. "Is there any air-conditioning in your house?"

"It doesn't need air-conditioning," Hope said. "These old houses, they were meant to keep out the weather."

"The weather is ninety-three degrees and humid as hell," Jason Battlesea said. "Do you at least have ice? Lots of nice big ice cube trays full of ice?"

"Of course there's ice," Hope said, but she didn't sound certain.

"I've got Jack and Mike coming over. Mr. Demarkian here wanted them on hand. I'll have them pick up some ice at Lanyard's or somewhere. You've got to take care of yourself."

Hope was still looking out the window. Her eyes did not look glazed, but they did not look focused, either.

"It doesn't matter," she said finally. "I'm all right. I'm going to be all right. I just need to sit down at home and rest for a while."

Gregor pulled down the visor in front of him. There was a mirror clipped onto the back of that. It made it much easier for him to see Hope in the backseat. He got the side of her face, now fading from the flush. She looked, oddly enough, very cold.

Jason Battlesea had pulled into yet another road. This one distinctive in that most of the houses on it were right up next to the pavement. They were also all old. He pulled up in front of a small brown one.

Hope got her door open quickly and started to get out.

"I'll be all right," she said. Gregor was tired of hearing it.

"I just need to lie down," Hope said. "I need to lie down for an hour and then I can talk to Mr. Demarkian."

Gregor sighed. "You know you can't lie down for an hour," he said, "and you know I'm not going to let you."

"Why not?" Jason Battlesea said. "Do you want to kill her?"

"I don't want her to kill herself," Gregor said, "and that's where this is going."

"Hope Matlock is going to kill herself," Jason Battlesea said.

"No," Hope said.

"I don't think you are either," Gregor said, "at least not as long as we're here. But I'd really like you to tell me why you killed Chapin Waring and Kyle Westervan before you decide to give it a shot."

Hot air was coming in through the open passenger door. Hope put her face in her hands and bent over.

It took a little while before Gregor realized that what he was hearing was sobs.

2

When they got her inside, the first thing Gregor could think of was how small the house was. It wasn't square-foot small. Gregor could tell from looking at the outside that no matter what size the building was when it was first erected, it had been added on to over and over again through the years. There was a lot of it sprawling out along the road and back toward what looked like a stand of trees.

It was the rooms that were small, the ceilings lower than the modern custom of at least eight feet, the total dimensions cramped and strictly limited by thick walls with doors in them.

They came through the front door directly into the living room. There was a great wing chair near the fireplace. Jason Battlesea helped Hope Matlock into that, and she went without protest. She was bent over when she went into the chair. She stayed bent over once she was settled in it.

Gregor looked around and saw that there were papers and books everywhere, as if someone had taken the contents of a small office and thrown them over the furniture without caring where they landed.

Hope had stopped sobbing, but she was still crying. Gregor could see her shoulders going up and down above the face she still had hidden in her hands. He walked through the living room into the dining room. This room, too, was full of papers and books. Nobody could have found a place to eat at the dining room table.

He went through the dining room into the kitchen. This room was just a mess. There were dishes piled up in the sink. There were bags of chemicalized snack foods on all the counters and on top of the refrigerators. On an impulse, he opened the refrigerator. There were things in there in bowls that looked like they might have been there for a decade. He opened the little freezer compartment above that and found big bags of something called Pizza Rolls, a stack of Swanson Hungry Man TV dinners, and a big bag of frozen chicken nuggets.

When Gregor got back to the living room, Jason was waiting for him, scowling. "You can't go looking around the place as if you owned it," he said. "We don't have a search warrant."

"I wasn't searching for anything," Gregor said. This was actually true, although beside the point. "I was just noticing the obvious. Aside from some on the dining room table, that don't look as if they've ever been displayed anywhere, there are no photographs."

Hope looked up at the two of them.

"I know what you're going to say," she said. "You're going to say it was wrong of me to kill Kyle. With Chapin, and with Marty—"

"Marty? Jason Battlesea asked.

"I told you we were looking at the wrong crime," Gregor said. "Chapin Waring wasn't killed because of the robberies, or at least not directly because of the robberies. She was killed because of the murder of Marty Veer."

"Marty Veer died in an accident," Jason Battlesea said.

Hope was staring at a small window on the other side of the room. "I grabbed the wheel," she said. "We were in the car, sitting right next to each other, and he was drunk as hell, and I knew, I knew from seeing the tapes on the news, I knew what they were doing. Chapin and Marty. Chapin and everybody. I'd seen it coming for months. I wasn't stupid. But then they started to air those tapes from the banks and I could see what they'd done. And they'd gone out and done it deliberately."

"I expect this makes sense to you," Jason Battlesea said.

"Of course it does," Gregor said. "Look at those tapes again. Chapin Waring is wearing black and a mask, but not doing much to disguise her identity. Martin Veer is not only wearing black and a mask, he's padded up in odd places to make him look bulky, and to almost force him to walk in a way that wasn't natural to him. The point wasn't just to make sure nobody recognized him, but to make sure that if somebody thought they did recognize him, it wouldn't be him they'd recognize."

"They did it on purpose," Hope said again. She rubbed her hands together and blew on them, as if they were cold. "I didn't know about the robberies, but I knew there was something going on between Chapin and Marty. There was always something going on between Chapin and everybody. You'd think she had enough in her life without having to go after everybody else's boyfriends and without staging one drama after another in the long soap opera that was Being Who Counted at Alwych Country Day, but Chapin could never relax. And I'd started to see the signs all the way back in February. That she was looking to get rid of me. That she was trying to get Marty to dump me and take up with her and then she'd pick him out another girlfriend she'd like better."

"I take it you knew about the robberies before the police did," Gregor said.

"I knew the first time I saw one of those security tapes on television," Hope said. "You couldn't miss Chapin. She wasn't even really disguised, just *obscured* sort of, enough so that if you didn't know her, you wouldn't be able to describe her very well. I never understood why nobody else saw it but me."

"Maybe they did," Gregor said.

Hope sniffled. "The night of the last robbery, after those people died, that night Marty was crazy. Marty wasn't like Chapin, you know. He wasn't a good person, not really, but he wasn't like Chapin. He wouldn't do just anything for the rush. So when I heard that two people had died, I was expecting something. And I got it. Marty started drinking early. He had a flask, and then we went to a roadhouse in New York State because, you know, in those days the drinking age over there was eighteen. And he was just drinking and drinking and going crazy. And I kept trying to talk to him. And then he got sick. We were on our way out to the car, and he bolted around the side of the roadhouse and got sick. And I went back there to talk to him."

"And?" Gregor said.

Hope shrugged. "And I went back there and I waited for him to stop heaving and then I asked him. And he was too drunk to play around with it. He just told me right out front. About how I was completely sickening, as far as he was concerned. I was completely ridiculous, prancing around, pretending to be a debutante when I wasn't anybody and my family wasn't anybody and never had been, and all those things. 'Prancing around' was how he put it. And even at the time, I thought it was ridiculous. I mean, he was nobody and his family was nobody, too. They were more nobody than my family was. They didn't even have the history. His father had just made a bunch of money in kitchen fixtures. But it wasn't Beach Drive kind of money. It wasn't Waring and Brand kind of money."

Gregor was getting tired of standing. He pushed some papers to the side on the sagging old couch and sat down. "Did you tell him all that? About his family not being anybody?"

"I don't know," Hope said. "I think I might have tried. But I was drunk, too, and it was late and everybody was yelling at us to go and I was feeling a little crazy. Because there wasn't anybody else. I didn't have other friends. I didn't have a place to be or anything like that. I had college, but I didn't have anybody there and then when I went to grad school later, I didn't have anybody there. And I didn't know what I was going to do. So I think maybe I just got back into the car and sat still and didn't say anything."

"I don't understand," Jason Battlesea said. "What did she know as soon as she saw the security tapes? What could she have known that the police wouldn't have known at the same time?"

"Marty Veer wasn't disguised just to be disguised," Gregor explained. "He was disguised deliberately in order to make him look as much like Hope as possible. He was bulked up in ways to make it seem as if it was Hope committing the robberies along with Chapin Waring. Hope and Marty were close to the same height and they had similar body types."

"He wouldn't have liked her so much if he'd heard what she said about him when he wasn't around," Hope said. "She was always going on and on about how he was 'squat' and how you could really tell what class people were in from how tall they were and how lean and it was like racehorses or something. She didn't really like him. She didn't even like him a little bit. She was just playing games with him to get rid of me, and once she was rid of me she'd have found a way to get rid of him. She'd have killed him if she had to."

"But she didn't kill him," Gregor said. "You did."

"I just grabbed the wheel," Hope said. "We were driving, and we were going faster and faster, and Tim was completely furious about it, telling Marty to stop and slow down and all that kind of thing. But Marty wasn't slowing down, and we came around Clapboard Ridge on the curve there and I thought if I could just make myself do it, if I could just make myself move for once, we'd all be dead and it wouldn't matter anymore."

"You did expect you'd all be dead?" Gregor asked.

"It seemed like the most likely thing," Hope said. "We were going very, very fast—crazy fast—and I was right there on the seat next to him and I leaned over and grabbed the wheel and just pulled at it. I pulled and the car just spun off the road. We did a complete circle, like some kind of carnival ride. And we spun and we spun and then we hit a tree, but we did it kind of sideways, not head-on. And then I heard the smash and I looked up and for one second Marty was just there, and then his head exploded. It did. It just blew up."

"Jesus Christ," Jason Battlesea said.

"I think I must have passed out," Hope said. "I thought we were all going to be dead. And then we weren't. Then only Marty was dead, and Kyle and I had bruises, and I think Kyle had minor broken bones in his arm, and everybody in the back was all right. And there we were. And everybody was saying it was an accident, and blaming it all on Marty, and I didn't see any reason not to let them."

"But other people had seen what you'd done," Gregor said.

Hope nodded. "Kyle had seen it but he didn't say anything then," she said. "He was on the other side of me, so I knew he had to have seen it. I didn't realize Chapin had seen it until later. After Marty's funeral, I mean. Just before she ran away. She came here after the funeral, really late at night, and my mother—you would have to have known my mother. This was Chapin Waring coming to the house. My mother would never have believed that a Waring could do something really wrong. Chapin came and we went upstairs to my room to talk and then she just sort of laid it all out. She said she'd been sitting in the middle in the back and she'd seen everything I'd done, even if Tim and Virginia hadn't, and she could call the police right that second and I'd go to jail for murder. My whole life would be ruined. I wouldn't be able to go back to college. I wouldn't even be able to stay in Alwych, because everybody would know I'd killed him and they'd hate me for it. And I thought that that was true. Almost everybody liked Marty more than they liked me."

"And that," Gregor said, "is when she asked you to hide the money."

"This house was searched," Jason Battlesea said. "It was searched by the local police and it was searched by Federal agents. Granted, it was before my time, but are you really trying to tell me that two sets of law enforcement officers couldn't find a stash of over two hundred and fifty thousand dollars in cash in a house this size?"

Hope looked contemptuous. "They came in and searched," she said, "but they searched like it was an ordinary house. I was afraid when they first came, because I thought they'd find it, too, but they never got near it. I don't think it ever even occurred to them."

"What didn't occur to them?" Jason Battlesea said. "How isn't this an ordinary house?"

"In the seventeenth century, most people here didn't have access to banks as we know them," Gregor said. "A lot of people didn't think the banks they did have access to were safe. It wasn't unusual for people to build into their houses some kind of hiding place to keep money and other valuables in."

"They'd have found it," Jason Battlesea said.

Hope got up off her chair and went to the fireplace. The mantel was made of a thick plank. The surround was made of what seemed like the same wood, but polished.

Hope fiddled with a space just to the left of the surround itself. A big hunk of wood came off all at once. She put the hunk of wood on the floor and reached into the opening. Her arm went in all the way up to her shoulder, and when it came out she was holding a bound stack of one-hundred-dollar bills.

She put them on the floor in front of her and looked around, at nothing. Then she went back to her chair and sat down again.

"It never even occurred to them," she said again. "They didn't even ask. Maybe they didn't really take me seriously. By then everybody knew it was Marty and Chapin who had done the robberies anyway."

Jason Battlesea went over to the fireplace and looked into the hole. "Jesus Christ," he said.

"It isn't all there anymore," Hope said. "I burned some of

it. I never liked having it here. The television news kept saying that the money was worthless because the police had all the serial numbers and if anybody ever spent any of those bills, they'd be caught right away. It didn't even feel like real money to me. But then my parents died and I kept trying to make a living and it kept being so damned impossible and I'd take some of the money out sometimes and look at it. And then I'd burn it, so I wouldn't try to use it. She said she'd tell the police what happened in the car if I ever used it."

"And she'd come back every once in a while to remind you of it?" Gregor asked.

"Not right away," Hope said. "It was maybe ten or fifteen years. And then she'd show up all of a sudden and ask me to go over to the house. And I would, because I was afraid not to. And she always had a way to get into the house so the alarm wouldn't go off. And it was just like that. I thought she was going to ask for the money someday, but she never did."

"But something must have changed, this time," Gregor said.

Hope nodded. "She wanted to come back home, that's what she said. She said she didn't care if she had to spend the rest of her life in prison, she just wanted to stop all this and come home, and she was going to tell the police everything so that it could all get worked out and she wanted me to know that. I don't know what she expected. I don't know why she would have thought I'd just listen to her and nod and let anything that was going to happen happen, but that's what she must have thought. So I said I had to go to the bathroom and she said the water wasn't on and I said it didn't matter anyway, and I got the knife from the kitchen and I came back in. And I stabbed her. And she had a gun. I stabbed her and she sort of reeled back and then the gun was there. I don't know where she kept it. But it was there and she started shooting up the place and I just ran. I thought she'd follow me, but she didn't. She just kept shooting at the mirrors and then all of that just stopped. And I didn't know what to do. So I just waited. And there was no more noise.

And I went back into the living room and she was dead on the floor. And then I just sat down and tried to think."

"You sat there?" Jason Battlesea said. "With Chapin Waring dead on the floor?"

"I sat there until somebody came around," Hope said. "I don't know who it was, but I could hear them walking around on the terrace and in the bushes. I waited until whoever it was went a little bit away and then I went out through the kitchen and then across to the beach."

"Angela Harkin saw her shoes through the glass doors to the terrace," Gregor said. "The curtains were a little ruffled, and she saw a woman's feet in espadrilles."

"Everybody out here wears espadrilles."

"I thought Angela was imagining things," Jason Battlesea said.

"I wouldn't have killed Kyle if he hadn't said all those things about how we should tell the whole story and bring an end to it," Hope said. "I really didn't think he remembered seeing anything at all, and then he came to talk to me and said he knew what was going on, because he just knew, because he knew about Marty. I don't even understand why he did it. He called me just after it happened and asked me to hold some things for him and said he'd pay me to hold them, some tapes he said needed to be secret, but then he changed his mind. And all that time, he didn't say anything about Chapin or about Marty and I just thought he didn't know. We had the crash and the shock and he didn't remember. But then he started talking about how I'd never feel right unless we all told the truth about everything, and I just didn't know what else to do."

"Well," Gregor said, "you could have told the truth about everything. You'll have to now, whether you like it or not."

Hope shook her head.

"I'm not going to have to say anything," she said. "Just wait and see."

EPILOGUE

The face was missing wrinkles, as though the aging process had stepped out for a cigarette break and been hit by a bus.

—Keith Snyder, in *The Night Men*

It had been Father Tibor's idea that he could foster a cat better than either Bennis or Donna, and the decision nearly brought all three of them to blows. They were hardly calmed down when Gregor reminded them that the cat was going to go to live permanently with Hannah Krekorian as soon as Hannah bought the equipment she thought she needed to keep it. Hannah seemed to believe that cats required a great deal of equipment, some of which could only be obtained by going into the heart of Philadelphia and consulting a cat feng shui advisor.

"Do you think she'll redecorate the entire apartment if the feng shui advisor says she has to?" Donna asked.

"She didn't redecorate the apartment when there'd been a dead body in it," Gregor said. "What in the name of all that's holy is a feng shui advisor for cats?"

"Well, Krekor," Father Tibor said, "the principal foundations of feng shui—"

"I know what feng shui is," Gregor said.

"I am working on the principle of financial fraud," Father Tibor said. "Do you think when this is settled with the cat, you could sit down with Russ Donahue and me and figure out what Federal agencies we're supposed to be contacting? Russ says we can sue, but it would be better to get somebody arrested."

"They're trying to foreclose on three whole houses they don't even have mortgages on," Donna said. "Russ told me about it last night. I don't understand how they can do that. I mean, if they don't own the house—"

"They think they own the house," Tibor said. "They have digital records."

"But the digital records are wrong," Gregor suggested.

"I think somebody just invented them and now here we are," Father Tibor said.

"I want to hear more about the murder," Bennis said. "Isn't that what we started with? Gregor was telling us about the murders, and then—"

Gregor twisted around in his chair. He made a face as if the chair were uncomfortable, but that wasn't what his problem was. The cat was climbing up his right leg. It was digging its claws in as far as they could go to get a good grip on things. The claws went right through the fabric and into his skin.

"There really isn't much to tell," Gregor said, trying to remove the cat without also removing several inches of himself. "Like most of these things, it was easy enough when you looked at it the right way. And I had an advantage. I knew who the murderer had to be before I knew how to look at it the right way."

"You mean you did one of those things where you knew the murderer right from the beginning?" Bennis asked.

"No," Gregor said. "I did know, from the beginning, that there were only five people who could possibly be serious suspects. I knew that from the notes, before I ever got to Connecticut. It's not always safe to rely on notes, even good notes, but in this case it was fine. Then there were three possible people. The other two—Virginia Brand Westervan and Tim Brand—were right out of it."

"They had alibis?" Tibor suggested.

"Heavy-duty alibis," Gregor said. "Virginia Brand

Westervan is a United States congresswoman running for the United States Senate. On the night Chapin Waring died, she was attending a fund-raiser at this place called the Atlantic Club, and before the fund-raiser she was doing events, appearances, and meetings all day long. Tim Brand is a doctor who runs a free medical clinic."

"For poor people?" Donna asked.

"For poor people and anybody else who walks through the door. He was at the clinic himself all evening, and before that he was on his own, but he was visibly on his own. He went to Mass. He went jogging. And then," Gregor said, "I met the two of them. They're fraternal twins. They might as well be identical twins as far as personalities are concerned. They're both absolute moralists. They have two entirely different codes of morality—well, maybe not entirely, but you know what I mean—but they're the same personality type. If either of them had known where Chapin Waring was, he wouldn't have killed her. He'd have called the cops and turned her in."

"So," Bennis said, "it couldn't be those two. It could have been how many other people?"

"Well, up to the murder of Kyle Westervan, there were a few," Gregor admitted. "There was a woman named Caroline Waring Holder, who was Chapin Waring's youngest sister. There was Evaline Veer, who was the sister of Martin Veer, who was Chapin Waring's accomplice in the robberies. There was Kyle Westervan himself, part of Chapin Waring's little group, and Hope Matlock, who was also part of Chapin Waring's little group."

"All right," Donna said, "but then Kyle Westervan died? And that changed everything?"

"Absolutely," Gregor said. "It was the medical examiner's reports. Chapin Waring, who was very short, was killed with a downward thrust of a knife. Kyle Westervan, who was very tall, the tallest person in this case, was killed with an upward thrust of the knife. Even if you look at Kyle Westervan's murder as committed entirely separately, and by another person than the person who killed Chapin Waring, that immediately leaves out Virginia Westervan and Tim Brand, because they're both very tall. Neither one of them would have thrust upward if they'd been stabbing the man in the back. They'd raise their arms up and then thrust down. That left Caroline Waring Holder, Hope Matlock, and Evaline Veer—and Caroline Waring Holder isn't exceptionally short. She's not exceptionally tall, mind you, but the ME's report insisted that the knife was thrust upward, that it entered the body going up. And for that, you need tiny."

"And that left you with?" Bennis asked.

"Evaline Veer and Hope Matlock," Gregor said. "They were the only two who were physically able to have committed both these crimes in the way in which they were committed. And once I had that, it was only a matter of figuring out which one of them would have wanted just those people dead. And it was something Evaline Veer said to me that finally made it click."

"What did she say to you?" Father Tibor asked. The cat had gone over to him and was now sitting very calmly in his lap, as if he'd never dig a claw into any human being anywhere.

"She said," Gregor said, "that when she looked back to thirty years ago, she saw a different crime than everybody else did. She didn't think about the robberies, which weren't very important to her, even if she admitted that her brother had had a hand in them. She was talking about the accident. And she did think it was an accident. Everybody did. Evaline Veer just thought that it was a crime that Marty's friends hadn't stopped him from driving when he was that drunk."

"Well," Bennis said. "They should have."

"They certainly should have," Gregor said, "but the alcohol wasn't what made Martin Veer crash. What made him crash was that Hope Matlock grabbed the wheel and made it turn until it had to crash. And three people saw her do it: Martin Veer, Chapin Waring, and Kyle Westervan. Chapin Waring was in the backseat but in the center, so that she was looking right over Hope Matlock's shoulder. Kyle Westervan was on the other side of Hope."

"And they knew she had done it deliberately?" Father Tibor said. "And they did not tell the authorities?"

"Chapin Waring was on the run nearly immediately afterwards," Gregor said, "and she was able to use what she knew to get some help to get away. I think Kyle Westervan just felt sorry for Hope. He always felt sorry for her. If he hadn't felt sorry for her, she would never have been able to kill him."

"She killed him because he felt sorry for her?" Bennis looked doubtful.

"I didn't say that was *why* she killed him. I said that was why she was *able* to kill him. He knew she'd killed Marty, but that was nothing. He thought she'd been drunk and a little crazy at the time, not that it was something she'd done deliberately. But he also knew she'd killed Chapin Waring, and he had to know that one was deliberate. You'd think anybody with half a brain in his head would have known better than to let that woman come up behind him."

"I'd think anybody with a brain in his head would have known better than to meet her in an empty parking lot in the middle of the night," Bennis said.

"Hope's explanation for that is that he'd been helping her out, on and off, for years, and when she called him and said it was an emergency, he didn't even think about refusing. I don't know if that's true or not," Gregor said. "Whatever the reason was, he came. And then, like I said, he felt sorry for her. He saw her as—what she actually was, to an extent. Small. Out of shape. With the start of a heart condition. Weighing close to five hundred pounds. I don't think he was capable of being afraid of her. Which meant—"

"Which meant that she killed him," Bennis said.

"Which meant that as soon as his back was turned, she just stepped right in, shoved the knife in his back, and gave him one good, hard push." Gregor shrugged. "When I first heard the story of those robberies, I thought I had two sociopaths and four fairly decent people. It was really three and three."

"Which was because Martin Veer had disguised himself

in a way that was supposed to throw suspicion on Hope," Bennis said. "He padded himself so that he sort of looked and walked like her so that if there was ever any interest in him, he could lay it off on her. Do you really think he could have gotten away with that?"

"Probably not, in the long run," Gregor said. "But I don't think Hope Matlock was worrying about whether or not the ruse was going to work. She was just furious and panicked because it was being done at all. It meant that he was about to dump her, and she was about to be dumped out of the clique she'd spent her life getting into and keeping herself in. So she grabbed the wheel and pulled, and she was never the same again. Everybody remarked on it. She went through the motions of getting herself a life, but she never carried through with any of it."

"Did she really burn a hundred thousand dollars?" Donna asked. "That's what they said on CNN, but I'm not sure I believe it."

"I think the actual tally was forty thousand," Gregor said. "She would pull money out of the place she'd hidden it and burn it in the fireplace. She was poor to the point of pain, and she had to do something to keep herself from spending any of it. Because once she spent any of it, the law would have been down on her like a ton of bricks."

"And you think it makes sense that the police never found it?" Father Tibor asked. "Police searches are very thorough, Krekor. The police are not idiots, and in this case there was also the FBI."

Gregor shrugged. "It was not the kind of place anybody would have expected was there. You'd have to know something about seventeenth-century Colonial architecture. And my guess is that Hope Matlock was actually way down on the list of probable suspects right from the beginning. And, as I've said, Hope Matlock never spent any of that money. Chapin Waring got luckier than she should have been with that. Although she did work at it."

"By going back to Alwych and talking to Hope Matlock

every once in a while," Bennis said. "They got lucky there, too."

"Not really," Gregor said. "Plenty of people are out there who have been fugitives for twenty years or more. Eventually, the police lose interest. They'll look into it again if somebody comes up with a credible lead, but if you can go a decade without being caught, the chances are good that you can go forever if you don't come to the attention of the police for any other reason or you're not picked up by *America's Most Wanted* so that your neighbors start poking into your business. And she was in New York. Her neighbors probably never noticed her."

The doorbell rang. Father Tibor got up and headed toward the door. It was pushed open before he got to it, and Gregor made a note to himself to lecture the man, one more futile time, about why you had to keep your doors locked when you lived in the city of Philadelphia.

Father Tibor stood back, and a small woman with frizzed gray hair came marching in, dumping a huge pile of packages as soon as she reached the coffee table.

The packages did not land on the coffee table. They landed everywhere. Hannah Krekorian looked at them and said, "I'd better ask the Ohanian boy to help me get these over to my place. I'm pretty certain I've got everything we'll need. I got the sweet little thing a day bed and a night bed. The psychologist I talked to said that was absolutely essential. Otherwise, they get confused between naps and bedtime, and they never learn a proper schedule."

"She's going to get a cat on a schedule," Donna said, whispering.

Hannah went over to the couch and got the cat from where it had settled after Father Tibor stood up. Then she wrapped her arms around it and gave it a big kiss on the head. The cat looked as smug as the one that was supposed to have gotten the canary.

"I'm going to call him Tolstoy," Hannah said, "because he's a genius, and geniuses should be named after geniuses."

"Do you think she got him a cat IQ test?" Donna whispered.

"I think," Gregor said, "that cat knows a sucker when it sees one."

2

That day on the Connecticut shore was slightly windy, and slighty muggy, and slightly wet. Caroline Waring Holder pulled into the driveway of what she knew would always be called "the Waring house" and cut the engine to her Volvo Cross Country. There was a hearse already in the driveway. The sight of it made Caroline want to scream.

"They're bringing an urn," she said out loud and not bothering to hide it. "They have to bring an urn in a hearse?"

The front door opened a little wider and Charlotte stuck her head out. She brightened when she saw Caroline.

"There you are," Charlotte said. "Cordelia and I have been just frantic. Whatever took you so long to get here?"

"I'm right on time," Caroline said. She went up the walk and then through the front door, past Charlotte and into the foyer. Cordelia was in the foyer, looking grim.

"We've been lucky so far," Cordelia said, "but how long can you expect that to last?"

"I'd give it another five minutes at the outside," Caroline said. "Somebody will talk if they haven't yet. Where did they put the urn that they brought in the enormous hearse for no reason?"

"It's in the living room," Charlotte said. "I put it on the fireplace mantel. The mirror is still broken, but it seemed to be the right kind of place."

"Why are the people from the funeral home still here?" Caroline asked.

Charlotte and Cordelia looked at each other.

"Well," Cordelia said. "The man said he'd just stay around to help, you know, if we needed anything."

Caroline counted to ten. "Get rid of him," she said. "Get rid of anybody from the funeral parlor and anybody who isn't us. If they followed my instructions about the urn, I can carry it myself when this farce is over."

Cordelia and Charlotte looked at each other, and Charlotte hurried at the door.

That was something she would never have, Caroline thought. She would never have that mental telepathy her older sisters had shared with each other, that ability to have entire conversations without words.

She went into the living room. The space above the fireplace where the mirror had been was still ugly and still raw. The blue white marble urn on the mantel right in front of it was just as small as she had asked it to be. Caroline put her hand out to touch it, but she felt nothing. What did she think she was going to feel? Chapin was dead, and Caroline had to use everything in her body and mind to keep herself from adding, automatically, "finally."

Charlotte came into the living room, looking strained. "He's gone," she said. "Don't you think that's going to look a little odd? Aren't people from the funeral home usually there when there's a service going on?"

"I don't care," Caroline said. "I just want to wait out the suitable interval, and then I want to get out of here. Where's Cordelia?"

"I'm here," Cordelia said, coming through from the same direction Charlotte had come. "He's left the driveway. I watched. There are other people in the driveway, though. Some of them have cameras."

"I don't care," Caroline said again. "Let them sit in the driveway and stew. God only knows they ought to mind their own business."

Cordelia sat down on one of the couches and smoothed the knees of her black dress pants.

"So here we are," she said. "And it's over. Can you believe it's over?"

"I can't believe we got away with it," Charlotte said. "Thirty years is a long time. It's practically forever."

"We were very careful," Caroline said. "We never saw her. We never talked to her. We never even really wrote. I was so surprised when I found out she was in New York. It hardly seemed possible. None of those places I sent the envelopes to was ever New York. None of them were even in New York State."

"She probably had that man running around, picking things up for her," Cordelia said. "Did you see him on television? Could you believe Chapin would ever know anybody like that? Well, it was Chapin. It is odd, though."

"My oldest sister robbed five banks and killed two people," Caroline said. "That's odd enough for me. I want to make sure we all get what's going on here. We're going to sell the house. We don't need it anymore, and Chapin doesn't need it anymore, so we're going to get rid of it. And I truly hope to never set eyes on it again."

"She let that man come into the house and take our family pictures," Cordelia said. "Isn't anybody bothered by that but me?"

"There is no free lunch," Caroline said. "She had to pay him with something. She needed his help. Let it go. Sell the house."

Charlotte straightened up a little. "Yes, of course. We'll sell the house. We'll have to get it cleaned up and repaired. I wonder what she was thinking, shooting it up this way. And the report on the news said that Hope was in the house when she did it. When Chapin did it. Hope Matlock."

Cordelia sniffed. "Well," she said. "The Matlocks. I don't see that that's all that surprising."

"That's true," Charlotte said. "Most families who've been here since the *Mayflower* are very well off by now, it's the natural progression of things. If the Matlocks weren't, you do have to assume that something was wrong."

"You could tell there was something wrong about Hope in elementary school," Cordelia said. "She didn't even look like a human being half the time."

Caroline looked from one of her sisters to the other. *Our older sister planned and carried out five bank robberies and killed two people. And she didn't need the money. She did it for kicks.*

Caroline got up and walked out into the foyer, away from the talk.

This was not her home in the way it had been home for Charlotte and Cordelia and Chapin. This was a place that she had always feared and been, just a little, ashamed of. She was not ashamed of her sister Chapin. Sisters were sisters. You could hate them, but you couldn't ever let them go. That was the difference between people like the Matlocks and the Veers, and people like the Warings. That was the difference between people like the Warings and everybody else in the world.

The foyer was cool and dim and wide. There were sounds coming from just beyond the front door that let Caroline know that reporters had arrived. She imagined the fuss she would cause if she went out and told them, "Once every year or two, I got a letter with an address in it, and I sent a key and the security codes to that address, so that Chapin could come here. I didn't know why she wanted to come here, and I never asked. I never saw her myself, but I wish I had. If she were still alive, I would go on doing it for her."

Yes, it was amazing, really, that they had gotten away with it. But people did get away with these things. Sometimes they never stopped getting away with them.

Caroline passed through the foyer into the dining room, and sat down on a chair, and started to cry.